# The Cinder Pill

*A Dark, Sexy Comedy About Dealing With Depression*

Gwen Holsapple

GEEBA
productions

# Mile One

The worst hangover I ever had lasted three days. I was in a fog of forgetfulness and pain for three days, until the irritating and incessant ringing of the telephone finally stopped, and the door started banging instead. I knew it was the photographer from work. I answered the door because I was tired of the wet, musty smell of my bed, and I was afraid that my legs and my lungs might actually stop working if I didn't start using them again soon. Also, I knew that she wouldn't go away. Maybe she was right. Maybe it was time to stop talking to myself and try talking to somebody else. I was stuck anyway. My brain was going around in unending, unresolved circles, and now my entire body was joining in on the ride.

My body started talking to me. It had spoken to me many times before, but I wasn't listening. I didn't want to. I don't know if I particularly wanted to this time either, but I had no choice. My body was shouting and it wouldn't shut up. It spoke to me first by taking away all of my strength. Every last ounce. I couldn't walk down the hallway to pee without my breath coming hard. I couldn't stand without feeling weak and dizzy. I could feel myself swaying. I couldn't lift a glass of water to my lips without watching my hand shake, and I couldn't even keep my eyelids open as I called into work to tell them I couldn't make it in that morning, I was too ill. I even tried twice. I thought my body was just being a nag, so I called in the first time to tell them I would be late. Two hours later, my body's voice would not be put off any longer. It really meant business this time. It took away all of my strength so that I would be forced to listen. That's when I called into work the second time to confess that I just couldn't make it in at all. I lay back down. I was at the mercy of the voice, and the voice continued.

It tortured me with varying bouts of coldness and sweat. My heart pounded up through my neck and into my ears, where it made my eardrums vibrate with an annoying steadiness. I had to reposition my head over the pillows so that my ear could hang over an empty space between the pillow and the mattress. This way, with my ear suspended, the sound couldn't bounce off the sheets and come back up and make my head bob back and forth. Then my heart moved on and pounded around my head like a thick halo. It stayed there all day.

I heard mysterious, sharp little pains every now and then. Mostly from my lower abdomen, where my intestines struggled, and from under my left breast, where my heart pumped alternately between fast and slow. The painful tenor of the sheerest poison soaked up my veins and soddened my limbs. The sound caused me to flinch involuntarily and to moan and rock and curl up in a tight ball. My arms were dead, and my legs had the dull ache of bruises and a pulled muscle that was taking forever to heal.

This went on, through a thin consciousness of day, night, and time, for three days. I called in sick three days in a row. After hanging up the phone every morning, I crawled right back into bed, getting up only to force enough water down my throat to keep my blood in liquid form. My body told me that it was going to die. That it was already dying, and that if I wanted to savor any more of life and the world, I would have to stop trying to drink myself to sleep.

Sleep, sleep, that beautiful, magical, and ever elusive thing. Sleep used to be a sweet and desirable state of delight. When did God decide I was done with sleep? It didn't matter that I was young. It didn't matter that I liked to eat well and even liked to exercise. My body was going to die anyway because these compensations weren't fair. It meant it. I believed it. This time I had to listen.

I could do this. My body was very strong. I knew this well from the volume of abuse I had heaped upon it. I took advantage of my strong body and its ability to recover by abusing it over and over again. Someone else might be dead already. But not me. Not yet. I got up and answered the damn door.

Helen was standing there with a steely look of determination in her eyes and a foot in my door. She grabbed hold of my arm. Decked out in full, black motorcycle gear complete with buckles and zippers, it was clear that there would be no getting around this soldier. Her long, brown hair was dramatically tousled, and her cheeks were slightly flushed from her ride.

"I made you an appointment up at the hospital," she said. "I want you to talk to somebody. Can you make it?" I nodded and made her let go of me so that I could change my shirt. The fresh shirt I put on was already damp when we walked out into the street.

The good thing about living smack in the heart of the city is that you can walk almost anywhere you need to go. Sometimes my car stayed parked in the exact same spot for weeks. We walked quietly, side by side, up the five blocks to the hospital where we both did a lot of work for the staff in almost every department. The graphic design firm we worked for used to be a part of the communications department. Another good thing when you're working with a hospital is that you can get whatever medical attention you need at just about any time you need it. It's a definite clique. Helen had found a psychiatrist to see me in the evening, on the same day she called, at a big, important, metropolitan hospital complex just by knowing somebody who knew somebody else and so on.

It was cool and dark outside in the early October night as we walked. The layer of sweat accumulating on the inside of my shirt was already sticky and caused me to shiver. Helen marched me up the steps and into the back entrance, across the lobby without so much as a nod to the security officer that we both knew, and upstairs into another cool, dark place. She delivered me like a package to the middle-aged woman inside the office, watched the door close and sat down in the waiting room to block any attempt to escape. I sat down in the room with the woman with the perfectly coiffed hair and the appropriate suit and the predictably large jewelry with barely a sigh. I don't remember her face very well. I think she looked a little bit like Margaret Thatcher. It didn't matter. I'd been there before and it was always the same. The same dim, cool, quiet room with plenty of books around. The books are often shelved right up to the ceiling, just so you know that you are in knowledgeable, well-informed hands.

Sometimes there is water gurgling softly from some cheesy, "picturesque" rock sculpture in the corner that is supposed to invoke an atmosphere of Asian serenity. Sometimes the sound just comes from a machine on the floor. Things are everywhere, objects and ashtrays and plaques and just *things*. The couches and chairs are always comfortable. I have to give them that. The shrinks' appearance is always a cross between a suit and a hippie. Their clothing is expensive, neat, and pressed, but their hair is too long or the earrings too big. They have to be businesslike with the prices they charge, but they want you to admire and trust them as well. The questions are straight out of the book, but their reactions can range between anger and boredom when they don't get the answers they are equipped to work with. I'll start at the top, and this will be quick:

**Shrink #1.** A heavyset German woman with a hard look to her face and a helmet of short, white hair. She was the Chairman or the President or the Head of the Psychology Department or something like that, so I really ranked. It was my freshman year in college, and she was trying to explain to me why I was being asked to take a semester off and get my act together before even thinking about returning to her precious school. She then proceeded to lecture me on my duty to my parents, my community, and the school, and how the acceptance of these duties ought to whip me right back into shape and cure me on the spot. I remember the anger in her face as she leaned toward me and spat, "How could you do this to your parents? To this school?" I, myself, wasn't sure exactly what I had done at the time, and I had no answers to her questions. Completely clueless and lost, all I knew was that it was me with the bandages on my wrists, and her laying the guilt trip all over me because of it. I wasn't offended. After all, I had lots of experience with this method of attempting to grind people into obedience simply by growing up in the Catholic Church. I wish I had been a little more self-aware, and had been able to tell her just how well I expected this method to work for me, but it didn't matter.
I knew I would never return to that school.

**Shrink #2.** I went to a new school and was straightaway assigned to this gentleman on conditions of my acceptance. This man was my most favorite in appearance. I swear to God he could have come straight out of a Woody Allen movie right along with his set. He was thin, with a Vandyke beard, wire-rimmed glasses, and a perfectly tailored dark blue suit. His desk was wide and shiny and deep, and he sat behind it way, way across the room from little me, seated on an equally long and wide couch at least 15 feet away from him against the wall on the opposite side of the room. He would remove his glasses and lean back in his chair and actually steeple his fingers in front of his face, as he looked me over with concern in his eyes. He steepled his fingers. I'm not kidding. By this time, I had taken the prescribed semester off and had plenty of time to reflect on the inappropriate behavior of Important School Shrink #1. If either of these two docs knew anything about psychology, then I was Sigmund Freud. This guy was so completely inane that I wasted no time washing my hands of him after completing the required number of sessions. Once again, the reaction was anger. He unclasped his hands, returned his glasses to his nose, and leaned a whole foot closer to me over his impressive desk to shout, "You cannot quit therapy! You are running away from your problems!" "Running away from your problems." Those where his exact words. I'm still not kidding.

**Shrink #3.** A peace offering to my parents for so quickly dumping Important School Shrink #2. She had her own private practice in a ritzy section of town, and charged an exorbitant amount of money in accordance with her location. I swear I think she was my absolute favorite of all. Let's call her Dr. Shocker. Dr. Shocker had me wait in a tiny anteroom while she shuffled the patient before me out a door on the other side of her office so that we wouldn't have to see each other and be ashamed of where we were. Again, in the tradition of great comedic movies everywhere, Dr. Shocker actually had me lie down on the infamous couch while she sat across from me with her pencil and pad and a very loud, ticking clock facing away from me on the little table beside her chair.

She said absolutely nothing.

It became a test of wills. Sometimes she sighed audibly. Sometimes I peeked over and caught her chin nodding down toward her chest, her eyelids looking heavy. There was one session when neither of us said a single word. Not one word, until the blessed minute hand hit the 50-minute mark and she said, "Time's up." Then she ushered me out the back door with a look of relief in her eyes behind those plastic owl frames, and her thin lips set in a tired line.

The main thing I remember about her sessions was the clock, ticking away my parents' hard-earned dollars, and the expressionless, pudgy, bored form of her body trying hard to stay erect in her chair. Everything else is now blurry or white and nonexistent, except for her thick black glasses, the dry red line of her mouth, and the never-ending tick-tock, tick-tock, tick-tock of her clock. The clock would get louder as the hour went on. It was very much like the old man's heart buried beneath the floorboards of Poe's imagination. Either one of us could have been the dead man in the story, but at least she was getting paid. I went home and told my parents I was sure I could make do with the free counseling center appointments available to the students on campus.

**Shrinks #4 and #5.** This dynamic duo ran a group counseling session every week in a cute little cottage on the edge of the university campus. I voluntarily attended, because by this time I was getting so little sleep I felt ready for a NASA experiment on the ability of the human body to continue functioning in an environment of almost complete and total sleep deprivation. I would stun them all, and make the cover of *Time Magazine* as the real-life person who never slept. Top scientists from around the world would want to meet me and study me and fall in love with me because I was making them famous.

The campus group consisted mostly of young women who talked about almost nothing besides food, how they felt about their looks, and whether or not they were attractive to boys. I was there because I was worried I might actually be insane. My insomnia was not getting in the way of my schoolwork. It seemed impossible that I was even standing on the amount of sleep I was getting, and yet I was still on time for every class and making decent grades. I wanted someone to assure me that this was somehow normal. Shrink #4 was a super tiny, petite brunette who could not possibly have weighed over 100 pounds, and Shrink #5 was an obese, balding, bearded male. Seriously now. They seemed very nice, but an underweight woman and an overweight male in a room full of vomiting co-eds? I graduated from college and got a job and swore never to bother with professional psychology again.

Now I just had to shake off Ms. Thatcher here.

"How are you feeling?"

"I've been a little depressed. I'm not sleeping very well. I guess I'm just a little overwhelmed with work and everything."

"Do you feel as if you might hurt yourself? Are you having any suicidal thoughts?"

"No, I'm just really tired. Work has been crazy."

"What do you do when you're feeling overtired? How do you like your job? How are your personal relationships going? Are you worried about anything in particular? Do you feel this? And do you feel that? And what, where, when, why, how, okay?"

"I'm okay. I'll be fine. Thank you for your time. No, I don't think I need to make another appointment or see anybody else. I'll be fine, thank you again." Same old, same old, piece of cake. Rivulets of sweat were dribbling down my body, one drop at a time, from my armpits down to my waist like a Chinese water torture. As she sent me on my way, I wondered why she hadn't brought up the issue of alcohol. I must have been reeking of booze all over her office. I could smell it, the sour air, wafting up from my chest. She didn't mention my smell, my sweat, or the three days I had called in sick to work. Her eyes were squinty and watery. She seemed fidgety, impatient, and a little red in the face as well. Maybe the boozy smell in the air was coming out of her, not me. In retrospect, I believe that perhaps she, herself, was drunk at that exact moment.

Helen walked me home.

"How do you feel?" She paused. "Do you think you're an alcoholic?" Helen was my number one drinking partner at the time. She was available at any time and any place for any reason, so there was no way I was going to admit to being an alcoholic to her even if I thought that I was. She was obviously a little afraid of this as well.

"No, I'm just letting myself get really depressed about this job and always being broke and my love life and JC. You know how he sucks. He's so difficult. I can't even think straight when he's around."

"Tell me about it," she sniffed. "You have got to stop doing him, and we have both got to get out of our jobs." Then she laughed. She may have been making a little more than me as the only photographer in the firm, but it couldn't have been much more. There were only six of us: four young women and two, older male partners.

"Will you make it into work tomorrow?"

"Sure, sure. I'm fine now. We'll go out after work on Friday and talk." We were already at my apartment, the second floor of a rowhouse in a "good" part of the city. She had parked her motorcycle right in front, so she only had to pause for a moment.

"Okay, see you tomorrow." Helen was always so easy. That was the great thing about her. Everyone else was much, much too complicated.

I walked up the front porch stairs and turned to watch as she drove away. Back in my room, I stripped off my shirt and changed again into a clean, absorbent gray cotton rag. I looked down at my torso as the shirt waist dropped down. Yeah, looking a little flat, white, and weak down there. Back in the bed, I lay down and propped my head up on two pillows, closed my eyes, and started thinking.

Okay, major changes need to begin right now. Not only to keep everybody off my back, but to keep from accidentally killing myself. Things were getting serious and the brass was getting involved. I had to be different now.

A different person completely. Different goals, more long-term goals, different attitude, different strengths, different resolve. What could I do, right away, right now to get this going? It came to me in a true epiphany. My eyes opened to the ceiling.

I needed to become a long distance runner.

I ran track and field in junior high and loved it. Well, in reality, I ran track and field in junior high because my circle of warmest friends demanded my participation and there wasn't much of an alternative. Girls' soccer had not yet exploded onto the scene, and the only alternative for spring was girls' lacrosse, played with heavy, flat, wooden sticks more suitable for a street fight than for the capacity to capture a high-speed missile. Then there was that natural boundary rule of the playing field. In other words, there were no boundaries. Might as well just drop the stick a few yards out and keep on running straight home, pop open a Tab, and hit the couch until dinnertime.

Track it was. During a track meet, we screamed at our teammates, shoulder to shoulder, with our arms locked together over the fence on the sidelines. In good weather we piled close together over the bleachers, and in bad weather we huddled beneath them, discussing our dreams and jitters and the oncoming summer. Those friends of mine went on to college, marriage, and everyday life with the joy I had lost still secure on their faces as I whirled out into the endless night alone.

Running it would be. Becoming a long distance runner would solve everything. It would clear out my head, make me tired enough to sleep, strengthen my body, force me to continue setting goals, and spiritually catapult my ass out of my poverty-level job. I could do this.

Figure it out. Where would I do this? It would be easy. There was a big university down the same road as the hospital, and the big university had a stadium, and the stadium had a track. I was good at going around in circles. I could run after work. It would be rush hour, with plenty of headlights and traffic to light me up and keep me safe on the dark city streets along the way. It was only a few blocks away, just like everything else on the north end of town. Was it locked up? Could I somehow just blend in? Would it be monopolized by the track team? Figure it out tomorrow. Right then, I just needed to close my eyes.

I knew I was feeling better already, because I immediately started thinking about sex.

# *Mile Two*

I made it into work the next day. No one in our eccentric little group was unduly distressed about my short disappearance, and no work had gone undone. The four of us girls were always freaking out about something or another between deadlines. Shit, once Sandy was so wiped out after being the lead designer on a major catalog job that she didn't show up for a week after it went to print. The week after that, she showed up in pajama pants and fuzzy slippers.

I spent most of the morning downstairs in the basement on the photography floor. Literally, flat out on my back on the photography floor. We worked out of a rowhouse in the "bad" part of the city just a few blocks down the street from my apartment. That's all it took, just a couple of blocks to cross over the line between good and bad. 25th Street cut horizontally across the north end of the city like the Mason-Dixon line symbolically divided the states in the Civil War. I lived above the line, in the 2800 block where preppies, scholars, and punky artists walked and giggled outside my bay window on their way to the university shops. Down on the corner of the 2500 block, the prostitutes were still on the corner at 8:00 a.m. People were drinking on stoops, kids were fighting in the street and once a guy got shot in the rowhouse right next to us during the day. We heard the gun shot through the walls. We didn't leave work until late that night. We were shaking in our shoes, and the ambulance and police cars were too creepy to pass.

The top two artists were, naturally, upstairs. They got the covers and the big name advertisements. I classified myself as the "graphics grunt." I worked on the second floor, running up and down three flights of stairs between photography in the basement and the other two elitists upstairs. I got the inside of the catalogs, the text flows, the leftover film runs and most of the old hospital clients. Doctors are pretty unenlightened about graphic design. They all thought I was wonderful. They were also always in a hurry and always last minute and always so grateful. My job swung back and forth between overload and down time. Right now I was down. Down on the basement floor while Helen was in the darkroom in the back of the house. The lights were out, but the light table was on as always, casting its eerie, smooth glow over the room, keeping me calm and still. The revolving door that lead through a tube into the darkroom swished open every now and then, and Helen's black combat boots strode softly past my head as she came into the room to grab another roll of film. Then she swished back out. After awhile I got up, arranged my flowing, flowered skirt down over my tights and went upstairs to get some work done. First things first. As always, check the incoming emails for horrific bombshell deadlines that might necessitate a duck-and-cover operation.

First email, whoa.

What the hell? How the . . .? What the . . .?

There was an email from someone I hadn't thought of in years. It's a man I know in California. I can't bother thinking about a man on the West Coast when I'm having enough problems here, on the East Coast. That man was damn fine as I remember. Why is he . . .?


**CAL:** Hi, Grace.

Sorry I've been out of touch. I'm not very good with computers and emails. I got your address from your friend Melanie, I hope that's all right. I'll be flying into Baltimore this Christmas to see my parents. I'll be there until the twenty-seventh of December. Any chance we could arrange a little reunion? It'd be great to see you and some of the old crew.

I hope this finds you well. I completely understand if you're not up for anything, but I would love to see you. You can also reach me on my cell phone: 323-555-xxxx. Hope to hear from you.

Xx


No. Fucking. Way. There is no way I can see this very fine man now or later or forever with the way things exist in the universe as it stands. I am way too out of it. I can't even think about trying to look pretty for someone I used to have a crush on a million years ago. I don't even want to see any of my old school friends who live less than an hour away. Plus, I'm completely tied up with getting away from JC, the crazy, hot, dark artist on my block, who would probably choke me down in a jealous rage if he even knew I was receiving this email. *Why* was I receiving this email? It didn't matter. I wasn't even going to think this through.

**Grace:** I'm afraid it's just not in the stars that we see each other this time around. I won't even be in the old neighborhood over Christmas, because my family will be out of town. Also, I'm so sick with bronchitis I've had to cancel everything this week and I just linger on with these antibiotics. Missing a lot of work and don't want to get anyone else sick. Feel bad about missing your guest appearance from the other side of the continent!
Have a wonderful Christmas, and let's BOTH have an excellent New Year.
Love Grace

**CAL:** Man, Grace. I'm so sorry to hear you're feeling so bad, although your attitude is amazingly positive. I send you all my warmest thoughts for your recovery, and I hope you're able to enjoy the holidays at least. We WILL meet up down the road sometime. Maybe you and the gang will have to visit me in beautiful Los Angeles some day. Take care of yourself. A big kiss and a Merry Christmas to you.
Xx

Oh, boy. I'll deal with Melanie later. I'll deal with everyone later. Right now, even more than ever, all I can think about is trying out the track. Just have to tie up some loose ends and get out of here. One thing at a time.

Back in my apartment, I'm throwing clothes off all over the floor and putting on more old, gray cotton sweats. I need to invest in some color. I really, really hope I can sneak onto the track without being a student at the university. I've decided that I'm going to run one mile today. That's easy. It's only four times around. Better walk to the track so as not to waste any energy running there, just to be sure I can run the mile.

On campus, the entire stadium is lit up like daylight. This is good because I won't get mugged, but bad because I don't want anyone to see me. Then I realize that no one is going to see me. The track has at least a dozen or so people running, jogging, walking, and sprinting around it, and not a one of them appears to belong to each other or to a team. They look like regular working people, not students. They are not paying any attention to each other. There is one team there though. It's the lacrosse team practicing in the middle and taking some pretty wild looking shots at a goal pointed directly onto the track, just a few feet away from the runners. Why don't they point that thing towards the infield for target practice? Oh well, I never did think of lacrosse players as having too much sense, and at least I could look at their legs to keep me going. I find a gate that opens into the track, check my mark, and plod out into the first lap.

I think maybe I'm taking some of the tiniest steps ever taken, definitely sucking wind right off the bat and blowing snot on top of it, but what the hell, I'm here. I had layered up my body and willed my unmotivated ass out the door, and I was going to do this. My mind was perfectly set. I am going to run this mile.

After one lap, I'm already looking for some kind of diversion to take my mind off my lungs. Look at legs - no, no, too much effort to turn my head. Looking down I see all kinds of stuff. There's an open condom wrapper beside the rail on the track. Beautiful. There are beer bottles and soda cans and other trash around the outside edges. Guess the students do their partying on the outfield before their screwing on the infield.

My chest is constricted and my legs feel weighted and I'm eating my hair in the wind that I'm sucking. I've only run two laps. Looking up at the backstretch of lap three, it looks like the longest road I've ever seen, trailing off into oblivion. That's okay, oblivion is where I want to go if I can get there without hyperventilating first. My steps are so small. My knees are jarring up into my hips. I think even a toddler can take bigger steps. I look up in my misery and see something white in my lane. As I come upon it, I see that it is a pair of undies. See-through undies on the track, smack in the middle of my lane. Jesus, there must be some serious sex going on here after the stadium lights go out. See-through underwear, condoms, and beer bottles. Jesus H. Christ, I'm trying to workout here. I hop over the undies in disgust and use that feeling to struggle onward into my final lap.

Now, wait a minute. How had I missed a pair of sexy, transparent undies on my first two laps around the track? How could they suddenly appear like magic in lap three? And why did they look exactly like a pair of mine that I'd worn a few nights ago with JC? I figured it out in a stunning moment of agonized embarrassment. The underwear must have been stuck inside my sweats with static cling from my last laundry day, and had shaken out onto the track in the second lap. Holy crap! The smutty, sexy, indecent underwear in the middle of the track was mine! How do I get it off the track? That stuff is expensive, I'm not going to leave it here. Did anyone see it fall from my body? I risk a quick glance over my shoulder and no, no one seems to appear horrified that they are running closely behind a whore, but they are running way too closely behind for me to pick up the underwear unnoticed.

Impossibly, my unexpected panic goads me into picking up the pace in order to gain some distance between myself and my fellow fitness seekers. I fly around the upper corner of the track and hurl into the final backstretch, probably running about three miles an hour in reality, and do a neat reach down to scoop up the panties and tuck them under my sweats without looking around again. I exit the track at the nearest gate.

Walking home, I'm heaving a bit and feeling pretty rung out. This was not a very good start, but I'm already thinking about trying again tomorrow. I know I'll be back.

# Mile Three

The Morning Dread. I wanna be dead. I wish I were dead. I need to be dead. Dead, dead, I wanna be dead.

My friends are drifting away. My love is drifting away. My spirit is already far, far away. Nightmares. I have nightmares. I woke up a thousand times during the night, relieved to roll over and see the glowing numbers on the digital clock telling me that it was still the middle of the night, and not time to start a new day. But then it's 6:00, and then it's 7:00. Waves of anxiety, fear and depression move in for high tide. It's time. Time to fuck up another day. I'll perform poorly at work, scraping away hour after hour for a shred of creativity to throw out at the clients and keep them at bay until I can deal with the deadline. Then I'll go out after work and drink to escape my self-loathing. But wait, remember? You're going to go to the track again today after work. You promised yourself. Start with your cardio. Tomorrow is another day to dread.

Look at me at work. Walking around, smiling at people, saying kind things, being funny, and pretending that I'm a human being. Pretending that I'm a real person. Laughter is coming from the third floor "Cover Girls" upstairs. I'm drawn to go up even though Sandy doesn't see me and Mandala sees right through me. These two are a striking and unusual pair. Sandy is from way down South, but has absolutely no trace of a southern accent. Her skin is lily white, her hair a natural auburn with strawberry highlights, her figure is slim and her appetite is just like a li'l bird, as Mammy would have required. She dresses like a hobo and swears like a sailor. She'll talk to her clients on the phone with a voice that is low, modulated, honey sweet and convincing.

The minute the handset hits the base, she says, "Kneel down and blow me motherfucker," and placidly returns to her keyboard and screen. She's always the first to figure out all the cool new tricks in Photoshop and beyond. She can name that font in two notes. I call her the Font Goddess.

Mandala doesn't swear. In fact, she doesn't say very much at all. She's a Cover Girl in looks as well as talent. African-American and Baltimore-bred, she looks at everyone with the calm, yet flaming eyes of Samuel Jackson in *Pulp Fiction*, or in any movie he's ever made really. She even has his cute little nose. I have accused her of being his secret love child which may have elicited a tiny smile, I'm not sure. It's hard to tell with her. She dresses perfectly, every day, from head to handbag in designer wig-outs that are especially incredible to behold after we've been up all night on the phones and on the boards. No deadline can faze her, and her hairstyle is painstakingly, amazingly different every day too. She knows everything that is happening to everyone and how they are feeling and how they will react and exactly what they are going to do next. It's uncanny. She's a witch. She can put out pages of logo designs in the same time it takes me to come up with one or two on a single page. If the client doesn't like them, she puts out five more in a day without flinching or chipping her nail polish. She is the Logo Queen.

My favorite thing about sitting around with these two is listening to them argue. They sit at their desks, facing opposite sides of the room, and have an argument without raising their voices or their eyes, or missing a beat on their keyboards. They disagree like a flowing stream, free from rocks and rapids. When they don't disagree, Sandy lets go with a string of expletives and Mandala speaks a few words or gives a low hum. Now, I've reached the top of the stairs and I can see what they are giggling about.

Mandala's fastidious person has long taken offense over the working girls we have to step around on our way to work in the morning. Her light, expensive perfume clashes sharply with the aroma of the neighborhood. This will not do. She has taken a swath of leftover poster paper and printed out a sign that reads, "MANDALA'S HO WASH, $1," and pasted it up on the front of her desk. At first she began to paste it up in the window, but Sandy gently reminded her that, "You can get your own skinny ass shanked in the vestibule if you like, but the rest of us bitches don't need to put our lives on the line while trying to make it into work." Mandala explained that she planned to hook up a hose on the corner fire hydrant and wash them all down one at a time for a buck apiece. I suggested that maybe she could turn the hose on our salesmen too, but never mind. The aftershave signal is good. The aftershave signal is how I know I didn't beat the bosses in when I'm late for work. When the air in the front vestibule is soaking with cologne, then I'm forewarned to sneak in as quietly as possible. This is easiest for Helen, whose steps lead down to her basement studio without having to pass a single workroom. The rest of us are upstairs. Half the time we don't even know if Helen is down there. Even if she is there, we can't ever reach her because she is always in the darkroom. Maybe that's why she and I get along so well. I am psychologically in the dark in every room every day.

It's time to leave work and hit the track again. Perhaps I can manage a mile without dropping any lingerie this time.

At home the answering machine is blinking. Damn. JC is supposed to be tied up with a mural job in Washington for the next two weeks, but I'm pretty sure it's him. It's time. It's been almost a week since we last fucked each other's brains out and entertained the neighbors while in progress, no doubt. I'm feeling the void, but I'm all holy and determined and committed and may as well pretend I didn't see that blinking button and not even hit it. I hit the button of course. It's him.

"Come over," he says. That's all he has to say, and his low, dangerous voice sends a flutter down to my knees. Yeah, I know that some girls like the bad boys and all that. Whatever. But this boy is worse than bad. He's so damn dark and sexy, and talented and sexy, and sexy and sexy. Black, thick, curly hair. It took me over an hour to trim his hair once, it was so thick. Heavy, heavy black eyebrows over dark amber eyes. Fine hands and feet, hairy black forearms, with his sleeves always rolled up. Tight little ass. Paint stains all over him. Always looking at me with those eyes on fire like dusky, promising jewels. His eyes were always ready.

His studio was cluttered with metal shelving units full of paints and supplies. There were so many large plastic buckets on the floor, soaking so many dozens of brushes in turpentine, that it was hard to stay in there too long without feeling as if you were going to swoon or pass out. His back room wasn't much better. His back room was the bedroom, which he lovingly dubbed "the Womb." The Womb was so small that you couldn't take two steps away from the full-size bed in the center without hitting a wall. There was a bathroom on the east side. The natural wall on the north side of the room was pulled even farther inward because he had cut it apart in sections to store paintings behind the drywall in a makeshift closet. Stereo equipment covered the west wall, farthest from the doorway, and drawings in frames covered the rest. You could lean over the far side of the bed without straightening your elbow to change a record. For some reason, the bedroom ceiling was lower than the front studio's eight-foot-high, traditional city ceiling, emphasizing the overall feeling of claustrophobia in the Womb.

At the bottom of the bed he had a tiny, black-and-white TV on a small table, with an old VHS recorder on the floor underneath. He owned several VHS tapes, but only one of them wasn't porn. This single, unsullied tape was a copy of Ingmar Bergman's *The Magician*. JC's TV was too small to watch a foreign film, because the subtitles got cut off at the bottom of the screen. In order to watch this foreign film on the miniature screen, he attempted to offset the vertical hold to flip over so slowly that we were able to catch a bit of scene, then subtitle, then scene, then subtitle, and so on, like an up-and-down tennis match. But we were cool, you know, because we were watching Ingmar Bergman in the first place.

It was hard to concentrate on anything besides sex in that room anyway. Keep in mind that the TV was at the foot of a man's bed. A man who appeared so dangerous in the flesh that I felt completely safe while cutting across a Baltimore City alleyway with him. You do not want to see this man in an alley. Anyone who sees JC in an alley will immediately take a turn and walk the other way, no matter what they're packing.

Once, we were walking down some questionable streets in New York City, and we had gotten a little lost. We were staying in the Paramount Hotel along with JC's painting buddy, Alphonse, because the Edison was unavailable during one of our yearly trips to visit the bigger museums. JC painted in oils. His personal style was risky and intentionally offensive, while his official commissions were mostly high-class forgeries for middle-class homes. His body was small and muscular, and appeared ready to explode at any time. His best friend was a six-foot-five, 280 pound black man who specialized in delicate, miniature watercolors. JC was all black hair and eyebrows and wearing a hoodie. Alphonse was all big and bulked up. I walked between them in a black mini skirt, tights, and boots. I wore a magenta, cashmere scarf wrapped around my head and lower face against the cold. Not a one of the shady characters lounging back in the recessed doorways of the closed shops made a sound in our direction as we passed. I think of that scene sometimes and wonder if the shadow people were just wondering how much I cost. I must cost an arm and a leg with that kind of protection, eh?

Anyway, the TV was at the foot of a man's bed, the man was someone a hardened hoodlum wouldn't fuck with on a New York street, and I never, ever, figured out what *The Magician* was supposed to be about.

Better not call JC back right now. Stay focused. I was finishing up the laces on my shoes when the phone started to ring again. Ignore, ignore, and out the door before the answering machine picks up and I feel obligated to listen. I'm free.

On the track, I'm scoping out the situation before going through the gate. Hmmm, some of the same people, but mostly not. Good. A new little group of four, obvious athletes are warming up and stretching out at the straight end of the oval track, in the place where the sprinters begin and the hurdles are locked up. Military-looking guy, must be the coach, strolling around among the human shapes on the ground and talking to them. As I watch, they gather themselves up and take off at a smart clip into the first two lanes. I'll be staying away from them in lane three. The only reason I don't hug the fence in lane four is because I understand that walkers have rights, too. Okay, let's get this over with – just four lousy laps. Enter the track. Once again, I'm breathing hard before I've even finished lap one. I'm so slow that my heavy, high-ponytailed braid doesn't even fly behind me. It flops over the front of my right shoulder and stays there. I flick it back behind. The running team comes flying by in lane one and I admire their strides. The coach is running with them, talking as easily as if he were conversing over a martini at lunch. Up close I see that he is not an old soldier. His hair is buzzed and glinting gray, but it's obviously a premature gray because his face is unlined. Hmmm, he's not bad looking. This will be a better view than the little lacrosse boys' legs on the infield. They remind me of a bunch of muddle-headed storm troopers, and I can't see their faces anyway. Yes, I'll watch the pack of four for inspiration instead.

Great, now they are lapping me again and I've just begun my second lap. They are running like the wind. I try to pretend I am running like the wind, too, but my braid stays solidly between my shoulder blades, lightly patting me on the back as I shuffle along. I am not running like the wind. Maybe I am running *as* the wind, like the doldrums over the Atlantic Ocean, that is. I look over into lane four and a walker appears about to pass me. Maybe I should have sneaked into the university pool instead. A person could get lost in all that soothing, chlorine blue.

No, no, I really want to do this. I want to watch the world go by, and even as I think this thought, the five thoroughbreds in lane one slice diagonally across the track and fly out the gate onto the campus lawn. That's right, it's fall. It must be the cross country team and not a few members of the track team. I watch them disappear over a hill and trip a little on my own feet. My breath is coming pretty hard now. My legs are tired and sore from yesterday, and I'm just plodding along. I remember the word "*form*" only when my knees knock together and my feet skid on the ground. Energy slumping, optimism waning, shaking and sweating, but I'm done.

I stand upright against the depression sliding down from the sky and falling flat upon my shoulders as I walk home. No endorphins for me today. Guess I could call JC, but I'm so very tired. I think of the energy level it takes to keep up with him, and he will just have to go on hold.

Really, really down now. Oozing despair and drowning in weakness. Maybe I won't hit the track tomorrow. I'll do a little strength work instead with some old workout videos. Try to perk up.

# Mile Four

<u>The</u> <u>Morning</u> <u>Dread</u>. I wish I were dead. I wanna be dead. I wanna be dead.

Here is a general rule to follow: whenever the words "I wish I were dead" pop into your head, then you'd better just take the goddamn Xanax. Don't wait. "I wish I didn't exist," . . . along the same lines. Take the Xanax. "I wish I were asleep forever" or "I wish I were happy" can be worked around, I suppose. Yet another good thing about working with doctors and hospital people is that you can get almost any drug you need or want or feel like trying without too much hassle. You don't even need a prescription most of the time. The docs just have all this shit around. So I'd scored some Xanax from a GP friend of mine on the south side of the hospital, but I'd been afraid to try it for weeks. I was afraid until, in a moment of weakness, okay, in a moment of absolute panic, I popped one down and discovered its magical properties. It was like Jesus in a jar. I'm not saying it's any kind of happy pill or anything like that. Nothing works on me like other people swear it works on them. I'm immune to cures. I'm just saying it threw some water on the fire for awhile. It tapped on my brakes, but it didn't really make me feel any happier.

I'm a true believer in nature versus nurture. My mother used to follow me around in the night, wringing her hands when I couldn't sleep. I turned to her in the dark and said, "Go back to bed. It's not your fault," but parents never want to accept that. My mother couldn't accept the fact that I couldn't be fixed. I was just born this way. My Italian grandmother was depressed every minute of her life until her death at age 95, and my Slovak grandmother hanged herself in the attic, so there you have it. Mom kept trying though. She was a true believer too, in doctors and drugs. She and I share a good, strong, genetic trait of never giving up.

Yes, I've had a long and disastrous history of antidepressant use to go along with my parade of illustrious psychiatrists. I'll make this list even quicker: Prozac = suicidal mania, Zoloft = absolutely nothing, Wellbutrin = edgy eyes and upset stomach (but at least I stopped smoking), and Effexor = out-of-body experiences. The person I became during those out-of-body experiences got into a lot of trouble, but we don't need to go into that right now.

Prozac was my favorite. On Prozac, I felt like tearing at my hair and rending my clothes. If there had been any ashes around, I would have rubbed them all over my face and stuffed them into my mouth. I became downright biblical on Prozac, and as a result, ended up as a guest of the state for a few days.

The point is that I've never met an antidepressant that didn't end up leaving me worse off than before. Not one of them worked, but always, always along came that inborn, unavoidable, inevitable, and involuntary desperation that forced my starving synapses to seek relief, any kind of relief, anything that could make them shoot off a little longer.

The Morning Dread was coming on slower and slower these days since I stopped drinking a six-pack a night. It began around 4:00 in the morning now, instead of 1:00 or 2:00. I still woke up at 1:00, 2:00 and 3:00, but I was able to stay in bed with some peace in the knowledge that I didn't even have to think about facing the day yet. When 5:00 a.m. rolled around, the panic started creeping in, and I had to make a decision. To pill or not to pill? I couldn't be all tired first thing out of the gate, so often I'd take half a pill. That way I could get up and still make it to work on time.

If I take nothing, I lie in the dark in the quiet of a nothingness so profound it hurts. I listen to my chest pounding and my ears ringing. I listen for the first sounds of birds and traffic to cheer me up. I used to hate the birds, signaling me, mocking me, forcing me to get up and function for another day. I used to wish I had a sawed-off shotgun propped up beside my bed so that I could march outside and shoot the first chirper on sight. Watch its dead little body plop down to the ground at my feet with satisfaction, and then go back to bed. I used to hate the sounds of traffic for the same reason, but now I kind of liked the cars. The cacophony of the morning rush hour morphs into the shape of a machine in my brain. The machine starts a little spark. Then the rushing sound, the whooshing, the whistles, and the wind scour out a pathway in my foggy morning brain like a bottlebrush in a laboratory test tube. The sounds scrub open a tunnel, and I can get out.

After work, I rummage around my shelves until I find Tom Holland's *Total Ab Workout*. This is great. All I have to do is lie on the floor for half an hour or so, and I don't have to suit up or fix my hair or try to act normal while secretly gasping for air around other people at the track. I pop in the disc and roll my yoga mat onto the floor.

Tom appears on the screen and looks straight into my eyes and wants me to get started right away. He wants me to roll down slowly on my mat and relax that neck. Tom is breathing so low and heavy and steady I can practically feel his breath on my neck as he guides me through the exercises.

When I glance up at the screen, he is staring right back at me with smoldering eyes and a slightly wicked grin. His face feels like it is hovering right over mine. His voice is crooning, low and breathy, while his eyes continue to look up at me, or sideways at me, or down at me from whatever position he is holding. His eyes are glinting with suppressed gaiety, and he knows what I need.

He wants me to bring both knees over to the side and hooooooold. Gooooood. Then he wants me to flip over onto my stomach and hooooooold. Excelleeent. Almost there. Then he wants me to straighten my arms and legs and hold it, hold it, hold it, aaahhh. He wants me up on all fours, reaching and holding, and back onto my back, and goooood. Flip over onto my knees, push back into my hips and squeeeeeeze. I have to *work* those spinal erectors. Hips up, relax that neck, and now he wants me to finish up with a nice hard one. He's almost there, almost there, it's goooooood, excelleeeeeent; and, You. Are. Finished.

Jesusfuckingchrist, I'm calling JC right now. I am all sweaty and ready. Motherfucker never picks up the phone until he hears who it is. Pick up! Pick up, motherfucker!

"Where have you been?"

"I've been working late and going to the track actually. I've decided to start running again."

"Yeah, right."

JC is the most insanely jealous man I've ever met or seen or read about. He can take anything at all and turn it into evidence that I'm seeing someone else besides him. I put on mascara, I must be having an affair. I'm wearing a jeans jacket and sneakers to work, I must be having an affair. I'm wearing a skirt and boots to work, I must be having an affair. I can't come to the phone at work or I don't pick up on the first ring at home, I must be having an affair. Girlfriends, family, clients, or cousins, if I'm out anywhere without him, then I'm having an affair.

The best one was when I came back from shopping with a large, store shopping bag, but the bag wasn't entirely full of stuff. I must be having an affair. I still can't quite figure that one out. Did I buy a boatload of sexy clothes, and then quickly empty those clothes out of half the bag to hide them from him while leaving a few things in the bottom? I don't know. I still haven't figured out how the store's lack of smaller bags in stock can reveal that I'm having an affair.

"No, really. I'm tired of drinking all the time and never getting any sleep anyway. I think I'd like running. I used to run in high school. I've decided to go up to the university track a few times a week."

"Yeah, right. Who did you meet? Who told you to go up there?"

"Nobody! I just want to run. Do you want me to come over or not?" No time for small talk, my vagina is snapping like a downed electric wire.

"Yeah, come over."

Thank God.

# Mile Five

Sunday. Don't want to do anything. Just stay curled up in bed or lie straight and stare at the ceiling while I listen to my heart pounding blood. Listen to myself exhaling and count off the seconds in my head to keep my breathing regular. Three counts in, softly, three counts out, heavier.

Three in, three out. Feel the air rushing out on my chest. The birds outside are riotous, but I can't get up to shoot them. I lie like this for hours. I'm always through with any kind of actual sleep before 6:00 a.m. It's after 8:00 now. A cloudy Sunday. Get up to eat some breakfast and make some lists.

Number one on the list: stop picking holes in your skin. Stop picking at yourself, period. Surprisingly, I manage to mop the hardwood floor with some Murphy's oil soap later in the day.

Monday. Standard issue 6:00 a.m. panic attack. Started breathing to the rhythm of my heart hitting my ribs: in for two, out for two, pound two-three-four. Got it down to one slow breath in, pound two, deep breath out, pound two. Get to work. Do your job. You can wallow in your breath later.

Tuesday. 6:00 a.m. Chest tight, too agitated to count. Birds squawking and cars tooting on every scale outside like an orchestra warming up. I get up to get ready for work, but the effort is just too much and I fall back down. Curl up in a ball. Traffic sounds thinning out now. Bitch! Get up and get out the door.

Wednesday. The morning meditation, which is actually an attempt to avoid a full-scale panic attack before the crack of dawn was different today. My heart wasn't pounding, but my brain was. I breathed to the count of the pounding in my head. Then my ears started ringing. No birds. A fly started buzzing against the window and butting its head into the unreachable light over and over again in frustration. I know how you feel, buddy. I gave up trying to avoid the fact that it was morning and crawled across my bed to kill the fly. Couldn't catch him. Gave up again and got up for work. I've got to find a better purpose in life besides getting through the day. Then maybe I could stop fearing the morning. The Morning Dread. Go run.

Thursday. I wish I were dead. I wish I were asleep. I wish I could be asleep forever. I wish I didn't exist. I wish I existed in a world of sleep forever. I woke up at 4:00 a.m. and tossed and turned for hours with The Morning Dread. Then, when I was just too wide awake to stay in bed a moment longer, I got up and cried.

It's after work on Friday and I'm back at the track. As I approach the gate, I spy the cross country coach from the night before leaning over the chain link fence that surrounds the track with his forearms resting on top. He is right beside the gate door. Great. I don't want to pass him. I am unworthy to pass this dreamboat in the flesh and yes, sure enough, as I slow down my approach, I can see that he has light blue eyes and what have got to be dimple dents in his cheeks. He's not smiling. He is watching his quad of runners intently as they lope past in lane one, but I can tell he would have dimples if he smiled. I am standing still.

Get a move on, girl. You are not even present on this earth to this man. Like all of the other athletes at the track, he is not looking at you. You do not register. No one is looking at you, ever. Just waltz on by and choke on your mile and go home in disgust and, quick check, are my panties on my ass? Yes, now avert your eyes, shoulders back, chin up, you're at the track after all. Looking up I see that his pack of runners have exited the track at the lower gate, and he is already gone from his position at the upper entrance to join them as they float up above the earth over the campus.

Entering the track. I feel slightly energized after that silly little panic. I launch right off on lap one. I'm in a kind of haze. The overhead lights are bright in this dark fall evening, and they have that eerie, dissipating glow about them. The track seems shiny and new, despite the usual trash deposits and the grinding, sweaty slams of lacrosse bodies all around. I'm even faster than one or two people in the lanes.

Feeling okay. I am coming down the last stretch of lap one when the screaming sound of my name jars me out of my head. I look over to the stands and there are three little black boys, screaming my name and grinning with delight as they hop up and down on the bleachers. "Go Grace! Goooooo, Grace! Yeeeaaaggghhh, Grace!" they giggle and scream. What the fuck? Stay calm. I feel a lame grin overtake my face as I trod on by. They're still screaming. "Go, Grace! Go, Grace! Go, Grace!" Okay. What's going on? Do they belong to Mandala? Is she in charge of them for the evening, and exactly what kind of joke is she playing on me? She is a subtle joker. She watches everything in her quiet way, then sits back and sums up the world in one horrifyingly accurate sentence. Has she followed me from work to the track in order to quietly support me? Is she a closet athlete behind those five-inch heels?

No way. No athlete could possibly live in designer stilts every day and then run without ripping her shins apart at night. Plus, I bet she'd look perfect at the track, and there is no way I could be missing her glamorous presence nearby. She would be shining in Saucony, naughty in Nike, or all over in Adidas. She would gleam and beckon like the Statue of Liberty, calling all weary runners to rest upon her silvery spikes. She can't be here. Besides, she barely gives me the time of day at work. I'm boring. She gives and receives the stacks of marked-up proofs I deliver without removing her eyes from the computer screen. She is too cool for my school, and there is no way she is arranging some sort of sisterly support of me here, in the night, away from all mandatory professional courtesy. I don't have any other African-American friends downtown.

I have just about convinced myself that I imagined what I heard when I rounded up the stretch to begin lap two. The little boys abandon their bleacher games and fly up into the air again. "Go, Grace! Go, Grace!" I finally look behind me. There is a middle-aged lady behind me with a beautiful smile on her face, and her eyes are looking up to the boys in the stand with so much happiness it was infectious rather than painful, as it usually is when I see someone capable of smiling in such a way. She's dressed all crummy, just like me, in loose, faded, once-colorful cotton without logos or wicking technology.

"Is your name Grace?" I ask, over my shoulder. She smiles and nods at me without speaking. "Mine, too!" I shout through an answering grin. I finish my mile slowly, but easily, with my ersatz cheering squad at my back. On the walk home, the sadness sets in. Those beautiful babies will never be mine. I can't even take care of myself.

The phone is blinking as I trudge into the front room with the exposed radiator and the glorious, righteous Baltimore bay window crowned in stained glass flowers. There is even an angel to go with my window. She looms out from behind the potted plants on top of the window shelf where I sometimes sit, her pale pink gown in full flight with her banner waving an old Latin message and one wing broken off. JC found her in the alley trash of the church I live behind in my block. Yes, I live directly behind a Catholic church. I mean, directly behind a Catholic church. I could shoot the BB gun over the cans we stack up in the backyard and hit a real stained glass window. Freaky. He hauled her in one day with a piece of the missing wing in his other hand and said, "You're a sculptor, fix her."

My second floor back porch looks smack into the blank white stucco of the church's back side, and on Sundays all the upright, uptown Catholics go to church in their BMWs and netted hats. They park their shiny black cars, legally for the day, in front of the church. I have to look past my peeling paint, and my fire hazard of a back porch stairwell to see them. I look past the mountains of trash in the alley with the furry little shapes running back and forth. Past the drifting tide of the homeless and the misplaced as they make their daily treks up and down, north to south, and back again. We're all back here, right behind you silky blonde people, right here behind you, but you won't see us. That's okay. I have your discarded angel in my front window, where she is looking out for me. You threw her away. She didn't deserve that.

I hit the blinking red answering machine button. It's JC. I call him back.

"Come over."

"Okay, I just have to take a quick shower and I'll be right over."

"Why do you have to take a shower? Where have you been? With some salesman from work? You're always late from work these days. I'm not stupid."

"No, no, give me a break. I was at the track. I'll only be a few minutes." This was not an exaggeration. We lived in the same block. What I see in the back alley, he sees, and sometimes we sit on my tiny square of a back porch between the stairs and barbecue food on a miniscule hibachi grill and watch it all together.

"Yeah, right. So, who is it? That asshole from the hospital? One of your doctor friends?"

"I was at the track! Do you want me to come over or not?"

"Yeah, come over. I'm not stupid."

Yes, you are. But your hands are so warm and your brow is so dark and your hips are so lean and you are so very talented that I don't necessarily need any conversation right now. I just need a shower. Maybe I don't need a shower.

"I'll be right there."

JC has left the foyer door unlocked. I turn and lock it behind me and then hear him opening his apartment door as my boots knock up the wooden stairs. He stands back and watches me as I breeze through the front room and straight into the narrow kitchen. I'm holding my breath to avoid being fumigated by the turpentine, I tell myself. I'm really holding my breath against the tension in the air. I open the ancient fridge and grab two Busch Light cans from the fully stocked bottom shelf. He doesn't have much other food in there, just a half a loaf of bread, some kind of lunchmeat, a few eggs, and a million condiments. Both of the beers are for me, because I can tell by the look on his face that he's going to start an argument before we settle down on the bed in front of the TV for the night. I snap open the first beer and start chugging as the interrogation begins.

"Where have you been? Who are you working out with?" He is scowling and the air around me feels really heavy. I can see he's all pumped up and ready to go. My heart begins to speed up.

"I told you. I've been trying to get to the track on a regular basis and – "

"Yeah, I bet you have. With who?"

"I'm telling you. With nobody. I just feel like I want to run and – "

"Bullshit! Who told you to meet him there? Who are you meeting there?" JC is pushing me up against the counter with his mere presence, without touching me at all. I've almost got the first beer down, and I need the feel of the alcohol in my veins to brace myself for our regular ritual of greeting each other with a fight.

"I'm not meeting anyone at the track."

"Since when do you run?" First beer down. Now I can slow up and think a little with the second one.

"I told you, I used to run in high school and I tried jogging some in college. I just feel like I'm not in shape at all. I want to get in better shape."

"For who?"

"For myself. I've been very depressed lately. Exercise is supposed to help with that, you know, improve your mood."

"Who are you getting in shape for?" His scowl is so black it's ridiculous.

"Fuck this shit, I'm out of here." I can drink alone. He grabs me around the waist as I start to move past him towards the front and pushes me back, lightly, against the counter.

"Who are you getting in shape for? Just answer me."

"I told you! For myself, asshole! You'd better get over it damn quick, because I don't intend to stop. I want to run! Get off me!" He's pressing me so close to the counter that my back is starting to hurt against the edge.

"Are you trying to hook up with some other runners there?"

"I'm trying to hook up with a whole boat load of sailors who just docked under the stands. Get away, I'm leaving." He steps back and positions himself squarely in the doorframe to the front room so that I cannot pass.

"*What?!*" I scream at him, and turn to go into the bedroom. I know the neighbors in this building just love us. And how does he always do that? How does he make me hysterical and screaming when I didn't do anything wrong? Then he turns my hysteria into an admission of guilt. He's going to move in for the kill now, but no. He opens the fridge and grabs a beer for himself and follows me into the bedroom. He's calm now that he's gotten me all upset. It always works that way. It's like he feeds off of it. The crazier he can force me to get, the happier he becomes. It feeds into his personal power trip. How do I keep handing him this food? Why can't I stand strong? Why can't I walk away? What the hell has happened to The Womb?

"How about I go to the track with you?" he says slyly.

"Whatever. Who cares? Come along. Why didn't you fix the bed?" Sounds like maybe he's done for awhile. The Womb is even smaller than ever. The headboard and baseboard of his hideous, dark wood missionary bed are stacked up against the wall behind the mattress on the floor. The sides and slats are in a pile on the floor by the stereo shelves. There is barely anyplace to put my feet down to step around anywhere. Scooting sideways past a chair with a broken arm beside the broken door to the teeny bathroom shower stall, I plop down on the mattress on the floor. I'm looking up at him. He's looking down at me from the broken doorframe to the bedroom, and his face is relaxed now.

He's diffused. He doesn't want me to leave. His expression is still intent, but his anger is no longer pulsing out into the room. Well, maybe just a little. He's always angry, but there isn't any room for anger in here. There isn't any room for anything other than whatever can be done on a mattress.

"We split the wood on the sideboard at the bottom there." He's pointing to the lower left front of the mattress. "I have to glue it and brace it over the weekend. I might have to get some new wood." I look over to the side slats on the other side of the mattress and see that one of them is cracked and split halfway down its length. The old T-shirts we use to tie each other up with are still hanging off its end. JC sees me looking at the T-shirts and smiles.

"How about I go to the track with you next time?"

"Sure, sure," I answer with a concerted, casual air as I take inventory around the room. The arm of the chair is broken and hanging down to the floor from a screw at the back. We broke that when my thighs were slung over each side. We broke the door frame when I was bracing myself against it as he took me from behind. The door to the shower stall is long gone. JC has towels thrown down in front of the cheap metal stall to sop up the water when he takes a shower.

"You know, you're never going to get any of your security deposit back."

"I'll fix everything." He's beside me now on the floor and he's sucking on the back of my neck and picking at my top. He's so warm. His body is like a furnace in the night. I'm always so cold. He's pulling me backward. Well, at least he's good for something.

I woke up in the middle of the night with JC, and I was tense. Exhausted and tense at the same time. Last night I was so upset, and then we were making love. He was badgering me and then holding me and then sleeping so soundly beside me.

He's snoring away, not a care in the world. I felt like a ping-pong match was going on in my head. It felt like my body was trembling, just waiting to explode, but when I looked down at my body, it was still. I was screaming inside. I felt like I was really going crazy. The top of my head was spinning. My scalp flew off like a little boy's propeller cap, spewing primary colors into the sky -- shut yourself off. Shut it off right now. I can't shut it off. I think I'm really going insane.

I had decided to go running whenever the craziness set in, but you can't go running at 3:00 in the morning. Do something. Do something. I can't handle the depression. I slunk out of bed and walked very slowly and softly to the refrigerator. I eased open the door and pulled out a beer. I muffled the sound of the tab snapping open with a washcloth on the counter and quietly chugged it down. I eased back into bed and started thinking. JC hadn't moved a muscle.

Okay, so you can't always run when the sadness starts sucking you down, and you can't always sleep. You can't always drink, because the poison will kill your every dream. Shut yourself off for a minute. Empty your mind. Empty yourself out. This won't work. There's nothing in there. I can't feel anything.

I can't feel myself.

I'm not here.


Sunday morning and I'm walking back to my apartment after spending almost the entire weekend at JC's, drinking, walking around town to get more supplies, and staying holed up in his room with the TV on, day and night. How does that man fall asleep in that stuffy, small space with the constant buzzing sounds and the darkness all around? It's like a tomb, instead of a womb, and sometimes I feel like I am being buried alive in there. Now I'm alone again, and ashamed that it's always the same: the rocking of my body and the dropping of my head. The acid words I remember muttering or shouting from the night before, causing me to hate myself. The pain that courses through my body with its screaming blood, and my desire to moan and not exist. I just don't want to be here. I don't want to be me. I want to be asleep all the time and not be me. I can't deal with anything. I dread every morning, every day. My blood is screaming.

Back in my place, I'm sloppy and hungover and looking at my wreck of a space. Shaky, sick, and smelly, I force myself to drink a few cups of water to anchor my swollen brain. I drink the last two Bud Lights in my fridge in an effort to equalize my outraged body. I drink more water and fix some breakfast. Exist today. Stretch and hold yourself together and try to exist. Go on now.

I force down some breakfast in small bites between pacing back and forth. Shivering and stalking about, I'm already thinking about going out and buying more booze. No, no, no, you have a full day of pretending ahead of you tomorrow at work. I have to edit and scan and proof and talk on the phone with confidence in my voice. I have to convince people that I know better, and that everything is going to be all right. The clients aren't usually very hard to handle. They want to be convinced. It's the marketing people who are downright crazy. I actually *do* know better than them most of the time. This is a scary, yet hopeful, thought; that I know how to do something better than somebody else. That is just too sad and weird, but the thought makes me feel just a tiny bit better, for a moment anyway.

The day is worsening. I ate some veggie bacon and bread with cheese, and it only increased my nausea. I leave all the dishes in the sink and go lie down. Head and chest throbbing. Shakes setting in heavier. Better not eat any lunch. Maybe get out the door for a run. It's cold outside, but the sun is shining and you're wasting the day. Run away the craziness. I'm fighting with my feelings now because I can feel that I'm going to demolish another day.

The afternoon is drifting away. Try to get up and clean the kitchen. I stay in bed and try to read a little. I'm almost halfway through the day. I can start counting the hours until it is night and I can try to sleep again. It doesn't look like I'm going for a run, and the realization brings me fully awake and my inner jangling becomes extreme. On a scale of 1 to 10, I give my scream factor a 9.5, only because I haven't actually screamed yet. Calm factor is zero. Desire for nothingness is a 6, with hate and dejection both coming in at a solid 10. I know I am wasting the day, but I've still got to get through it. Exist onward. Know that you will definitely run tomorrow.

It's 4:00 p.m. now, and I'm not going to make it. I can feel my nerve endings snapping and burning inside my head. I can actually feel my synapses misfiring. Anxiety and despair are topping off too high. I suck. Why am I always this way? Why can't I just stop?

It's Sunday, and the liquor stores are closed, so I have to walk up to the pub and buy beer for two dollars extra at the packaged goods store. Back on my bed, I pop open the first can and take stock:
I drank through the last wedding I attended and was in pain all the next day. I drank through the last birthday party I attended and had the same result. The last baseball game, the last art show, and the last Friday after work.

The holidays are coming up. Will I drink through Thanksgiving and Christmas and New Year's? When is the last time I had a good time with the beer? I can't remember, and yet I persist in my misery. Have I ever had a good time out drinking beer? I must have, but sitting here thinking hard, I can only recall a couple of times offhand. There must have been more, maybe. And yet this is how I plunge onward. Can I really be so stupid as to die this way?

It's 6:30 now, and I'm halfway through the beer. I am testy, and still rocking a bit on the bed with a book lying open and unread on my lap. The alcohol is not working in any way, shape, or form. Not at all. Better suffer through the rest of the evening without drinking any more beer. It isn't working anyway. Scream factor is still high. Calm down. Make some dinner. It will be time for you to go to sleep soon, and you can dream about running tomorrow. A bad run is better than no run at all, and you can always dream that it will be a good run.

# Mile Six

At work on Monday morning, I can already hear the two ladies upstairs talking as I shut the front door. No smell of cologne. I peek down the basement stairs, but it's pitch black down there and it is obvious that Helen isn't in yet. On the second floor, I pass the empty executive rooms, drop my stuff in front of the main computer, and proceed around the room, booting up all the equipment. As everything starts humming awake, I drag myself upstairs to the third floor.

"Good morning, girls. How was your . . . " I see that they are both already on the phone, so I shut up and sit down to wait. Sandy hangs up first.

"Motherfucker. It's Monday morning and that cocksucker can't even let me take a piss before calling about his pages." She rolls her chair back; hitches up her baggy sweats under her oversized, faded, striped men's sweater; and shuffles out the door to the bathroom.

Sandy is sleeping with an artist, like me. He is older, like my guy, and he constantly berates her for her lack of talent. Throughout these tirades, she seems utterly immune, unlike me. He is trained as a graphic designer as well, so he can really get into some specific detail about her supposed shortcomings as an artist.

When he's hanging around the studio on days when we have to work late, I feel like smacking him sometimes. He just sits there in the corner, and criticizes her every movement every chance he gets. Her face shows no reaction. She just keeps working. He's not even in a real graphic design firm. He works in a lousy sign shop. I bet he just can't stand it that her print work is so much more substantial than his, but I don't have any room to talk. Lucky for me, JC is a painter. I'm not even sure he knows how to turn on a computer. His criticism of me as an artist lacks a lot of technical knowledge. He still thinks that you cut and paste copy on a drawing board with an exacto and some red film.

I look over at Mandala, who glances briefly back in my direction while continuing to talk softly on the phone. She is wearing a slick, shiny black, patent leather bolero over a furry purple shell. Her miniskirt is flat black leather and covered in brilliant silver zippers. Her long legs, in purple tights, disappear into equally shiny, black patent leather platform shoes with zippers that match the ones on her skirt. Both of her wrists are covered in a good three inches of bracelets, and one of the rings on her left hand is so huge that she has to tap at her keyboard with her middle finger straight because she can't bend her knuckle.

Her hair is a triumph of Baltimore, tall and braided into a dozen different coiled sections, all piled on top of each other. This, along with her shoes, makes her look about six feet tall, even while sitting down. Somebody should snap her picture, or something.

Mandala never talks about who she is dating, and no one ever shows up at the door to pick her up. We know she is seeing someone, because sometimes we overhear snippets of her phone conversations about a certain guy. Sandy probably knows who she's dating, but I'm way too intimidated by her absolutely, always perfect appearance to ask her any personal questions. Finally she hangs up the phone and looks over at me.

"Mandala, do you have any friends or relatives who are into running? Like, running up at the track at the university?"

"No, why?"

"Nothing, I just saw someone that made me think of you the other day." She shakes her head briefly and dismisses me as her eyes go back to her screen. I head down to the basement, where I can hear that Helen has finally arrived. She is stowing away her helmet and jacket as I enter the main room.

"Hey! How was your weekend?" she asks as she turns to see me.

"Okay, I guess. Did you go out on Friday night? Sorry I bailed on you. I'm too broke to buy beers out this week. I just hung out with JC all weekend." I see her face fall a little.

"Are you okay?"

"Yeah, I'm okay, just a quiet weekend. What did you do?"

"Oh my God, you're not going to believe this. Well, you know those guys in the suits we keep seeing go in and out of that rowhouse across the street? The guys that look like businessmen or something? Well, you know I had to work late getting some prints up to the hospital Friday night, right? After you guys left, I ran to the corner store to get something to drink, and I was coming back up the street when I saw that one guy who always has his jacket off and his tie undone going into his place too. He stopped and asked me what all of us girls were doing over here. I told him we were wondering the same thing about them! Turns out they're an accounting firm, totally boring stuff.

Anyway, we started talking, and he asked if I wanted to go out for a drink. I told him I had to finish up some work, so he came over here with me." I already knew the rest of the story. Helen got married right out of college, and filed for divorce a few months ago. Ever since she moved out of her house, she's been humping everybody in sight. I know she's doing at least one doctor up at the hospital, a newspaper reporter, any guy she feels like picking up in a bar, and now the guy across the street. She's rattling on.

"We did it in front of the light table right here, and then we went out and I stayed over at his place. I shouldn't have done it with a guy who works right across the street, right? Now I have to see him every day, and I'm not even sure I like him. Plus we didn't use anything and his place didn't look very clean. Now I'm freaking out that maybe I caught something. I'm going to call someone I know in a clinic at the hospital and get some tests done. I think I'd better do that now. I don't really know that guy from the bar last week either. I don't even have his number. I'm really freaking out here. I think I may have caught something. Will you walk to the hospital with me?"

"Sure, sure." My turn to walk her to the hospital. I wonder if there are any decent guys in this entire city and why is it that none of us can find them?

Helen and I made up a work-related excuse to be at the hospital all afternoon. I left her with her confidante in the HIV clinic, went straight home, and changed into my sweats. I got to the track earlier than usual, so the overhead lights weren't on yet. There was no lacrosse team in the middle, and only a couple of other runners on the track. This is cool. I like this.

I start running, thinking about my last weekend all the while. My pace picks up and stays steady. I don't want to be around JC anymore. It's always destructive. It's not making me happy. He doesn't even love me. I start dwelling on the insults and the suspicion and the force of his presence. Before I realize it, I've completed several laps and I feel like I might even run more than one mile.

I hate drinking. It doesn't taste good anymore. I'm not having any fun. I start thinking about the hangovers and the hopelessness and the wasted sunshine. I finish a mile and am surprised to realize that I can go on.

I'm thinking about death and destruction. I am running to avoid thinking of ways to murder JC and get away with it. Euphoria isn't waiting for me at the end of this run. Visions of sugarplums are not dancing in my head. I'm having visions of violence instead. Anger is fueling me, and it is doing a mighty fine job. I'm going to leave some blood on this track, but it won't be virtuous blood. I keep going, and going, until I have to stop to walk in the last lap of a two mile run. That's okay. I still covered two miles on the track. I just caught myself smiling. Wow.

I'm on fire. I am practically marathon material. Now that I can run two miles, the possibilities are opening up. I don't know the university campus very well, but I know there's a road that cuts down around behind it from the bottom corner of the block where the stadium sits. A road full of trees. There are no parks nearby unless you count Wyman Park Dell, which is a frightening arena of unleashed dogs during the day and a thriving drug den at night.

I get in my car, sacrificing a primo parking spot as I pull away to figure out where that road goes. Left turn after the track, hmmm, it's rather winding and beautiful. It's also pretty deserted for a school road. I can see something down a hill on the right. What is it? A part of the university? It's something about outer space research, says a sign I can't finish reading as I drive by. I wonder where I am headed. I see a busy cross street coming up. Holy cow -- it's 29th Street. This street runs right in front of the art museum and would end up dumping me right out on my block. This is awesome. Now I've just got to loop around again and measure the mileage. I reset my odometer to zero at the top corner of the stadium block and start driving the course again. It is just under two miles at the spot where I would peel off to go home. What if I drove north, back up the block to the corner where I started measuring . . . yes! It is two miles exactly. So, if I get bored on the track or the track is too crowded or the lacrosse balls are whizzing by like torpedoes, then I can try out this very scenic, though still slightly scary, new course. It will be too dark to try it out at night. I'll have to wait for a weekend. Now I've just got to drive around for 20 more minutes to find a decent parking space.

As I drive around in circles, yes, more going in circles, I try to think through my options logically. I really can't give that course a go on a weekday evening. Even if there was lots of traffic, with headlights and people in their cars, there would still be long stretches without sidewalks, and several hidden turns where a car could zoom around push me off the road. If I want to run on the weekend, then I'll have to forego partying with JC and Helen on either Friday or Saturday night.

Helen won't mind. She never minds. Her dance card is so full these days that she doesn't even ask me what I'm doing after work anymore. JC will be a different story. He'll never buy that I don't want to go out on a Friday night.

I like the track more and more. The weather is getting colder, and the lacrosse boys aren't there anymore. Maybe they have some sort of restriction on practice time during the off-season. The runners aren't always there either. Cross country season must also be over. The semester will end next month, and all the wide blocks of the university campus seem to be simmering down in preparation for winter and the holidays. The track is wide open and lit up like a flood zone.

I finally get to run on the inside lanes. I'm not struggling as much or bored anymore. I'm not bored because I have created "The Atomic Theory of Running."

Now that I could run more than eight laps, staying stuck on the track was becoming a little monotonous. Let's face it. It's not as bad as an indoor treadmill, but unless I could relax enough to zone out and fade away into a semi-trance, then I was just counting the circles, and I was getting really sick of that. If I got into a really good groove and spaced out, then I ran the risk of forgetting where I was with my lap count. It can happen. Then the run that was supposed to release my tension and turn me into someone else becomes both monotonous and annoying. I want to know how far I've run, and this requires remembering the number of laps.

The solution came to me in a dream. With a little imagination and an open attitude with regard to actual facts; I decided to transform my surroundings to accommodate my captivity. Instead of driving an hour or so out of town just to find a new park or some woods, I came up with "The Atomic Theory of Running." College chemistry came in handy after all. Anyway, it goes like this:

My journey begins after work, as the rush hour heats up and the sun is going down. The university track is shielded from the road by a cement wall of bleachers that cause the sounds of traffic, construction, breathing, and birds to blend into one warm, low humming note that fills my ears and sets the scene.

Now I am not merely a runner on a boring old track. I am, instead, a perfectly formed piece of the universe and an instrumental particle of all that exists around me.

I am an electron.

The playing field in the center of the track is the nucleus, and the four lanes represent quantum levels, or shells. I start out in quantum level one. After each lap I become "excited" and jump a quantum level until I reach quantum level four, when the power of the nucleus pulls me back in toward the core where I begin my orbit once again in the ground state. This is an excellent way to keep track of mileage as well. One series of quantum level jumps equals one mile.

Wavelengths of light flow from my flopping hair strands as I fall in toward the nucleus. My energy level swells as I prepare to jump again. Sometimes another runner will be in my path, or I hear one overtaking me from behind. These powerful cosmic rays force me to evacuate my shell prematurely and leap to the next quantum level. This is okay. It is simply the nature of the scientific world. When I've finished my orbits for the day I am, naturally, in quantum level (lane) four. I break away from the hold of the nucleus by colliding with yet another cosmic ray, and spiral out into the campus portion of my run in a spectacular nuclear reaction.

I am a neutron now, but not for long. The long, winding finale of campus curves will deliver me into my final state. I entered the atomic field as a negatively charged subatomic particle, and have left it a positively charged ion. I am well.

My stress and anger or fatigue and worry have all melted away, and my mind is free to imagine that all of the good things in life will come true. My dreams are formed and my heart is full.

I love running, wherever I may land, even if it's in the middle of a 5:00 traffic jam.

One morning at work, I climbed the stairs to greet the ladies on the third floor as usual and sat down for a spell. I was in a rare, good morning mood, and still a little high from my run the previous night. In a moment of absent-minded excitement, I explained to Sandy and Mandala about "The Atomic Theory of Running," and how it works to make a run more enjoyable. They both stopped working and turned to look at me like I was crazy. Not "Oh, isn't she cute" kind of crazy, but seriously, certifiably crazy.

Note to self:  don't ever tell anyone what is really going on inside your head.

# Mile Seven

Thanksgiving weekend came and went without trauma. I didn't feel like drinking much, so I didn't have a hangover. This may be because I was shamed into sobriety on Thanksgiving morning.

I woke up in JC's bed, and the TV was on as usual. JC had gotten up before me. I focused my bleary eyes on the set and saw a morning news segment with a bunch of runners out in the streets at 7:30 a.m. Some of the runners were even dressed up like turkeys. They were all smiling and jumping about like it was the greatest idea in the whole wide world to get up at the crack of dawn on a holiday made for gluttony and run a 5K instead. I'm thinking, "You've got to be kidding," in the direction of the set, but I'm mostly ashamed to admit that I was too scared to sign up for any of the running events around town. I don't know why. I know I can manage the distance of a 5K by now, but all the crowds and the fuss are intimidating. I'm getting used to owning the track and half the campus these days. I liked being alone.

Anyway, I had to get up and get over to my aunt's house for the feast, and I still had a dish to prepare before driving for an hour due south toward Washington, D.C. I had to shower and dress up and pack the car with food. I had to check the map and leave plenty of time for the drive. I wanted to get there early and hang out with my cousins for awhile. I had a million excuses, but no real reason why I couldn't run a few miles on Thanksgiving morning if I really wanted to.

I was too chicken to run a turkey trot. How great is that?

Christmas wasn't so bad either. There is never enough money for presents, so I go to the grocery store every year and buy about a hundred dollars worth of baking ingredients and give out homemade treats instead. I have everyone covered and I get pretty fancy too: Yugoslavian nut horns and kolacky for the Slovaks on my mother's side of the family; biscotti, Italian knots, and chocolate totos for my father's side. I buy cheap baskets and brightly colored tins from the Dollar Store and fill them with the cookies along with some cheese and Boston brown breads.

The freezer in my dinky kitchen doesn't work. It won't even freeze ice cubes all the way, so I have to set aside every available minute in the week before my mother's annual Christmas party to do all the baking since nothing can be frozen in advance. The system has been honed down to perfection over the years.

Start with the biscotti, because who can tell if biscotti has gone stale anyway? The next night, the Boston breads are boiling for hours on the stove while the cheese breads are in the oven. Totos and knots can dry out for a day or two, but the nut horns and the kolacky have got to be fresh, so I save them for the last day before the party. Slovaks must be a bunch of masochists because all of their desserts are such a pain in the ass to make. Who the hell makes cookie dough with yeast? By the time I finish rolling out a hundred tiny triangles of dough into sugar for filling and rolling and baking, my lower back is aching like an old lady's from leaning over the rolling pin. All of the fillings need to be ground and prepared from scratch, too. Martha Stewart and my grandma could have been besties. Nah, I think the Italians have much more fun with dessert. I can sit around and roll chocolate balls for hours with my stereo playing, and making biscotti is so much easier than it looks. La Dolce Vita!

Oh, yeah, my family never leaves town over the holidays. I totally lied about that in my email to Cal. It was weird and strangely exciting, though, to think of him just a few miles away in our old neighborhood while I was hanging out with my multitude of cousins again for yet another family party. It was almost tempting to pop over to his house on some fabricated pretense. Not really, no, it was just a thought.


Christmas is the one time of year that JC drives out to visit his own family. Normally he has no contact with either of his parents or his many brothers and sisters. He tunes up his '65 Mustang fastback for the trip. Usually he doesn't drive it anywhere, he just keeps borrowing my car when necessary. He pays money to use another person's garage a few blocks away so that the cops will stop towing his precious baby to the impound lot on Pulaski Highway every month. The car is never illegally parked. It just sits around in one place for too long I guess. JC swears the cops keep trying to steal it, so he ended up hiding it. I know that JC loves his Mustang more than he'll ever love me, because he has nightmares about losing it all the time. He only has dirty dreams about me, and treats me like an easily replaceable commodity.

The car rarely runs well, if it runs at all. On our very first date, before we both moved to the city, he called me to ask me out and then, after I said yes, he asked me if I could drive, because his car needed some work. He allowed me to tip at the Mexican restaurant we went to as well. I should have known right then and there that this relationship was never going to go very well. He asks me out, asks me to drive, and allows me to tip. Brilliant.

Then I moved into Charles Village to be closer to my friends and work, and suddenly he finds a place in the same block within a couple of months. How could this not clue me in even more? His beauty and his talent and his confidence were blinding me. These traits appeared exotic enough to lure me in, but his nasty side came out quickly once we ended up almost living together. The façade of sincerity crumbled quickly once he had me in his clutches. He saw my heart fall into his hand and his whole personality changed.

On one of those first nights we were in bed, holding each other, all alight because we were living downtown, working as artists, and falling in love. Suddenly he heaved a heavy sigh.

"What is it?" I asked.

"We have to talk about something. I've had problems with this in the past and I know how it goes. I don't think you should hang out with your male friends anymore. It always leads to problems in a relationship. I don't think we can have a relationship unless you get rid of all your male friends," he pronounced with finality. This came totally out of the blue. JC had never made any sort of comment about any of my friends before.

"What do you mean? Half of my friends are male. I have a lot of them. Half of the population of the world is male, how is that supposed to work?" As a matter of fact, my previous apartment situation involved two male roommates who were very old friends of mine with no love interests involved whatsoever. JC knew all about it, and had never even made a lascivious joke. I remember, my two friends used to gripe when we all went out for drinks in one car. They said I was ruining their prospects for the night, because the single girls always assumed that I was with one or the other of them. I was instructed to step away when told, and go hang out with the leftover one. I was a wing woman, and we all had a great time together. I still talked to both of them a lot and JC knew this, too.

"It doesn't work. I trusted my last girlfriend with her male friend. Time went by and she ended up sleeping with him, and it happened before, with another girlfriend, and I know that it just doesn't work. We're not going to make it if you keep hanging out with your male friends."

"I'm not your other girlfriends." I was getting a little pissed. "And it's not my fault your other women cheated on you. I've had male friends all my life. I never hung out with just a crowd of girls. What am I supposed to do? Call them up and say I can't see them anymore?"

Turns out this is exactly what he expected me to do, and foolishly, I did it. JC had a great habit of hitting me over the head with this kind of crap right after we'd made love. He knew how to hit when his prey was most vulnerable. He could easily kick a man when he was down. He was pretty rough during the actual lovemaking, too. The finger bruises all over my thighs were sometimes embarrassing in the summer when they could be seen from under my shorts. Of course, all of these bruises were my own fault for being so damn sexy. If I weren't so damn sexy then he wouldn't get so carried away and hold me so tightly. Foolishly, I believed this, too.

I'll never forget the surprise and concern in my favorite ex-roommate's voice over the phone when I called to cancel our next night out, and all future nights out forever.

"Are you serious? Can't you see that this is totally wrong and really messed up? You can't be serious. Is he really serious? Can't you see that this is dangerous?" At this point I almost started crying because I could feel the pain in his voice pouring out over the phone line. I could feel the fear, too.

"Yes, I know it sounds fucked up, but I'm in love with him and I want to make it work. I'm sorry. It's what he wants." Long pause.

"This isn't right. This is wrong. I don't think you should do this. Do you really want to do this?"

"Yes, I'm sorry, I need to do this for now. It's what I want." Another long pause.

"Okay, if it's really what you want," he sneered skeptically. Then his voice softened up. "Be careful. Take care of yourself."

"I will, thanks for understanding." There was another pause, and we both hung up. JC smiled curtly from the sofa where he was watching me make the call. It didn't matter in the long run. Next I couldn't hang out with my girlfriends either because they were all a bunch of nymphomaniac, cheating sluts who would have a bad influence on me because I had no mind or character of my own. Then it was my family because they all disliked him and they were misguided liars who would try to tear us apart with their tricks and schemes. It was my bosses and my clients and the people I looked at on the street. It was vendors and mailmen and store clerks. I couldn't be trusted to do anything right or go anywhere without him. I scrambled constantly to deny my faults and reassure him of my devotion. It's amazing to me now, how stupid I was.

On New Year's Eve we decided not to go to a mutual friend's annual party in a room that she rented at the Belvedere Hotel. The year before, it had taken us over two hours to get a cab to pick us up and take us down. Technically, the Belvedere is within walking distance, but not in the dead of winter, at night, with heels on. Then we couldn't get a ride back until nearly dawn, and we were so wiped out for the rest of the day that we couldn't remember if we'd had a good time or not.

This New Year's, I became aware of the day at about 9:00 or 10:00 in the morning. I felt a queer sense of being awake, while convinced that I should still be asleep. My edges felt sharp, but at the same time, my insides felt blurry. I was a piece of neon pop art, with a black-edged contour, and an impressionistic painting inside.

JC and I had shared champagne and beer in front of the New York City telecasts the night before, and watched the actual fireworks over the Inner Harbor during commercials. We could see the fireworks downtown from the third floor landing of JC's fire escape.

I felt surreal and sharp as I awoke, despite my tired and confused gastrointestinal tract. Was I keen or was I dreaming? Was I tired or was I wide awake? We had eaten a boatload of junk food during our private celebration on the mattress and the rooftop. Caviar and crackers, cheese and wine, beer and chips and popcorn and whatever else struck our fancy. Surely I wasn't in any condition to go for a run on New Year's Day, but that was precisely what I was thinking. I couldn't get it out of my head. I knew the city would be deserted, at least on the north end, where we lived. I knew I would have the whole campus to myself, and it was dry and there wasn't any snow on the ground.

I rolled over onto my back with my forearms over my head, and thought about my new shoes. Ahhh, yes, I had gotten new shoes for Christmas and some other very fine gear from my family. My mother took me out to the sports store and bought me a pair of Saucony Hurricanes on sale for about eighty dollars. They were last year's model, and eighty dollars was the sale price. I kid you not. My old shoes were Saucony Shadows, and I loved them and cherished them like they were little brown puppy dogs. I had never gone out explicitly to buy a running shoe before, and I'd bought my Shadows just because they were on sale somewhere for only forty bucks. This price was still high for me, but they turned out to be worth every penny. I wore them for about a year before I even got onto this idea of being a runner. They were an ugly brown, the previous year's leftover color on top of leftover model number, but so damn comfortable I could swear I was running on a trampoline when I first got them. I couldn't believe it. I put them on and the shoes just started walking around the store all by themselves, dragging my body along like an afterthought. They fit my foot perfectly, and at the time I had never even heard of the brand before, I was just looking in the clearance corner as usual. They were like magic when I slipped them on. I was Cinderella.

Make no mistake about it, I had tried to be hip and wear some other big brand name shoes in the past. Those other shoes were heavenly and fairytale unreal at first too, but the heaviness of my bone structure or the lack of dedication in my footfall seemed to squash them down out of the clouds in just a couple of months. My first pair of Sauconys didn't give up on me like that. They were still holding onto my soul a whole year later, but now that I was determined to be a real runner, I felt that I deserved some new shoes. I let my mother buy them for me for Christmas like we real grown-up, dead-broke runners do.

Now, here's how it goes with my mom: she never does get over the fact that I'm not worth as much as she thinks I am. From shrinks to shoes, my mother will scrape every penny from every pocket of every coat she owns, and then volunteer for some overtime to spend more money on me. We were in the sports store. I was eyeing up the Hurricanes just because I was already in love with my Shadows, and I was guessing by the price tag that these Hurricanes were even better, if that was even possible. My showing interest in an item of clothing is all the incentive my mother needs to throw some more money at me. She asked the salesgirl to go look for my size, while brushing off my frown at the price tag in a brisk and authoritative fashion like I'm the fool in the room. She hates that I shop in thrift stores, and always look like a leftover flower child. I tried on those Hurricanes and I was transported to Mars. It's impossible to describe, honest to God. I put on those shoes and they just took off running for me.

My younger brother gave me a hoodie with his school logo emblazoned across the chest, and it's so thick I believe I could run around Alaska in it. I imagine it makes me look like I belong on the university track. My older brother bought me a set of three pound hand weights, because I was astonished to discover that I couldn't do a single regular push-up. I'm embarrassed to admit that the three pound weights felt heavy to me. They were all rushing in to support my new fitness kick, because that's what they always did; support whatever notion came into my head. They were the exact opposite of JC.

I went back to thinking about my new shoes, untried and jittering like Mexican jumping beans in their crisp, new, tissue-filled box at home.

On impulse, I bolted up to go for a run before JC was awake enough to bully me out of it.

# Mile Eight

There is no such thing as punishment to a runner.

Last night, I stuffed my face like I was at an all-you-can-eat Chinese buffet. Ah, well, maybe I will run later this week and salvage myself, I thought. I will run hard and good. I will force myself to have a "good" run as reparation for this indulgence.

I left JC with a kiss on his sleepy cheek and a promise to return very soon. I changed clothes quickly in my apartment, and ran straightaway to the university campus in that half-baked, glazed-over, semi-zone-out phase I find myself in quite often when I'm running. It's a miracle that I take the right steps and slow down to stop at stoplights at the intersections. It's the same sixth sense that navigates and keeps me from colliding into parking meters and road signs when I run.

I took off on a carb-packed, glucose-encrusted flight that was nothing akin to punishment. It was easy! My spine was straight and my head was high. My feet didn't fumble on the terrain and I had a smile on my face. Maybe overindulgence is worth it once in a while. I flew, and found myself gracefully extending my arms out to my sides like the princess, newly transformed into a swan in *Swan Lake*.

I thanked God for the speckled light between the tops of the trees, and the sparkling darts of sunlight that pierced me as I ran through the backwoods of San Martin Drive. I do honor You, I said to the Creator. I honor You with my body, whether I'm hurdling down a grassy slope or dribbling chocolate down my chin. I said, "Thank you, God" out loud. Thank you for giving me this morning, these legs, these lungs, and this run.

I think this is how runners pray.

The next day. I'll never understand it. Why I wake up every morning with a serving of depression. Here's your morning serving of depression, Ms. Doe, like a scoop of ice cream in a perfect parfait dish set in front of me by the butler on a tray as my eyes open for the day. The dread hits my chest and I don't want to get up and eat it. I don't want to be awake. Then the anxiety kicks in, and I have to get up or go crazy. Nothing needs to be going wrong. Nothing bad has to have happened. I don't have to be worrying about money or anything, it's just there, waiting for me, every morning.

Sunday. No sleep the night before. Seems like none at all. Only dreams, interrupted by getting up every two hours to pee. If I were drinking, I would wake up rocking and crying. Instead I just jiggled around and then got up to pace the floors. I could see the sadness in my face in the bathroom mirror as I passed the door. I could see it from the other room, even without my glasses on. Such a rotten night, I felt the tears rising up. I thought, what the fuck, I'll go out and run three miles, and I did. My knees started aching in the cold in mile three. Let it go. Let it all go.

Monday. Really down. Lying in bed, not wanting to get up as usual, and going through my options. I don't want to get up and face the day. I don't want to drink, take drugs, or see a shrink. I feel no hope or inspiration or joy. I want to hear nothing. I want to do nothing. I don't like being awake. I need to get to work. Try to exercise after work, because you are polluted. You are a toxic drainpipe painted over with some environmentally friendly, washable, colored paints. The next rainfall will wash away the bright exterior and expose the rusty old pipe that you really are. Get in the shower now. You've been in the same clothes for three days.

As soon as I entered the front hallway at work, I could hear Helen rumbling around downstairs in a frenetic fashion. This was odd, because we didn't have any major projects going on that I knew of. Most of our big clients had shot their wads with presentations and final reports before Christmas. January is generally a slow time of the year for graphic design. The big organizations all go crazy clearing their desks and spending the remaining budget money for the year before the holidays, and then they all need to regroup and come up with a new sales pitch over the winter. I smelled a man's cologne, but the entire building was silent as a tomb, except for the sound of Helen slamming drawers and moving things around. The whole 2600 block was dead as I walked to work. The whole city was dead quiet in the first week of January. I wondered what was up, and went straight down to the basement without stopping upstairs first to drop off my coat or boot up the room. Helen was white as a sheet and looked panicky.

"What's going on?" I exclaimed, startled by the sight of her pale face and distressed walking.

"I've got to get out of this place! I've got to get out of here now! I just want to quit!" and she stalked past me into the black tube and disappeared into the darkroom. I dropped everything on the floor as the cylinder door rolled around and jumped in to follow her. She was sitting crouched against the wall on the floor, and it looked like she was crying. I slid down the wall next to her.

"What the hell is going on? What happened?" I whispered urgently. The darkroom was two floors below the owners' offices upstairs, but for some reason I felt like I had to whisper.

"I got caught over the weekend. I was down here with Dr. Greene last night when Richard came in the front door. He heard us down here. I sneaked Dr. Greene out after I heard him go upstairs, but he just came down here this morning and gave me this big lecture on my professional duties and our relationship with the hospital and shit. I just want to quit, I hate it here! I need to find another job." Helen was crying softly.

"Don't quit! Jesus, we need you here. Richard knows that." Richard was secretly attracted to Helen. He was secretly attracted to all of us, and young womanhood in general, hence the lack of male artists in the company. Plus, men cost more.

"I can't quit now without another job. My divorce isn't final yet and I don't want to have to move in with my folks. I need to find another job first."

"We all need to find another job. But what's the big freaking deal? What do you mean he 'caught' you? We do late-night, last-minute shit for the doctors all the time. What's the big deal?"

"Richard hates Dr. Greene, you know that! He's always hated him, and how he jerks us around last minute all the time, then takes forever to pay the bills." Richard hated all of our boyfriends, too. So what? He fancied himself as the protector of his little harem, and he never really crossed any lines. No harm, no foul. Out loud I said, "No, I didn't know he hated Dr. Greene, and all of the doctors jerk us around. It's how their schedules work." The truth was slowly dawning on me, but I didn't want to suggest anything that would get

Helen even more upset. Dr. Greene was good looking, and had a rather sleazy reputation. He was known as a heavy flirt, and I also knew, from Helen, that he was thinking about a divorce from his wife and children at the same time she was going through her own divorce.

JC and I had run into them at the university pub more than once, late on a Friday night, but I just figured they were both working late together, and finishing up for the week with a quick dinner. JC disliked them because he knew they were both still married and to him, they were obviously having an affair. I worked with them both, which was a very bad influence on me, according to JC. I was sure to turn into an adulterous lunatic just by being around them. Since JC thinks that everybody is cheating on everybody else all the time, I totally brushed him off. Now the signals were coming in more clearly, but why wouldn't Helen have already told me if she was having an affair with Dr. Greene? I mean, Jesus, she told me all the gory details about her other conquests, and hadn't I just held her hand up to the HIV clinic a few weeks ago?

What's funny is that I always kind of wondered why Dr. Greene had never said anything even remotely inappropriate to me in light of his lecherous reputation. Sandy had said he made a bit of a pass at her during a project last year, and I'd overheard some stories from some nurses, but he barely looked me in the face when he had work for me, and he didn't smile at me either. It was almost insulting. Apparently the guy would hit on anything in a skirt *except* me. I rationalized that the hospital gossip was rampant and exaggerated as usual, but now I was thinking that he knew I was a close friend of Helen's, and that was the reason he was so careful around me. I probed a little more.

"What exactly did Richard hear? Did he come downstairs and see you two? How did he know it was Dr. Greene and not somebody else?"

"He knows his voice. We were laughing loud and we had some beers out on the counter and he came down after he heard us. They just shook hands and then he went upstairs and closed his office door and we left."

The buzzer on Helen's wall phone went off with an outside call. She looked at it sullenly and didn't move. I got up to answer, but she brushed up behind me and grabbed the handset over my shoulder. She started talking in a businesslike manner to whoever was on the other end, so I mouthed, "I'll be back" while pointing at the floor in case she didn't get it, and rolled myself out of the room.

I took the front stairway to my office so that I didn't have to pass Richard's room. The other owner, Preston, was the one with even heavier aftershave. He had an office door facing mine, but he wasn't in yet. He did most of the sales and footwork and was usually in his car. Even though he was Richard's partner, the business was Richard's baby and it was Richard who sat in his office worrying over the bills everyday, and how to keep our paychecks as small as possible. No overtime was allowed unless it was absolutely necessary to please a client. Otherwise, the atmosphere of a sweatshop during regular working hours was preferred.

I draped my coat over a chair and began the ritual dance of turning on the room. Then I tiptoed to the third floor, where I could hear Mandala shuffling softly around, to see if she knew anything more about the current crisis. Sandy was in North Carolina, presumably drinking and cussing away some vacation time with her southern belle friends. Good thing, because I really didn't want to hear her take on the situation just yet.

Mandala was organizing the flat files during her down time, and the shuffling sounds I heard were the heavy grades of paper being restacked between the drawers. She looked up as I entered. Her eyes were stony and her mouth was stern, but when she saw me her eyes softened up and she smiled slightly.

"You look nice," she said.

"What?" I replied in surprise. I looked down at myself. I was wearing my favorite short, black cowboy boots with diamond patterned black hose, and a long, black cotton tulip skirt. My sweater was a cream, black, and gold ski style. I wore medium-sized, thin gold hoops in my ears and my blonde, streaked hair was all blowsy out of my ponytail. The cropped bottom of the sweater swung wide over the snug skirt and made me look quite slim and shapely.

"Thanks! You look perfect as usual." Perfectly outrageous that is, in a shiny orange pantsuit worthy of a Paris runway. Every accessory she wore was the exact same shade of burnt orange. How the hell did she do that?

"You've been looking good lately," she said. Leave it to Mandala to notice an inner difference in me. None of the clothes I was wearing that day were new. The months of struggling to become a track junkie must be showing somehow, but I didn't have time to dwell on that right now. I walked into the room and took Sandy's seat behind the door. I pushed the door a little more shut and blurted it right out:

"Do you know what the hell happened here last night? Helen is downstairs crying and threatening to quit. I can feel the ice pouring out from Richard's office, can't you?" Mandala pursed her mouth and her eyes went hard again.

"Rick came in last night to go over some paperwork and heard her downstairs with Greene. He went down and caught them right on the floor." She rolled her eyes a little, like, what else can you expect from Helen? Mandala and Helen didn't get along very well. She talked less to Helen than she did to me, and seemed to disapprove of her more than she did the rest of us. She wasn't in Helen's confidence like I was, but she seemed to know everything there was to know about her anyway, just like she did with everyone.

"What do you mean on the floor? Making out?" Mandala just looked at me. "You mean fucking?" She nodded,

"He caught them right in the act."

"Holy *shit!* His floor! Did he tell you this?"

"Yeah, he walked away, but he wanted to fire her this morning. He got over it, because we have too much photography work in here and he'll need to find someone else first. He hates Greene, but we get a lot of business from him." She kept working as she talked.

"Hoooly shiiit. I better get downstairs and get to work. I better not slip up and let JC hear about any of this." I saw her smile knowingly as I rushed downstairs. She knew all about JC's evil self too, without being told. She didn't know any historic facts or world news or mathematic methods, but she knew how to divine the heart and soul of a person on sight. She was as illustrious as the sun and as open as the moon. She was one scary, smoky witch, but my fear of her was beginning to fade. I found myself admiring her tremendously, the more I hung around her.

The other salesman never showed up. The phones didn't ring. The three of us kept quietly to our rooms and left as swiftly as possible, one minute after 5:00, leaving Richard alone behind his closed door.

This will blow over, I thought as I walked home. I cringed as I imagined the scene in the basement, ugh! I don't know how this will blow over, but it has to. Richard and Helen go back a long time. She interned under him when he was the Communications Manager at the hospital, and he brought her back to us when we moved to North Calvert Street. We had all been together too long. Eeewww. I accidentally envisioned the scene in the basement again.

"Hey, you!" My head jerked up. JC was yelling at me from his front porch. I was so distracted that I had walked right past him without noticing. He walked down the front path to meet me.

"Where are you going? Why are you all dressed up?"

"I'm not dressed up, you've seen this outfit before. I'm just going home, work was busy." I could see him scrutinizing my face, checking my eyes to see if I was wearing mascara.

"Let's go get something to eat."

"I can't go out to eat today. I don't have enough money."

"Let's go to the market and get something to make here."

"Okay."

We walked the couple of blocks to the gourmet market and picked out a package of sushi and a can of Wye River crab soup. I grabbed a couple of other things I needed in the aisles, and we headed for the register.

"I've only got a twenty on me," he said. "How are you going to know what you owe me?"

"I'll pay for my stuff separately and just give you half of that."

"You won't get the change right. Add that stuff you're holding up in your head first," he told me, "so you won't make a mistake at the register."

"For chrissakes, I know how to count my change."

"No you don't, you're always getting ripped off. You just don't know it."

"Oh, for crying out loud, just pay for the stuff and I'll pay you back as soon as we get home."

"Here, give it all to me and I'll do it. You'll mess it up." At this point he was pulling my groceries out of my arms and we were next in line for the cashier. I let him because I didn't want to make a scene, but I was seething. I was so sick of this shit. I was sick of him treating me like a complete and total moron. According to JC, I was unable to: successfully negotiate a grocery transaction (I let the cashier rip me off on change and I always missed the sale items), put away dishes in the cupboards (wrong order, stacking, and rows), vacuum (I bump into the furniture and clog up the hoses), dice a tomato (too big or too small), season anything (never enough hot sauce), do the laundry (my loads are unbalanced and I waste so much soap), wash anything made of glass (I put too much pressure on the rag and I'll break it), select a CD to play (I'll knock the whole stack over), turn anything on or off (I'm not careful enough and I'll damage the switch), throw trash away (I'm wasting food), give anyone advice (he talks right over my words and berates my intelligence in front of them), dust anything (obviously I'll break stuff), or merely walk around his apartment (I'll walk into things and ruin them).

That last one is controversial. I did bump into things a lot. My mother must have hexed me with my name. That's okay, JC had plenty of new ones for me. I am a: mental midget, nitwit, McSimple, diseased face, moron, liar, douche bag, and total incompetent. As we walked back to his place, he explained to me exactly what I owed him and why, and I was so furious I handed over the money without adding it up for myself, just as he accuses me of doing. I did not want to fight tonight. I was still upset over the day, and worried that Helen might bail. On top of losing Helen, I'd be stuck in the darkroom for hours on end until a new photographer was found and trained. The other girls couldn't even do a basic film run, and there was no way Mandala was going to learn how to mix up a bucket of chemicals with twenty circlets of gold hanging off of each wrist. It will all blow over, I told myself again. In the meantime, tonight, do not let on that anything is wrong and do not fight.

We went inside, heated up the soup, and started eating on the bed in front of the news. There was no other space to sit, except for the broken chair. The only tables JC had were in the studio up front, covered with supplies and paintings in progress. When we were finished, JC took the empty containers and bowls into the kitchen and piled them up on the counter. The kitchen trash was already full and the place smelled like stale beer cans. He smashed and collected our empties in a sticky pile in the kitchen corner, between the wall and the stove, to load up in lawn bags and take to the recycling center for a few bucks. We would fill up the entire back seat and trunk area of my dented, red compact car, and the effort only bought us the price of another case of cheap beer. The smell stayed in my car for days, and it wasn't worth living with the smell, but every penny was a keeper to JC. I called him cheap and stingy, but he was proud of his miserly ways. He started bringing in the sushi containers and empty crab soup can to throw in the wastebasket on the floor near the mattress.

"No way," I hollered. "There's no way I'm going to smell that all night, or worse, tomorrow morning on top of all those rotten beer cans you keep saving."

"Then you'd better take the trash out." He saw me getting ready to protest and added, "I saw a mouse running around in here the other day, too. It walked right across the kitchen and stopped to look at me sitting in here. It wasn't even scared." He chuckled. Things like rats and mice and stink and dirty sheets didn't seem to bother him. He wasn't even manipulating me when he said so, but he knew I'd eventually snap and scrub out his greasy sink or moldy shower or refrigerator shelves, covered with congealed sauce drippings, because accumulating crud bothered me a lot. He told me I was just spinning wheels and wasting time when I housecleaned. Why make a bed when it was just going to get messed up again that night? He never set any mousetraps either. He told me that Buddhism had taught him that all the mice in his apartment deserved to live. He did hunt down and kill a rat in his front room with the BB gun once. I guess Buddha drew the line at rats, or else JC drew the line at rats eating his food. He'd gotten up one night and called me out of the bedroom. "Look at this!" I went into the kitchen and saw a big hole chewed out of a bread bag on the counter and crumbs were everywhere, sprinkled with big black turds the size of raisins. Another hole was eaten out of a banana sitting next to it, and you could see the big front teeth marks on the peel and inside on the fruit.

"Ahhhhhh" I yelped and started hopping up and down from foot to foot like Mr. Rat was underneath me at that very minute. JC will let all the bugs and vermin live in his place as long as they don't mess with his stuff. I knew he counted all his bread slices and eggs and slices of cheese to ration out for his lunches at work. He was pissed this time. This was no little mouse. He pulled out the mangled bread slices, sealed the bag back up and stuck all the food on the counter into the refrigerator, including the spice jars. Then he started examining the floorboards behind all the shelves of supplies in the studio, and found the hole in the front left corner of the room.

"Look at this," he said again, softly this time. I stepped rigidly toward him and peered into the corner. There was a big hole in the floor, just like in a cartoon, except this hole was surrounded with chunks of plaster, crumbs, and rat shit. Some of his paper drawings stacked nearby had the ends chewed off in strips. I knew he was mad now. His mouth went totally smooth and his expression was blank, but his eyes were radiating danger. It was that same look that kept homeless people and criminals away. He walked to another corner of the room and unsheathed his fancy BB gun. The gun looked like a real rifle, and sometimes JC would sit on his back porch with the gun across his knees as he drank his beer, just to send a message out to the homeless regulars in the alley.

"Are you kidding me?! You're going to hunt a rat down inside your studio?!"

"Yeah, I'll get him." I had no doubt. "And then I'll close off that hole."

I ran back into the bedroom and hopped up onto the bed, still on its frame at the time, and started keeping watch around the room.

"You can go to sleep," he called. "It won't come in there where there isn't any food."

Yeah, right. I turned the TV down low, but kept it on so that the room was still visible in the dark. I heard JC pacing softly, and then heard him sit down on the lumpy couch to keep watch. He was going to restore that lovely rosewood couch one day, just like I was supposed to restore my angel. We both had broken antiques all over the place. We were classy hoarders.

Sure enough, in less than 30 minutes, I heard shots fired and frantic animal claws scraping over the hardwood floor. My heart rate went up and I leapt to my feet.

"I got him." His voice was completely calm. I ran into the front room and hid behind his back, my eyes darting around the room.

"Where is it?"

"It ran behind that stack of canvases over there. I think it's still alive." He sauntered over to the large, shoulder-high stack of stretched canvases and leaned his cheek into the wall to peer down at the floor behind them.

"Yeah, it's still alive." He raised the rifle.

"Jesus!" I screamed and ran back into the bedroom. The sight of him taking aim with the rifle almost made me run screaming right out the front door and safely home to my own apartment.

Afterward, he followed me into the room. He rolled his eyes and shook his head at me, crying on the bed, like I was the crazier one of us two.

"Okay, I shot him, now you have to bag him and take him out." He was serious. He went back up front to start repairing the hole in the floor. I briefly thought about bagging the rat. You know, since I was a tough chick, city girl, and all that, but I started getting hysterical and weepy every time I approached the body with a bag in my hand. I don't know why. It didn't make sense. I saw plenty of live and dead rats all around every day, but I just couldn't bring myself to bag that pathetic, hunted down, murder victim in the front room. Why hadn't JC just blocked off the hole in the first place and skipped the whole, creepy horror film hunt? On the third day, the smell was finally too much, and JC took a shovel and scooped up the body and took it out himself. He didn't get too mad at me.

JC's comment about a new mouse in the house did the trick. I'd seen some droppings in the kitchen and knew he wasn't making it up. Now that the mattress wasn't even elevated from the floor, I envisioned the welcome little mouse guest silently pattering in the bedroom, peeking into my face as I fitfully slept, and maybe even tickling my nose with its whiskers as it checked me out. I hopped up without whining and proceeded to tie up the trash bags around the room.

As I stepped out onto the fire escape, JC called out, "Leave the back door open." I knew he was just making sure that he could hear me if I screamed, so he could come and rescue me if necessary. Gee, he really cares. I clomped down the stairs and across the little back lawn to unbolt the door to the alley. I left the alley door open, too, and stepped outside. I was about to drop the bags onto the pile on my left when I thought I noticed something strange.

The landlord had assigned three metal trash cans to each rowhouse he owned on the block. Painting the numbers of the house on the cans did not keep them from getting stolen, so he came up with the bright idea to chain the cans to the back gate instead, effectively preventing them from being lifted by the sanitation crew. The cans could never be hoisted up to be emptied, and so a mountain of trash was always beside the outside gate. They couldn't even pull the garbage bags out of the cans to throw them in the truck, because the homeless people ripped open all the bags looking for something to eat. The trash ended up strewn all across the alley. Sometimes the workers were able to skim a few, closed bags off the top, but most of the time I was looking for a stable, flat area on the trash mountain to pile up more bags without everything toppling over.

I couldn't find a flat spot. My eyes were adjusting to the night. I saw that the three cans had been pushed into a tight triangle with some two by fours and long metal rods arranged on top of them like a teepee. At the top of the teepee, carefully stretched out and perfectly positioned across the rods, was a pair of dark, lacy panties. The setup was a shrine, paying homage to the panties displayed overhead, beckoning the lusty, filthy, alley men to come and worship at this altar of the unattainable. My eyes became sharper, and I saw that the panties were a dark, midnight blue bikini crowned with a thick band of black lace and a little black bow on the front, right over the crotch. The panties were a perfect match to a blue and black lacey bra that I owned, with a little black bow sewn right between my breasts. The panties were mine, of course. Again.

I dropped my garbage bags to my feet with a gasp and took a step backward. Looking down at the bags, I saw a magazine lying open on the ground in front of the cans. Bending down to get a closer look, I saw a porno spread of a naked woman with huge, hanging breasts getting taken from behind by a heavily muscled man, both of them with their mouths open and their heads thrown back in ecstasy.

I totally freaked out. I shoved the garbage bags over the pages of the magazine and jumped up to unhook my underwear from the top of the poles. Looking around me in a sudden burst of fear, I saw no one and rushed into the yard to bolt the alley door behind me. Still looking over my shoulder, I almost killed myself racing up the stairs and ran breathlessly back into the bedroom to confront JC.

"Why are my panties in the alley?!" I screeched. "They were in the alley set up over the trash like a flag with a dirty magazine spread out in front of them! Did you throw my panties away?" I was in shock, thinking about some rapist stalking my movements from the alley behind JC's place, then sneaking into the apartment and stealing my panties as a warning that he was closing in on me. Then I remembered that no one could sneak up on JC.

"Oh my God. What are they doing out there?" I screeched on. JC's blank face broke into a leering grin. He started shaking with laughter and couldn't answer for a minute, but he was pointing to the wastebasket that always sat on the floor on his side of the bed. He breathed in deeply and answered, "They must have fallen off the bed and into that trash can when the bed was still on the frame. One of us bagged them up without noticing they had fallen in." His eyes were all alight with merriment, like this was the funniest fucking thing he had ever seen. "Then the homeless guys picked them out and had some fun." He was almost choking while trying to talk and laugh at the same time. His laughter was calming me down. I looked at the soiled panties hanging from my fingertip. They were stiff and crummy with white paste all over them.

"What the hell is all over them?" At this, JC doubled over and started slapping at his knees to gain some measure of control. I figured it out.

"Ahhh" I exploded. I ran into the kitchen and dropped them into a fresh trash bag. Then I stuffed that bag into an empty can and stuffed the can into two more trash bags and then stuffed that mess into an empty rice box and then buried the whole thing in the dirty tissues in the can in the bathroom. I was scrubbing my hands while JC continued howling.

"Holy shit," he gasped. "Fun times in the alley! All the homeless men are passing your panties around to jerk off in. What are you doing? Why don't you just wash them?"

"Are you *crazy?*" He thought about it for a second and then let it go.

"What was in the magazine?" I described the centerfold to him. "You should have brought the magazine in."

"Go and get it," I returned hotly, but I was starting to laugh now myself. That does it, I was thinking. First thing tomorrow, I'm going to bury that matching bra in the same way I did the pants. It's uncomfortable and itchy anyway. Then, no more sexy underwear. I am not having any luck with sexy underwear. It's expensive and useless and the gods are sending me some kind of sign. I'm going to drive out to Kmart or Sears and buy some Jockeys. I am never going into Macy's lingerie department again. Besides, Jockeys are cute and they suit my personality better. JC will never notice. All he wants to do is rip them off of me anyway.

Sexy lingerie is plaguing me. My life with inappropriate underwear is over as of right now.

# Mile Nine

Tuesday. I should have been left behind the caravan.

Seriously, in ancient times, I would have been left behind the caravan. I am the embodiment of hopeless, endless depression. I am not an asset to the common good. I am a useless, dead weight, sucking the life force from the tribe.

The moment my eyes and brain register that I am conscious, and that any chance of sleep is gone, my inner voice kicks into its mantra: I need to be dead, I need to be asleep, I need to be dead, I need to be asleep. My father would have raised his broadsword and taken care of that problem without further ado. My grim-faced mother would have carried me to the edge of the cliff herself. I would simply have been thrown away, left behind on the side of a dusty road while the caravan moved on. I am not a part of creation. I am a waste of a ration of bread. I am not a credit to my family. I don't know how to be alive. Evolution was supposed to have weeded me out.

I'm just so bad at life. I suck at it. I can't handle any emotion correctly, and I wince over the memories of every effort I've expended while trying to do so. I can't take another antidepressant, I'll end up locked away for sure. I've got to get up and get on with pretending. Get up. Shut it off, shut yourself off. Get to work and make some money, because no one is going to waste a skein of silk or twenty goats on you.

It was a frigid day outside on this winter morning, but that didn't bother me as long as I was inside my sauna of an apartment. For whatever reason, the subdivision of the old rowhouse caused my apartment to register nearly 90 degrees in January. I felt sorry for whoever might be living in an icebox on another floor, but I was very glad that the heat was included in the rent. I walked around my place in the evenings in a tank top, and if I had to wear makeup anywhere, I packed it in my purse and got to the venue early enough to apply it in a public bathroom before the event. Otherwise it would all melt off of my face before I even left my building.

On workdays, I set out my many layers of mostly black clothing the previous evening on the couch beside my front door, with my coat hanging on a hat rack behind it. I would roll out of bed, take a quick shower, and stroll around in my underwear until I had everything I needed together before I walked toward the front door, still half naked. If my hair needed washing, I always washed it the night before and let it air dry. There could be no running of a hot hair dryer in the Baltimore jungle that was my apartment. In front of the door, literally smack in front of the door, I would dress as quickly as possible and get myself out into the cold. At least the rowhouse at work was evenly heated.

Even more comical than my winter work exit strategy was my return from work routine. I would tear off my coat as I climbed the stairs, and strip so quickly the minute my door clicked shut behind me that Wonder Woman herself would have been impressed.

At work, things were still solemn and quiet. Helen stayed downstairs. The bosses, Preston and Rick, stayed tucked away in the back office most of the day, murmuring, whispering, and occasionally laughing softly. Sandy was still away, but due back before the end of the week. I actually had some proofs that I needed to get out for review, so I decided to keep to myself and get my work done, and get the hell out of there and get into a run, despite the freezing weather. I didn't care, I just wanted to get out of there and run. I would prove to myself that I was worthy of somebody's caravan somewhere. I felt a burning need to run in the cold today. My legs were itching to get at it.

Mandala came down briefly to eat her lunch with me. She told me that the boys in the back were writing up an ad for an intern-slash-assistant photographer to help Helen out with her workload. It was true, Helen had the steadiest and heaviest workload in our place, due to that fact that the majority of the doctors at the hospital were so old fashioned. They wanted black and white photos for their files, and then they just pinned or taped them up on the walls behind them during their lectures. That's why I was considered such a graphics guru to the specialists who were sending their presentations my way.

I was just phenomenal! As competitive as doctors are, the more they saw of the attention their colleagues were getting from my posters and slide presentations, the more they wanted it for themselves. Helen still did the bulk of the hospital work though, and had needed an assistant for some time.

I cleared up my desk, hit "send" on everything I could on the computer, packaged up the hard copy proofs for Rick to drop off on his daily trip past the hospital, and trotted swiftly home to do the superhero change in front of my door again.

I love running. It's weird to me that I found I loved running in the winter as much as I did in the fall. I had almost talked myself out of my October decision to become a long distance runner and save my soul, all future souls, and the balance of the universe for all eternity, because I figured I would just knock it off and be dead by February anyway. Luckily, my desperation knew no bounds that fateful day, and here I was, sans tech gear and looking more like the Michelin Man than an athlete as I took off for the track and its environs.

Layers piled on, a woolen headband wrapped around my head, Ivy League hoodie, Kleenex up my sleeve and snot already on the outside of it, I start out just as the sun is going down, leaving its pink and purple streaks along the horizon and I feel all right. I am enclosed and alone, and yet I feel safe. The evening is cold and quiet, and I make sure to run near enough to the road so that I can throw myself into an oncoming car versus being abducted into an empty Charles Street rowhouse if need be. You need to keep your wits about you downtown, no matter what magical thing you are doing.

After a couple of miles on the track, I decide to peel off into my campus loop even though it's probably pretty dark out there by now. There are so many headlights rolling by, and surprisingly so many runners on the track in this weather, that I believe it will be safe enough.

I take off in my positively charged state. I round the bottom corner of my loop and see pitch blackness before me. I feel something though, I feel surrounded by similar positive charges, and I confidently decide to keep going. I see shadows moving toward me and shadows moving on the opposite side of the wooded road. The shadows define themselves into the shapes of other runners, and we share the peace together as we pass and nod or smile with our lips pressed together against the cold. Some shadows stay enclosed, and that's all right too. I actually feel sweat forming beneath my armpits. Without fear of ice or injury, I pick up the pace a little. Okay, okay, to be honest I'm a little scared too, it really is pretty dark out here with plenty of places to get dragged into the woods, never to be seen again, and I'm only about halfway around the lower loop.

I'm getting near the end now, and my breathing slows down to a regular rhythm. There's a short patch of ground just before the parking garage that is always soft and downhill to boot. In the fall, it was thick and green with grass and surrounded by flowers. Now it is smooth and smells of the trees and air around it. This stretch of the run is called Nirvana. After I pass through Nirvana, I am safe amid the city lights again. I turn left and head down Art Museum Drive. I love running down this road most of all, with Wyman Park falling down to the right and the towering Ionic columns of the BMA overlooking me on the left. The columns are a cool blue-gray in the last evening light, and I feel as if I'm in another world. I'm in another century. I'm somebody else; someone startling or significant or pretty. I am not myself at all, and it feels good.

My heart is in a place of purity as I walk down the block to my apartment, when I look up to see JC standing on the porch. He looks like all the mass murderers I have just successfully avoided, and my heart seizes up a bit. His brow is black and thunderous.

"Where the hell have you been?"

"I've been running, obviously," I say weakly with my sweaty, snotty, sweatshirted arms held out to him in appeal.

"Bullshit! It's freezing out here! Who were you with?"

"Oh for God's sake, come inside before we both freeze. You can yell at me upstairs while we figure out some dinner."

JC is fuming behind me as my frozen fingers fumble with the key in the vestibule. My perfect karma is evaporating up the hallway stairs as we climb to my door. I can tell that the rest of the night is already ruined with the accusations that will drag on for hours along with the tired, repetitive excuses and explanations and the endless, endless fighting. I felt so very tired as soon as I saw his face standing there, waiting for me on my front porch. I had felt so electrified when I was walking down the block just a second before.

I have got to get rid of this asshole.

Once we're inside, I start wriggling out of my sweaty layers. My sweatshirt is only mildly damp, but the two shirts I'm wearing underneath are pretty soaked. My socks are disgusting. I don't think I'm looking very sexy, but you never know with JC. If I walk past him in any state of undress he usually grabs me, but he's not looking at me struggling with my clothing as he continues to harangue me to the walls and the ceiling.

"Are you absolutely nuts? Do you really expect me to believe you were running in this weather? It's like 38 degrees outside, and it's already dark after work. What kind of idiot douche bag runs around the city at night with ice and slush everywhere? Are you *trying* to get kidnapped? Oh ho! Some pervert would have some fun with you, you fucking simpleton!"

At this point I feel the need to stick up for my city a bit. It's true, in the months since I began running alone in my quest for inner peace, I have been naturally nervous and wary at various times of the day, but there are always so many cars around my area. If there aren't enough cars around, say, on a Saturday morning, I'm just a little more nervous because, even though it's daylight, I'm not sure a city dweller would respond to a scream as swiftly as a stranger in a passing car.

For example, one morning the previous summer, I was taking a big bag of trash down the back stairs when an alley cat darted out from under the first floor landing. Like lightening, the first floor tenant's dog pounced and caught the cat in its teeth. It started shaking the mangy gray bundle vigorously back and forth in its jaws while I started screaming bloody murder.

"*No!*" I screamed. "*No, no, no! Oh my God, no!*" The dog must have stopped to take a breath or something because the next thing I saw was the cat streaking over the fence into the neighboring yard and the dog, whom I knew quite well, was looking at me happily as if I had just popped down to give him a biscuit and a hug. That dog loved me. The irresponsible college brats on the first floor kept the poor guy outside all day in the awful heat, and I would often hear him whimpering and scratching at himself like crazy. I don't know if it's against the law to groom another person's dog, but I felt so sorry for the beast that sometimes I sneaked under their porch with an old hairbrush and brushed him.

I didn't feel sorry for him right then. I was horrified and scarred by what I had just seen. I had dropped the garbage bag again, I do that a lot. My hands were on my head, pulling at my hair in crazed distress as I started looking around for the reinforcements my screaming was sure to have called up.

There was no one in sight. The summer air hung heavy, wet, and quiet as it always does in Baltimore. There were dozens of windows open in back of the houses on my block, trying to catch the nonexistent whiff of a summer breeze.

So there you have it. A young woman screaming "No! No!" at the top of her lungs in the middle of the day with windows open all over the place did not even bring a face to a window. However, in all my years living downtown, I had never been robbed, accosted, or even verbally abused on the streets. Well, I got a couple of "mmm, mmms" if my skirt was short or an occasional beep from a car going by. One time a runner passed me from behind and murmured, "Nice ass" in a very polite way as he overtook me with ease, but nothing really creepy like what goes on in the suburbs.

In the nice quiet and safe suburb that my parents moved us to when I was about 9, I had some nasty little bits happen to me. I was riding my bicycle home from a friend's house for dinner one night when a man pulled over to the side of the road in front of me and walked around his car as if to open his trunk. I didn't think anything about it. I was only 10, and shows about serial killers weren't rampant on TV yet. I rode right on past. The guy gets back in his car, pulls around in front of me again, and strolls back toward his trunk. This time I can see that his pants are open and he is fondling himself in front of me. I rode up onto the sidewalk and cut across a neighbor's lawn to get home and tell my mom what had just happened. The next thing I know, the police are at the house trying to get me to describe the man while I bear-hugged the big, new Raggedy Ann doll I had just gotten for my birthday. Just think. I was only an arm's length away from being thrown into that trunk and living famously forever on the side of a milk carton.

Another time, I was taking a jog around the perfectly positioned mailboxes and tidy lawns of my neighborhood because I had foolishly allowed my best friend Melanie talk me into trying out for the junior varsity track team. A man pulls up slowly beside me as I'm plodding along and asks if I would like to join him for a drink.

"I'm trying to run here," I responded with irritation. What a jerk. He sped up and drove away as I realized that what I should have been more concerned about than an interrupted workout was the fact that I was only 13.

Next up, the pompous and preppy local high school. I can't even count how many times my girlfriends and I got flashed by masturbating men and penises from cars parked on the roads we used to walk home on after school.

We always fled squealing and giggling like the innocent little fools that we were. Looking back on it though, I can only come up with ewww, gross.

The winner for the all-time grossest comment ever thrown at me from a strange man happened during my senior year in college. I was bicycling into Towson from my parents' home. I always hated driving, and luckily there was a designated bike lane that covered almost half of the eight mile trip from the house to the university I was attending.

I was flying downhill on Charles Street, thinking about an upcoming test, when a trucker called out calmly from his window with an audible intake of air, "I'd sure like to smell that seat!" It was a warm day. I still cringe when I remember the low, measured, threatening sound of his voice. Involuntary reflex caused me to glance over and look into his face. It was radiating evil. I braked until the truck was forced to move ahead. Honestly, no one in downtown Baltimore had ever treated me with such a total lack of manners.

The worst thing that continually happened in the city was that my car kept getting hit when I wasn't even driving it. Other drivers kept banging it and denting it and smashing up against the bumpers while trying to parallel park. I was parked, facing west on 29th Street, when it got into a three-car pileup all by itself. JC hammered out the dents for me and tied down the trunk with some rope. Meanwhile, I kept collecting the insurance payouts instead of taking the car to a garage to get it fixed. I made a lot of money on that car. It was a mess to behold, but it ran like a clock. Needless to say, no one ever bothered smashing in my windows looking for something to steal. My car was bona fide city-proof.

I digress. Back to the scene at hand. I was finally naked, but still completely wet and starting to chill. JC became silent. I brushed off his tirade, walked away, and stepped into the shower. JC squeezed in behind me. That shower stall was full of dents, as well. It's too small for one person much less two. Some of the dents are from my elbows banging the sides while my arms are up above my head trying to wash my hair. Most of the dents are from the two of us just plain banging. He put his arms around me from behind and rested his face on the top of my head. His hands were touching me tenderly, for once.

"Don't go to the track in this weather, in the dark like this. Please don't do this again, or get me to come with you." He didn't call me any more names. He was pressing against me, holding me tighter.

"Okay," I said. I knew he was right. I'd find some more workout tapes to use with my weights in the meantime until the dead of winter was over. It made for too much laundry anyway.

<u>Wednesday</u> <u>Dread</u>. Not so bad. JC was beside me. He didn't have to drive to D.C., so he was able to spend the night for the first time in several weeks. His next job wasn't set to start until Monday. He would be doing some faux finishes and gold leaf in a bank building downtown, so he'd be around more often, I guess. I hoped it would be okay, especially after last night. He was tender instead of bruising, loving instead of threatening, and careful instead of cruel. I still went into the usual state of panic when my eyelids began fluttering open in the morning, but I jumped right on it with some meditative breathing. I didn't want JC to start freaking out all over again after a very sexy, almost wonderful night. I breathed in deeply, and imagined I was breathing out a blackened thread of toxin from each nostril as the air came out in a measured rush.

Breathe in, breathe out -- you're okay.

Breathe in, breathe out -- you're okay.

Breathe in, breathe out the rapid beating of your heart. Breathe in, breathe out the tiny pains around each temple and the uneven ringing in your ears. Breathe in, breathe out the burning sensation that runs along the base of your skull. Breathe in, breathe out the tense muscles and the twitching in your fingers and your toes. Breathe in, breathe out the shooting sparks within your brain. Breathe in, breathe out whatever you believe will stress you out at work today. Breathe in, breathe out -- you're okay. You're okay. You are going to be okay today.

I started easing out of the bed, but JC woke up and threw his long, warm arm over my chest and pulled me back in tight.

"I've got to get ready for work," I said softly. He pressed his groin against my hip and his hardness was burning under the covers. His big, fat, heavy balls were pressing against my ass. I can be a little late. A quick endorphin rush will set me up nicely for the day. When a person wakes up in such an overwhelming depression that she doesn't even know how to be alive, sometimes it only takes the smallest thing to enable her humanity to go on.

For example, I might hear somebody laughing in another apartment, and I know it's all right to be alive today. I walk to work and I see a tree that is shaped in a beautiful way, and I think that it's good to be alive just to see this tree. Quickies work well on almost every occasion. When JC has a few days of downtime, I try to get away for lunch just to run up the two blocks to his place and have a quickie to get me through the afternoon. Mandala can always tell when I do that. She never says anything, but I can see it in her eyes that she knows. Witch. Freaky witch. Horny toad Helen never notices a thing, but Mandala knows. Speaking of Helen and Mandala and work, I've got to get to it. I push myself out of JC's finishing cuddle and bolt to the bathroom.

"Sorry, I've really got to go now."

"Why? Do you have a date at work?"

Don't answer, don't answer, keep going. Don't let him ruin the morning. He can't ruin your morning unless you let him. See? I learned something from all that therapy.

JC has a terrible, casual habit of throwing out an innocuous comment at the moment I'm about to leave him, that is in reality a calculated dig designed to throw me into a flustered exit that will keep him in my mind for hours after we part. He is constantly dissing my job as nothing but a social gathering where the only things we do all day are plan what to eat for lunch and how to hook up with other men. Every time we're together in the morning, he waits until I'm heading for the door to get his final words in, and they are never words of love or encouragement. I won't hear, "Don't worry about that deadline, you know you can do it" or "That client is stupid, your designs are fantastic" or "Have a nice day."

Nope. It's more like, "Why don't you leave early and we'll go do something? It's not like you do anything at work anyway" and "Why can't you take my phone call? Are you too busy talking to your boyfriend? Bullshit, you don't have any real clients" and "Your work is stupid. Just spit something out and stop worrying about it. There's nothing to worry about. Your work isn't real art."

I've learned that when I leave him, even if it's after good sex, I have to be very meticulous and careful in my departure. Don't fling back any hot words in response, because they will only haunt you throughout the day and interfere with your concentration. Also, check and recheck that I have everything I need, because I always forget something when he's watching me get ready to go. Last, pick the least sexy of all the underwear you have left in your drawer. This never makes much of a difference, because JC thinks everything is sexy on me. This is not the compliment that I initially believed it to be. It's always an attack. I'm always going to meet someone and why does my underwear have to match my bra? Who is going to see it? I don't know about other women, but it feels kind of good to have matching underwear on, even if no one in the world is ever going to see it. It feels good to shave your legs every once in a while in the winter as well, so there.

I've also learned to impart as little of this subtle torture to my friends and family as possible. I avoid talking about him too much. My family already hates him anyway, because he doesn't buy me anything or take me anywhere and he's too old for me and his profession is far from secure and I don't warble on happily about him and I don't look happy in general.

Worst of all, the greatest affront to my large and boisterous family, an actual sin in my mother's book, is that he never shows up at any family gatherings. They never stop asking where he is either. I was sulking around the house one day after my mother had carried on too long about his antisocial behavior and my many excuses for his absence and the fact that I didn't seem very happy with him. She droned on, "What is it with him? Is it just the sex?"

"Yes, Mother," were the unspoken words that popped immediately into my head. "It is just the sex so shut up for a minute, will you?"

Ironically, JC's ego is so huge that he accuses me of talking about him all the time. Any problems he encounters with other people are all my fault because I never stop talking or complaining about him. In truth, I talk about him as little as possible, because it only makes me look like a complete and total idiot for staying with him. Talking about him will make my girlfriends give up on me, or at the very least stop going out with me, or maybe even stage an intervention. He doesn't treat me well, and why would I broadcast this news to the people who truly love me and still want me around? Intelligent, fun people don't enjoy hanging out with stupid people.

It's a fact.

# Mile Ten

At work, and almost on time, the sound of light footsteps bustling around the floors above me comes down through the ceiling. Thank goodness. Maybe the latest workplace scandal is blowing over. I climb to the second floor and get straight to work organizing my day. I hear voices along with the footsteps and go upstairs to say my hellos.

"That fucking cunt-sucking prick can eat me raw if he thinks I can have all these pages done by Friday."

Ah, Sandy is back. I didn't think girls were supposed to use the word "cunt." Whatever, we needed to get this place back to normal. Encouraged by my third-floor greetings, I go downstairs to see if Helen is feeling better. She is, but she is too busy to accompany me to the tiny local branch of the Enoch Pratt Free Library at lunchtime so that I can look for some exercise tapes. Helen genuinely does need an assistant, I rationalize as I climb up the building stairs once again.

First flight up from the basement, second flight past my room, third flight on my way to the sky when I notice that I'm not even breathing hard. Looking down at my body, I see that my belly is flat, thank you, Mr. Holland, and my thighs have a nice curve to them beneath my clingy black slacks. The scale doesn't register that I've lost any weight, but I've definitely noticed that none of my clothes feel tight anymore, and that I look better in them overall. My waist doesn't hang over my waistbands, even when I'm sitting down. Clothes that I used to wear as a last resort look good on me. My wardrobe has expanded without my having to spend a dime.

I enter the print room and see that Mandala's ever-expanding wardrobe will prohibit her walking with me to the library, even though it is only one block away. Her platform boots measure six inches, I swear. I ask her anyway and pick up a ruler from the drawing board to try and measure her shoe height. She laughs and kicks me away.

"How about you, sailor?" I say to Sandy.

"No way, no fucking way. I'm going to be sucking this client's cock from now until the weekend, and my ass will not be leaving this chair. I'm going to shit right in this chair, so back off or take a big, juicy whiff!"

"I can go with you," says Mandala. She can, too. It's always amazing to watch her walk around in her outfits as if she's wearing sweats and flats.

"Good, but we'll have to bring this ruler with us to fight off all the HOs who will try to steal your shoes. I can pop over there alone in the middle of the day."

"No, I'll go. I want to buy lunch at the corner deli, and my HOs will all be asleep by then."

"Great!" I am fearless in the city with either JC or Mandala at my side. I suddenly find myself in an excellent mood. I run back downstairs, making sure to pick my knees up high for better form, and meet almost all of my deadlines by noon.

In the front room of my apartment spa, I am standing in shorts, bare feet, and a flimsy tank top as I examine the disc I picked up at the library during lunch. Ms. Kathy Smith is cute, curvy, blonde, and long-legged. I have a blonde ponytail, too. She is oozing fitness all over the cover, but not grossly pumped up like the bulging, vein-popping biceps on the other female choices in the fitness section. Best of all, she assures me that her quick and easy, 20-minute sessions are all I need to see results. In just 20 minutes I will sculpt and tone, and I can do it at any time of day, every day, in whatever order I choose to fit my schedule. All l need are a set of hand weights and a mat or a carpeted floor. Check and check.

Let's begin with the larger muscle groups of the back and chest. We start with one-arm rows. I'm breathing nice and even. This will be easy, I mean, I can run much longer than 20 minutes, right? Uh oh, push-ups are next. Damn! After almost two months, I can still only manage about five full-plank push-ups before I have to drop to my knees and do the girly kind. No problem, 12 push-ups, done. Wait a minute . . . another set? No problem, I'll just start off wimp-ass girly. And up, six, up, seven, "Smiiile!" She's kidding. I'm already panting. I look up and see that she actually is smiling. Everyone in the video is smiling. What the hell? Okay, wait a minute, no rest break? What is she doing? She is doing "Super Setting." Apparently this term means to work out like a maniac on speed. She is moving way too quickly for me, hence the speed part. I can see she is sweating, but her face never grimaces or strays from that lovely smile, and she hasn't stopped yapping the entire time, hence the maniac part. No problem, no problem, I got this.

We're moving on to the arms now. We're working on the upper arms, the biceps. I can do this one. Tricep dips. My butt hits the floor at the base of my couch in the second set, and I have to take a little rest. This is my first time doing this video, you know. It's not unusual to take it easy in the beginning while I learn the moves.

Now we're moving back into the biceps, so pick up your heavier weights and *what the fuck*? We already did the damn biceps! She's trying to kill me. She's killing me, she wants me dead. Where's the box cover? I'm going to sue the video company and the distributors for my funeral expenses. My arms give out way before it's time for Track Two to take a break.

Track Two is for the people who choose to work out with heavier weights. They get to take a break in between sets instead of continuously pumping a lighter weight while waiting for the onset of cardiac arrest. I've decided I am going to have to stay on Track Two for the rest of this hour. I mean, 20 minutes. Can this really be only 20 minutes? I'm sucking wind like my very first mile.

I gulp down some water, nearly choking while trying to swallow and breathe at the same time as I watch Ms. Smith set up for her final muscle group, the shoulders. I get up. I will not quit. We're doing military presses overhead, and this is the "last muscle group we're working today, so push it!" she hoots in a high-pitched, merry voice. On the fifth press, my arms are visibly trembling and I stumble backward a step. That's it. That's it for me today on the arms. I can't believe this.

I skip over the lower body workout for the time being and move right into the bonus abs. This I can do. My spirit is not totally smashed, and my self-esteem rises up a notch, but I've got a serious problem here. I understand and accept that I've got to incorporate these strength moves into my lifestyle, but the whole time I was trying to keep up with the video, all I could think about was how much I would rather be running. I just wanted to run. We're moving into February now, and if this weather doesn't break soon, I'm going to have to figure out a way to sneak out for more runs without setting off JC. I need some more water. Where is some more water?

I got lucky right away, thank you, God. The very next Sunday was a balmy 49 degrees and full of sunshine. I layered up in my preppie sweats and headed off to the North Pole: that gleaming oval ground that beckons me like a bright, shiny Christmas gift sitting on top of the city. The track was completely deserted, which was not unexpected, but I soon found out exactly why it was going to stay that way. While trying to maneuver around my quantum levels, I was lucky not to pop a knee out of place with the constant lateral dodging required not to slip on the many piles of ice that the snow plows had left all over the track. The infield was perfectly clear, but the track was a bombsite. What a mess.

Then I remembered that this particular university only cared about lacrosse, even in the off-season. The campus loop couldn't possibly be any more dangerous than this. I jumped out of the gate after only one lap. Much better. The sun was so brilliant that even the dirty snow looked like a carpet of diamonds, and the slow pace of weekend traffic rolled by quietly with a reassuring regularity. I was the only person in sight. I really was at the North Pole, or maybe underwater in a hidden lagoon. I was covering my course at a pretty good clip and about to enter Nirvana when I spied a figure up ahead, coming toward me. I couldn't tell at first if it was a man or a woman because the sun was so bright that my eyes were half closed, and I was squinting downward to make sure I didn't step in anything obnoxious. The figure drew closer and I could tell that it was a man, with a pretty good physique, so I hopped up onto the curb to give him the right of way in the road. Besides, I was entering Nirvana anyway, and I always went down the middle of this fairway between the perfect landscaping and the manicured grasses and imagined I was someone else.

I prepared a passing smile of greeting to acknowledge a fellow runner on a mission. Our shoulders were near to passing. I lifted up my chin to flash him the smile and my heart skipped a beat. Oh My God and Holy Crap. It was the cross-country coach, and damn he was even more gorgeous up close. Shit. He smiled right back at me and his eyes didn't dart away from my face as he grinned. He looked like he was truly filled with glee to find someone out in the air as crazy as he was. We both laughed a little as we passed.

Goddammit! I just ran past an uber-hunk with dazzling blue eyes. Why don't I ever think to buy some nicer running clothes? Why do I always wear such baggy pants? JC says my ass is looking mighty fine these days. I'm tongue-tied. I almost tripped, but wait! I don't have to think of anything intelligent to say to Coach Cutie because he is going the other way. Whew. I'm going to call him Coach Cutie from now on because the initials CC = Cross Country. I am very hot and bothered. I am practically sprinting toward the museum. I don't even notice that I'm running like an Olympian, because my mind has darted off into a crazy flight of fancy.

Suppose, just suppose that I was all alone out here on this deserted campus road when I slipped on a random patch of ice, twisted an ankle, and fell to the curb. Suppose CC was running by and, *stop*. This won't work. He can't be running along to save me, because there cannot be a sizzling love scene in broad daylight in the middle of the frozen tundra.

Suppose, just suppose that he was taking a shortcut across the campus in his vintage, black Jeep Cherokee. As I'm hobbling over the curb, out of the way of the cars and into the grass, I can hear that a vehicle driving up behind me is slowing down.

"What the hell?" I think as I struggle to pull myself up off the sidewalk. "It's the serial killer that I always fear. This is how I'm going to die; at the hands of a serial killer!" There were no buildings on the strip of road where I fell, and no classes in session on Sunday. There must have been some form of humanity within a scream's range, but we've already gone through the efficacy of screaming in the city. Lowering my head and nonchalantly glancing away, I wait for the vehicle to pass. A small thump of panic hits my chest because I realize that, yes, the Jeep is definitely slowing down and, no, it does not appear in a big hurry to pass. Hopefully the driver is just a rubbernecker, wondering why a young woman is standing beside the road like a stork. I look up and peer all around. Not a soul in sight. The Jeep finally passes by, and then suddenly stops dead in the middle of the road. It is still in the middle of the road when the engine cuts off.

Major panic! My heart sinks down into the soles of my feet as a wall of warnings come crashing down upon me: "All that crime," "It's dangerous over there," and "Are you nuts?" The next words I see are "Crime Scene," blaring over a fuzzy photo of my corpse covered by a blanket on the evening news.

The driver side door opens. Seconds might be crucial. Should I scream anyway? Can I possibly outrun him? Of course I can't outrun him because -- a tall, slim figure steps down and I am paralyzed by the movement. There is something about his walk. There is something about the set of his shoulders. There is something about his rangy, strong limbs and the way his hips seem to stay still while the rest of his body is in motion that looks very, very familiar and I know exactly who it is. Why, it is Cross Country Coach Cutie. I had certainly spent enough time analyzing his tight little ass in those beguiling black running shorts to be sure. I finally looked up at his face. CC is approaching me with concern, and lust and desire and oops, getting ahead of myself in the fantasy here.

"Are you all right?" I stare at him, mesmerized by the intensity of those very light, soft, blue eyes.

"Hey," He was close to me now, reaching out to take me in his arms. "Did you fall? You're injured. Let me help you."

"No, no! I'm fine, I mean, yes, I did fall, but I'll be fine in a moment," I protest in a proud and unconvincing manner. I have to grab hold of his arms to steady myself. My ankle is throbbing, but I make a quick decision to ignore all pain, laugh adorably, and saunter off in an endearingly independent exit. Instead I fall flat into his chest. Ooomph, yes, it was as hard as I'd imagined. His chest, I mean. He takes charge now.

"Here, I've got you. Let's get you to my car and I'll drive you home." He wastes no more time. Without missing a beat, he bends his knees and scoops me up into his arms.

"Sorry," he says, "but you look pretty bad off and my car is blocking the road." He does not show the least sign of physical distress as he carries me off to his car like I weigh nothing more than a snowflake.

"Can you get in by yourself? Let me help you," and I feel the warm palm of his hand high up under my thigh as he helps me into the seat.

"I'm fine now. Really. How stupid! I shouldn't be running in this weather anyway. I turned my ankle, but the pain is already going away now, seriously. Thank you for offering to drop me off at my apartment, but I can make it on my own. I'll be fine in a minute. I only live a few blocks away."

He doesn't start the car, but looks directly at me and then down at my leg. He looks back up into my face. Our eyes lock. Good thing no one ever uses this road.

"Is anyone else in your apartment?" He still hasn't started the car.

"No, I live alone, but I'm sure I'll be fine and I'll just go and elevate my leg and I'll be fine, I'm sure," I ramble. He hesitates for barely a moment, and then his eyes become visibly less soft as he makes a decision. Abruptly he turns, starts the car, and pulls away.

"It's a Sunday, and it's early. Let me take you to my place and look at that for you. I've studied physical therapy. I'm a coach at this university, and I live right at the end of this street."

To *his* place? To a *bachelor* pad (hopefully)? The burning sensation in my ankle has somehow made its way up to my crotch. Again, I find myself whipping my head around in a jerky motion to look in every direction for some sign of life at the edge of the world.

Maybe he really is a serial killer! No one has seen me! They'll never find the body! I am an utter imbecile! I am ruining my own fantasy!

I close my eyes and breathe in deeply. I open my eyes to find myself back on University Parkway. I look over at him. He is staring straight ahead, driving calmly down to the end of the road and into the driveway of a large, red brick apartment complex. I take another deep breath.

"Isn't it nice to live so close to work? I walk to work myself." Pause, with forced composure and another quick check around the perimeter. "Do many of your colleagues live here?"

"There are some, but I'm new this year and don't know anyone who lives here, personally. Let's get you inside quickly."

The quicker, the better. Magically he transports me into his foyer with the same ease in which he got me into his car, and I hear the click of the door lock behind us.

His apartment is dim, with blinds drawn down against the streaming, morning sunlight. It is stone cold quiet and we are completely alone. The couch in the main room is covered with piles of clothing, and he notices me staring at it. Removing his jacket, he carelessly adds it to the top of the pile.

"Sorry! The place is as mess. You can sit on the end of my bed while I look at that foot," he says with a wholesome smile. He half-lifts, half-pulls me into the master bedroom and onto his bed. Not a trace of a leer.

We're inside, and the bedroom is warm. I feel beads of sweat rapidly forming on my forehead from the shock of coming in out of the cold.

"Excuse me, it's really hot in here." I'm struggling out of my arctic hoodie and I feel him helping it off, over my head. We toss it behind me, and turning back I notice that his forehead is shining too.

Suddenly, I am aware that I want him. Badly. I have to have him. Now don't be a fool, stop being a fool.

I am foolishly wondering what I'm supposed to do next, and I'm clutching nervously at the hem of my T-shirt and thinking about his T-shirt when I feel his face in front of me. He has dropped down to his knees and is leaning in closer. He is staring at me, his face a total blank. Then, without a sound, he pushes my hips back further on the bed and moves in even more closely than before. I can feel his body heat mingling with my own and I can smell him. He smells of fresh, warm skin.

"Sit here, like this on the bed," he says, and positions me with my feet dangling just above the floor. He leans down between my knees, pushes up my pants legs and peels off both shoes and socks. At this, I can feel my heart thumping so hard against my breast I can't believe he can't hear it, sounding out over his head across the room and bouncing back against the walls. He is touching my left knee slightly while gingerly holding and turning my left ankle. His hands are large and firm. He moves my left leg a few inches to the side and then turns to move my right leg outward as well, making room to brace his torso against the end of the mattress. This is too much! I feel a hard, demented, whirring tornado of heat and pressure ride up between my legs as my vagina twitches and erupts and I gasp out loud.

He looks up, his face remains impassive, but those eyes are asking me a question while his fingertips pause, one hand resting on each knee. Don't blow it. No time for shyness. I meet his gaze directly and answer, "I think I just had an orgasm."

Without moving his eyes from mine, he slides the fingers of his right hand lightly up my thigh beneath my sweats, and inserts one finger smoothly into my hot, wet, pulsating vagina.

"Yes," he replies, his finger probing deeper inside me, "I think you did."

Now he gets to work. His fingers are between my legs, stroking and caressing as he plunges two of them in and out. His face swoops down and he attacks my lips, moving and sucking and pushing me down onto the bed. His free hand cleanly pulls off the rest of my ridiculously oversized clothing and he pulls back sharply to take in the sight of me naked, on his bed. He is raking me with his eyes as he stands up in the full glory of his rippling, sinuous frame with his cock, rock hard and erect before me. He pulls his own clothing over and off. He leans over me again, gracefully, and begins working on me with his tongue and his lips and his hands all in communion as he travels from my lips to my shoulders, and hungrily upon my nipples down my abdomen to my legs. There he settles in with a purpose so intense I begin to wonder if it's possible to die from too many orgasms. I'm gripping the bedspread in my hands with tightly balled fists. I'm twitching and moaning and digging my shoulder blades into the mattress as he places both of his hands on the insides of my thighs and holds me open while he licks and laps and sucks. My body is wracked with spasms. I want to feel him, every inch of him, over and inside me. I grab at his shoulders, wanting to take the full size of him into my mouth and deep-throat him down until I am full.

Feeling my intent, he rises from between my legs and crawls up the bed on his knees until I can grasp his penis in my hands and shove it into my mouth. I grab at both of his buttocks in a caressing, forceful grip and knead them as I suck and swallow and dart my tongue out to savor his balls. My eyes are closed in ecstasy, but I can hear him moaning and grunting above me. The heat between my legs is about to burn up the sheets when he draws out of my mouth to lay over me and insert his huge, hot shaft inside me, smooth and thick and slow, forcing me to feel every inch of the entry. Now his long, hard body is melting over me, brushing my breasts and my neck with his body as he moves in and out. His lips are soft, but firm, and he exhales hot air into my neck and fucks me slowly and thoroughly and deeply. He is pressing into me, so deeply I can feel his balls smashing into my ass, just how I like it. He wants to grip me even tighter, I can tell, but he holds his large hands in check as he brushes them up and down over my body, touching and fondling. He doesn't want to hurt me.

Then he loses control. He slips out of me and pulls me down to the end of the bed by my hips. He flips me around so that I'm standing on my good leg, with my left knee safely propped up on the mattress to the side. He spreads my cheeks and plunges in with so much force that my chin gets scraped against the sheets. I lift myself up to brace against the thrust of his slender hips pounding up against my ass as his cock shoots up to my waist. I arch my back and offer up my ass in its full, rounded glory. He holds onto my hips like bicycle grips as he slaps and shoves himself into me, and I grunt under each thrust with muted, mewls of pleasure. I reach down between my legs and grab his balls. He falls

82

forward, flattening me onto the mattress as he shoots his steaming, milky gush all the way up to my throat.

He's lying on top of me, flaming skin and ragged breath and wetness from his mouth on the back of my neck to match the oozing lava flow tricking down between my thighs. He holds me from behind with his long embrace warming me like a stove. His breath evens out and he rolls onto his back, pulling my slim figure along with him onto his side. He closes his eyes, still panting lightly.

I'm panting. I'm panting in my fantasy and in real life as I open up my stride and finish off a four mile, double-loop run on this sparkling, frozen day.

"Ahhhhhh. Holy fuck. Holy shit. I, oh, my God, I feel wonderful. Jesus, fucking shit. I can't think."
 In a waking dream I am breathing contentedly into his shoulder. (I'm actually walking briskly home down St. Paul Street.)

"Are you okay?" CC asks me.

"Yes! Yes, I am so okay. I am so . . . good. I'm really, really good." We breathe together for awhile.

"So, you're okay. You are so fucking hot, you know. You're the only ass on the track worth looking at. I size up that big ass of yours in those black yoga pants every chance I turn around." (Never mind the fact that I don't own any black yoga pants.) My confidence is surging.

"Oh, really? You want to rip aside my tight black pants and stuff me up against the bleachers maybe?"

His face is smiling above mine.

"What else would you like to do?" I am feeling very bold. He doesn't answer, but his breath begins coming in harder again. No, wait a minute. It's my breath coming in harder.

Down the block I spy JC standing in the middle of the sidewalk with a market bag in his hand. He is staring at me with that distinctive black and thunderous expression.

I couldn't feel my feet hitting the ground as I walked slowly closer to him. I wasn't even aware that my body was in motion. I was on autopilot. I felt unable to prevent the oncoming crash.

Here we go again. How does this continue to happen? How is it scientifically possible for an endorphin rush of joy to flatten out so quickly? Yet, at the sight of his face, so unreasonably angry, I could actually feel my spirited and joyous blood run cold. I felt the warmth fly from my pores as my fantasy disappeared in an instant, and a heavy, tenuous sadness overtook my soul. I forced a smile back onto my face by remembering that *I just ran four miles.*

"Hey, whatcha' doin'?" I call out.

"Yeah, right. What the fuck are *you* doin'?" he spits. "I saw you leave over half an hour ago. What the fuck are you doing?" He is standing in the middle of the sidewalk, blocking my path.

"I just had the most amazing run. I ran four miles! I think I might want to enter a race or something in the spring. I felt like I was flying!"

"Yeah, I bet you did. With who? Who wants you to run a race with him? Who are you meeting at the track? Where have you been for so long? You really think I'm stupid, don't you?"

Yes, my brain is screaming. Yes, you are so stupid. I can't do this. I can't give up my little bit of joy. I won't give up this last little spark of joy from my run. Dodging around him, I race down the block and up onto my front porch while pulling out my key. I am swift in the clarity of my recent accomplishment, and I turn with a lightening resolve to lock the door behind me. I don't even stop to look at his face as I fly up the stairs to double-lock myself into my apartment. I ignore the banging on the door, and the subsequent ringing of my doorbell. After about 20 minutes or so, JC is either too smart or too paranoid to continue pursuing me from the foyer. He probably knows that someone in the building might call the police.

My phone rings all afternoon and evening. I don't budge from my bedroom. I just lay there, curled up on the bed. I am willing my mind into nothingness. I want my mind to be blank. I don't want t feel anything. I want to be nothing. I am nothing. I want to be asleep forever.

No sleep. I have to sleep. There are so many things to do tomorrow. There are so many deadlines at work. It's unhealthy not to sleep, especially when I need to concentrate in the morning. I have to be sharp. I'm expected to produce. I'm expected to function like a normal human being at work. You know, smiling and talking and standing up without trembling and all. I'm expected to engage and banter and negotiate. I'm expected to eat and look alive and remain calm.

I'm expected to navigate through the waterways of the world with an even keel, a sure hand, and a hearty heart.

The more I think about how important it is for me to get a little sleep tonight, the more I can't sleep. JC calls me a dolphin, because even when I appear to be sleeping, I'm never really asleep. He teases me, saying, "No matter what hour of the morning it is, if I whisper 'Grace,' you always say, 'What?'"

He is still calling me at midnight, at 1:00 a.m., and then again at 2:00. He knows I am awake.

# Mile Eleven

What a mess. The next morning I am a panicky mess. I feel terrible. I'm doing very badly. My head is full of hot, throbbing water. My eyes are backed with pain. My chest feels compressed, my breathing is shallow, and my heartbeat is wild. I have to keep reminding myself to breathe. I keep coaching myself to go on. I want to cry, but I have to get my face in order for work. I'm maxing out on depression. I feel hate. Stay calm. Breathe through this. Maybe I do need a doctor. Maybe I should call a doctor. This can't be normal, waking up this way over and over again. This has got to be very far from normal. I should call a doctor.

No! No, don't call a doctor. Doctors make you come into the office. They will put you on antidepressants. I can't go through that again. They will put me on antidepressants and I will end up wanting to die. Don't die. Don't call. Just survive. Survive today. You can do this. I hear a train rumbling by in the distance. The sound wraps around my head and pushes me out of bed. The sound of the train is just what I needed. I am up.

It's pouring rain outside, making even more of a mess. The sparkling leftover snow from yesterday is all gone, and the roadsides are ugly and icy. I decide to walk over one block, and then down two blocks to work instead of down two and over one, as I usually do. I'm just barely holding my thoughts together here, and I don't want to risk seeing JC for any reason. He should already have gone to work himself, but I'm not taking any chances. I just can't bear to see him at all.

At work we're nice and busy and it's good. I go downstairs to drop off my film, and Helen is over her head with packages lined up on the light table, machines humming and deadline checklists all over the place.

"You know, you really do need an assistant down here," I say. She tries to glare at me, but smiles instead. I go upstairs, just to say hi, and the two pairs of eyes don't budge from their screens as they grunt a reply. They don't have time for me, Helen doesn't have time for me, I don't have time for me, and none of us has time for JC when he starts calling just before lunch.

"We need to talk," he says.

"Not at work, we're really busy here. I can't talk now."

"We need to talk."

"I'm telling you I can't talk now. I'm hanging up." I hang up.

My phone line rings immediately. I answer professionally, just in case.

"Don't hang up on me. What are you doing? Is someone there with you?"

"No! Of course not." My voice is speeding up and rising, damn it! Why can't I ever remain calm? "Listen, we're really, really busy. I can't talk now. I really have to work. Please stop calling me. I'll talk to you after work. Aren't you at work, now?"

"They had to close the building early for some kind of heating problem. We were evacuated."

"Well, I'm still at work, and I have to go."

"Bullshit. You never work."

"I'm hanging up. Don't call back." He calls right back. Jesus H. Christ, are we toddlers in a sandbox? I don't want to answer, I want to let it ring, but someone else in the building will pick it up and page me. What to do? I think I'll just be honest. I'll tell the truth. It is always embarrassing to admit that you are a fool in love, but Helen already knows, and Mandala and Sandy know everything without being told, so what the hell. Mandala has already answered the phone and paged me when I appeared at the top of the stairs.

"I'm sorry, you guys. JC and I are in a bit of a fight, and he won't stop calling me. I've got two deadlines to get up to the hospital today. Can you answer my phone line for me?" Helen and the salesmen have their own lines, and never answer the studio lines unless they see that everyone is already lit up. I don't have to worry about them.

Sandy doesn't look at me; she just keeps working. Mandala's cool eyes look over at me, but she doesn't miss a beat as she reaches over to pick up the blinking line.

"I'm sorry, JC, but Grace is tied up on another line with a client and she'll be unavailable for awhile. I'll be taking her calls for her." Good girl! Keep him from trying again! "Do you want to leave a message? Okay, goodbye then." She hangs up and goes back to work with a little nod in my direction.

"Thank you! I'll never get any work done with his constant calling! Thank you!" I jog back downstairs and get straight to work. I want to concentrate and block JC out of my mind and get these jobs done so that at least I won't have deadlines hanging over my thoughts tonight.

My work is done and packaged up for the courier to deliver. I'm walking home in anticipation, and there he is, out of his door and standing on the sidewalk in front of his apartment before I can pass.

"Come in," he says. I may as well go in. This way I won't have to try to get him out of my apartment if he goes all ballistic. It will be hard enough to get out of his apartment, but not as hard as the other way around. We walk up in silence. I don't even have my coat off when he starts in.

"So, who is it? Who are you running off to meet with all the time? We have a problem here, and you need to tell me about it. Who are you seeing? I know you're seeing someone."

"The only person I'm seeing is the asshole in front of me. I am so sick of this."

"I'm sick of it, too! You and your lies and your other boyfriends. So who is it?"

"It's no one you asshole. I've told you and told you that I'm enjoying running again. I'm not going to stop running just because you have a problem. You're jealous of everything! You're jealous of my work, my friends, my family, and now you're even jealous of my running? You've got to be kidding me. What am I? A dog that you own that is only let out to pee and then has to come right back into the house? What the fuck? Am I not supposed to wipe my ass without informing you first?"

"We're a couple. Couples are supposed to do everything together. Why do you have to go places without me unless you're seeing someone else? So yes! You do need to tell me everything. How am I supposed to trust you if you go sneaking off without inviting me or telling me where you're going? If you can't tell me everywhere you're going, then we have a problem here. What are we going to do about it?"

"That is the stupidest thing I ever heard. I'm supposed to check in with you before I do anything? That's just ridiculous! What about you? Are you supposed to tell me every move you make every day?"

"You know I'm not a cheater. It's always been my girlfriends that go running around, lying and cheating on me." (Gee, I wonder why.) "You know I'm always here, waiting for you after work." (Boy, is he ever.)

"So you're supposed to be my shadow, everywhere I go?"

"That's what couples do. Unless you want to go fucking someone else."

"First of all, you are invited to all of my family gatherings. You choose not to come."

"They don't want me there and why should I have a bad time? I don't need to have a bad time at my age. I'm over that bullshit."

"So, what then? I don't see my family anymore? Just because you don't like your family doesn't mean I don't like mine."

"They're all a bunch of idiots. I don't know why you're all over them anyway. You must want to have sex with some of your cousins or something. You don't need to go over there all the time."

"Your hillbilly side is pure white trash, you know that? You're just disgusting!"

"At least I don't want to fuck my cousins."

"So, let me get this straight, you don't want me to see my family so much, and you don't want me to see my girlfriends unless you're invited to come along, and you don't want me to go running either? You don't want me to do fucking *anything* without you?"

"We're a couple! You're not supposed to! Why can't your friends talk in front of me? What are you hiding? You're all just looking for guys to fuck! Especially that Helen! That's all she does!"

"And God knows I have no brain in my head, and I will do exactly whatever the girlfriend beside me is doing. I haven't any mind of my own. I think I'll go up to the hospital and find me some doctors to fuck right now."

"You probably already are! I don't want you going out with Helen again at all -- not unless I'm invited, too."

"Well, I am going out with my girlfriends again, without you. It's impossible to talk around you. You are absolutely no fun. I'm going to keep seeing my family as much as I want, and I'm not going to stop running whenever I want."

"Then we have a problem here. Who is it? I know you're seeing someone. There's no reason to go out with girlfriends without me unless you're planning on fucking someone else. *Who is it?!*"

"*It's no one, I hate you!*"

I run into the bedroom and start sobbing. I mean, totally wracked with sobs. I'm so tired from work I just can't stop crying now, over everything. I don't want to fight. I don't want to leave JC, but I don't know how to stay with him. I'm not equipped to handle his stifling brand of power. I'm not swift enough and not nearly calm enough to handle his constant possessiveness. It's not flattering. It's just sad. I'm sad enough already. How did we even end up together? We're not at all alike. He hates people and I kind of like people, excepting myself, of course. We like to talk about art and history and films and music and lighting and angles and techniques; but even then, if I disagree or have an alternate opinion, the name-calling starts and I'm just stupid and I don't know anything. I can't figure it out right now. I didn't get any sleep last night. Work was demanding, and I just can't figure anything out right now. I continue sobbing so passionately that JC has stopped talking. I cover my face with my hands and I can't stop. I'm so tired. I am so, so tired.

JC sits down on the bed next to me and puts his arms around me. Usually, once he's broken me, he is content enough with his victory to drop the argument for the time being, but apparently not this time.

"Don't cry. I don't want to see you cry," he says softly. "Just tell me who it is."

"It's *no one!* It's *no one*, you stupid, stupid idiot! I want to go home." But I can't go anywhere just yet, because I've started to hyperventilate between sobs, and I can't get enough air in to stand up. Oh, he's happy now.

"Okay, okay, you're not going home. We'll stop arguing for now. Just calm down. Stop crying. I don't want you to cry." (Bullshit.) "Come on. I'll make us some dinner. Turn on the news and stop crying. We'll talk later."

"We're not talking later," I manage to choke out while still whimpering. "I'm not listening to you anymore."

"Okay, okay. No talking tonight. Just sit there, and I'll make some dinner." He goes into the kitchen. I sit and stare at the air. The TV is on, but I don't even see it. Everything in the room is a blur. I can't see anything. I can't think. I'm so weak. I can't even sit up, so I prop myself back up against the pillows at the top of the mattress on the floor. I wish he would fix this bed. It's creepy sleeping down here on the floor with the insects and the mice and whatever else runs around at night in a dirty, filthy, city apartment.

I'm so tired I don't talk as we eat. It takes every ounce of effort to chew. I'm just going to lie here, finish eating, and say nothing. At least he's not talking anymore. Maybe he can see in my face what I feel. It is not defeat that I feel. I feel surrender, but not to him. I feel surrender to whatever is left of my heart. I give up. I don't want to be here anymore. I'm going to be silent tonight, then I'm going to get out of here before work, and then I don't want to come back here anymore, ever again. Ever.

Tuesday. Savagely depressed. Furious fog and thunderstorms. It's a sloppy mess out there. No running and no motivation. Come on, come on, get out there and get messy. Get up. You can get up.

Wednesday. Drizzling and dripping. The freezing temperatures are here to stay for awhile. Despair, agitation, anxiety and listlessness are piling in and pushing me down. Stay aware. Stay calm.

Thursday. I had planned to do a 20-minute upper-body routine after work, but every scrap of motivation just dropped off a cliff as I arrived back home and I lay down on the bed again instead. So tired. Suck-ass tired. Not functioning. Just want to sleep.

Friday. I'm so tired. I'm so, so sad and tired. Infused with inertia, I wish to wallow in nonexistence. Every movement is a concerted effort. Concentrate.

# Mile Twelve

I can't run anymore. I don't want to run anymore. I can't do it. No, really, I can't go outside to run anymore. It's Code Blue all over Baltimore, and no one is going outside this February unless they absolutely have to buy some more toilet paper and milk before they die.

What to do? What to do? I'm going crazy stuck inside my tropical apartment. Somehow, I've managed to avoid JC without feeling intimidated about it for almost a week. He's not venturing out either. At work, the upstairs girls are working from their computers at home instead of risking their lives to drive downtown. Only Helen and I have been in these past few days to run film and answer the phones. We're working in shifts, so we don't even see each other or the owners. They're staying home and calling every other hour to make sure that one of us is there. It is silent and lonely in the rowhouse alone. The city is covered in ice.

Friday night. My apartment is silent and lonely as well. I am in a tank top as usual, pacing around. There is too much energy, but I'm not interested in my exercise videos. I'm tired of Tom Holland trying to seduce me and Kathy Smith trying to kill me. I've got to get out of here before I go insane. I need some insane cardio. What to do? What to do? On this, the coldest day of the year, it came to me in a flash of true inspiration.

I needed to go swimming.

Yes, yes, I know. Most people wouldn't think about putting on a bathing suit and jumping into a pool when the outdoor temperature readings were in the single digits, but I really needed to work out. I needed to get out. I needed to move. Going swimming was definitely the answer. How was I going to make this happen? I must know somebody at the hospital with connections to the university who could get me into the pool -- no, wait! I was an alumna of a university just a few measly miles to the north and could swim there for free.

My car was in good running condition. The pool was safe and indoors. I had gone swimming there regularly when I was in school, both during the day and in the evenings. I knew the area, the locker rooms, and the parking. I still had my old, black and gold Speedo racerback. Did I still have my goggles? I would start making phone calls tomorrow morning and find out about the schedules. Right now, I had to lie down. I closed my eyes and stared into the backs of my eyelids and thought about it some more. Cross training is good for you, right? We're not busy after hours at work in the winter. I could do this. I knew this was a good idea because I immediately decided to have an orgasm.

Ah, the trusty little tan plastic vibrator. It was inconspicuously plain, smooth, and unimpressive. The most generic version of a vibrator, I'm sure. I had plenty of top-of-the-line, gold-topped, Duracell AAs though. I might be broke and drink cheap beer, but I never skimped on the batteries. Ironically, I had JC to thank for my favorite toy. It turned out that he, himself, introduced me to his own emergency replacement system.

I had been sulking around, late one sultry, hot Saturday afternoon last summer in the meager shade of my sweltering bedroom while JC was downtown at a baseball game with an old college friend. I was pouting, because his friend had called him up that morning at the last minute with the offer of an extra ticket and he agreed. Since when did JC have any old friends? When I first met him, he didn't even own a telephone, and the only people he talked about from his past were the multitudes of women who adored him. And since when does this alien male friend show up with only one extra ticket? Of course I had to show support for any sign of positive social behavior from JC, but I didn't have any other plans for the day and I was left behind and I was bored. Bored and hot and stifled.

Breathing in the summer air of Baltimore is like sucking warm water up a straw through one nostril, and it's hard to get enough oxygen to the brain. It is hard to move around very much at all. I didn't dare to go outside and into the humid belly of the beast, so I was really bored. Slovenly, sluggish, sizzling, and bored. I ghosted around the rooms in the semi-gloom, and watched a few old movies on the television.

I rejoiced at the sound of my buzzer in the vestibule because I knew it would be JC returning from the game. He came into my bedroom with a smile on his face, yapping away about the game, the plays, and how the two of them had a walk around the harbor afterward.

"Look at what I got you," he said with excitement just bursting all around him. He reached into his inside jacket pocket as he was taking it off, and pulled out a small brown bag. I'm thinking booze, or maybe a game souvenir. He pulled out a slim, molded plastic rectangle and displayed the package to me face up. It still took a moment before I recognized what it was.

"What?" I yell out. "What? I told you I never wanted one of those things. You bought that right in front of your friend? Oh my God, I can't believe you. You and your friend went shopping after the game and bought me a vibrator?"

"No, no. Ben wasn't watching me the whole time. Besides, it's no big thing. He was buying stuff for his girlfriend. It was his idea to go into The Love Zone. You should just try it. What's the problem? Just try it?"

I was inorgasmic at the time. This never seemed to bother him much, but he had mentioned, more than once, that I should try using a vibrator. I guess this particular scenario should have shown me that he truly cared. Instead I was mortified.

"I can't believe you. You bought that for me in front of somebody else? I'll never be able to face this friend of yours. I don't want it, I'll never use it, put it away!"

He could see I was becoming unreasonably hysterical, so he quickly slipped the vibrator back into the bag and put it under his coat on the chair.

Later that night, we were drunk and having sex. I was blowing him with my ass in his face when I heard the crackling sounds of him trying to quietly open the package. There was a soft click and a low buzzing sound. I decided not to start a fuss about it because I was rather preoccupied at the time. Let's call it unconscious rationalization. Subconscious, maybe?

I used to be afraid to watch pornography, too. When JC finally coerced me into giving it a try, I agreed to allow his video to play, but I refused to keep my glasses on. I'm very nearsighted, so all of the action on the screen was a perfectly innocent, flesh-colored, moaning blur. No orgasms, no vibrators, and no porno for this good little Catholic girl. I had surely wasted a lot of prime time sex years before running into JC.

Again, it's always amazing to me to look back and see how stupid I was.

Monday night. I'm shivering from the locker room showers as I stand on the cold tiles around the pool in my skin-tight suit. My crumbling old goggles are dangling at my side. It was easy to get here. The period for public swimming doesn't begin until after 6:00 in the evening, when most of the school is closed. I flew up Charles Street and parked easily in an empty lot near the pool building.

Now comes the hard part. I have to jump in. I scope out the lane population for an acceptable speed circle without too much of a crowd and choose the lane second from the left wall. There are only two people in the wall lane, and they are rather slow, but I'm always afraid I'm going to bash my arm into the ladder on a backstroke in that lane. The second lane over has three people in it, and their speed is moderately consistent. I can always hang back on the wall for a lap if I start to get in the way. I've made up my mind, when one of the three swimmers in my chosen lane pulls out and smiles at me with a sideways nod of his head to the lane. He's done, I'm in, no more hesitation.

I quickly wrap up my glasses in my towel and set them gently on the edge of the bench behind me. I struggle into my goggles, trying not to pull them on too quickly and snap the strap. That would definitely break my resolve in an instant and give me an excuse to turn around and go home. I wait for the largest break between the two remaining swimmers, and I'm in with a quick drop into the water and a push off the wall.

"Fuuuuuucccckkk!!!" I scream underwater as I always do when the shock of the initial immersion hits me on the first lap. I also always wonder if anyone, under or above, can hear me doing that.

Even though it's been years since I last swam laps, I decided before I got here that I could certainly manage at least 20. I'm not completely out of condition. It takes me only a few laps before I feel myself falling into form. This is too easy. Perhaps swimming is like riding a bike. I wish running were like riding a bike, but that's okay. Suddenly, everything is going to be okay. This is where I need to be. I need to be inside this pool with my eyes and my ears underwater.

My senses need to be drowned and muted. I'm wearing water earmuffs. I'm absorbing water tranquilizers. I can hear a blast of music in the distance whenever I turn my head for a breath of air. The lifeguards are playing Stones. It spurs me on after every breath. There is chatter all around me, but I can't understand a single word. I don't want to understand or hear a single word that anyone is saying. None of it matters. It's all okay. I am wearing life earmuffs as I swim.

I finish 20 laps, and I have to keep going. How is this possible? I'm swimming and swimming and ascending the water line and floating up into another level of existence. I'm swimming up above the earth. I don't want to stop. I want a mile of water to rush before my eyes. I don't want to get out of the pool. I don't want to go home. I watch the blue water cut across the frame of my goggles and bubble all over my body and stream down my sides. The sight of my limbs moving underwater and the thick, black line rushing beneath me is mesmerizing.

The oxygen I steal pushes painfully against my chest as I try to hold onto it for as long as I can. I want to force the maximum of solitude into every stroke. The longer my head stays underwater, the more peace I can gather and hoard. I was becoming tired, but I was definitely in a groove. I began to operate as a machine. I became mindless and automatic.
And then I became an artist.

I was freed from civilization, society, convention, and dinner plans. I was dancing in the water. I felt my fingertips brush against my hips as my elbow broke the waterline and lifted up in a poetic arc of the most perfect port du bras. My wrist flipped forward as my hand followed in a graceful line to reach for that celestial center point above my head. Then I become all Tae Kwon Do. Knife hand into the water, reach and pull and tuck that forearm in tight down my torso before my fingertips reach my hips, and I become a ballerina again.

Legs keep fluttering, soft knees, hard thighs, and flowing straight ankles. Conduct the legs from the hips, the arms from the shoulders, tight in the core, and straight through the neck. Now I've got it all down. Now I am automatic, and now it is time. Now is the time that I forget about myself, forget my world, forget my family and my president and my country and Africa and the Middle East. I am transcending the water, even as I am the water. Flowing and flowing and evaporating until I am gone.
I didn't want to stop swimming.
I wanted to stay gone.


I finally stopped at the wall after over 50 laps. Not bad for a first plunge. I was panting slightly, and when I looked down my body to measure out my breath, my abdomen appeared almost concave with every exhale. Huh, I thought. I look positively slender. I was weary, but not exhausted, and pleased, though not quite happy. Never that, I laughed grimly to myself. I'm not even sure I know what "happy" really means.

Pushing myself up and out of the pool, I gingerly removed my goggles as I grabbed my towel and headed back into the locker room. Surreptitiously, I glanced down my body some more. The wet, black swimsuit was practically painted on. One, two, three, four . . . okay, I didn't exactly have a six-pack, but thanks to my personal video trainers, I most definitely had a four-pack, with a completely flat stomach beneath it. I felt like a shiny, sleek, skinny seal. There didn't seem to be an ounce of extra flab anywhere, and even my small, A-cup-at-best breasts seemed to stand out firmer, with nipples saluting the sky. I should do this more often. If only it didn't involve getting into a car and driving and parking and getting wet in the winter.

The moments between deciding to work out and actually doing it are very delicate sometimes. Oh well, I don't have to think about that now. I was done for the day. My mind felt calm and blank. I didn't need to think about anything else, except drying off and driving home. Damn, and parking. I speeded up the drying off. I hadn't thought to throw any underwear into my gym bag, so I pulled on my sweats over my chlorine-clean body and drove home commando style.

Parking in Charles Village, was at a premium on weekday nights. I knew I would never get a spot across from my apartment, so I sat back in the driver's seat and mentally prepared my list of acceptably safe side streets to drive around. A couple of circles and bingo! It's divine intervention. I find a comfortable spot on the side of 28th Street only one block away, diagonal from my apartment. God bless compact cars, I said to myself with a smile as I affectionately patted my dash. Holy shit. I smiled. I was still smiling a bit, probably from the shock of it, as I darted across the street to get inside.

I looked up, and there he was. Once again, there was JC, standing between me and my front door, with that solemn, black look of danger on his face. He must have been watching out his window for my car to reappear. I walked right up to him. There was nothing else to do. He grabbed me by the upper arm so tightly I could feel his thumb digging into my bone through my coat.

"We've got to talk."

"I've just been swimming. I'm freezing. I'm going inside, and we can talk later," I replied firmly. I am my own person. I have nothing to be afraid of.

I don't owe him any explanations. I'm only shaking because it's so cold out here and my hair isn't completely dry.

"You don't swim. Come on. We're talking now." He started pulling me up the walkway to his front porch. I tried to wrench my arm away, but he had me in a crazy, effortless grip of steel. It always amazed me how strong he was, considering his wiry build. He was like a Latin Bruce Lee.

"Let go of me," I hissed, because a couple of neighbors had come out onto the porch beside his. I saw someone walking down the block on the opposite side of the street from the corner of my eye as well.

He saw the people too, and knew I wouldn't cause a scene. We all lived in the same block and knew each other without actually knowing each other, like city people do. We acknowledged each other's presence as acceptable neighbors. We never spoke any words, at least not on a regular basis.

"Please let go. I want to go home. I'll talk to you later," I said as softly and evenly as I could.

"No. You're coming in now." He didn't want a scene either. He forced a lower tone into his voice.

"Come on, we're not going to fight. We may as well talk now. We're just going to talk." He was pulling me inside, and I was trying hard to make it look as if I wasn't being dragged. I didn't have much of anything left in me after that swim, and I could feel whatever I still had draining away. I was emptying out as we entered his apartment. I remembered something. A fleeting memory. Had I really smiled a short time ago, or had I imagined it? The door closed behind us. He attacked.

"Who are you seeing? You're seeing other people, and we're going to talk about it now. Who is it?" he demanded. "Look at you!" he snarled, taking in my damp hair and my gym bag. I knew he was thinking that I had just showered at my imaginary lover's place, and that my gym bag was some sort of booty call kit. That's the way he always thought.

"I'm not seeing anyone, and what the hell business is it of yours if I do? We're not married. We're not engaged. We don't even live together. It's none of your business who I see and when I see them or how long I see them!" I spit right back, knowing he would take these words as a confession. I didn't care. I'd had it. I couldn't take it anymore, this constant stealing and scraping away at any bit of happiness I managed to find. He couldn't have it anymore. He couldn't have my sorry, last little threads of joy.

"Now get away from me! I'm going home and I don't have to talk to you!" My blood was getting hot. My face was screwing up. Don't lose it, don't lose it. He saw my struggle, but he also saw my resolve and he reached out and pushed me backward. He pushed me! I reached out with both hands and pushed him back. I tried to jump around him to the front door, but he grabbed the hood of my jacket and pulled it hard against my throat. The zipper dug into my neck and I reached up to pull it away. I tried to twist out of his grip but he moved himself around in front of me again and pushed me down to the floor. I can't believe this is happening, I thought. I can't believe this. I started to get up and he pushed me down again. He dropped to his knee and pulled the front of my coat and sweatshirt away from me and looked down my shirt at my naked body.

"You're not even wearing any fucking underwear! What did you do? Leave it behind as a souvenir? Which ones were they? What color were they?" He was yanking my sweatshirt back and forth and making my head snap. He was grabbing at my pants and pulling them down, tearing the elastic at the waistband as he clawed at my hips. I felt panic setting in.

"Let go! Let go! I'll tell you everything!" I yelled. He eased back in anticipation, his eyes boring into my face. He let go of my shirt and his fingers loosened at my waist. I pretended to get up slowly, and then lunged for the front door. I had the knob in my hand and was trying to get it open, but he grabbed the strap of the gym bag that was still slung over my shoulder and yanked me away again. I screamed. He let go. I lunged again and got one arm out the door when he jumped up and grabbed my other arm from behind.

A door opened across the hall. A young man was standing in the doorway with worry and concern on his face. I couldn't believe it. Someone had answered my scream. All three of us were frozen in position. I saw his eyes go over my face and into the face of JC, standing behind me in the half open door. I saw him hesitate. I burst into tears and started gasping for breath.

"Do you want me to call the police?" he asked shakily.

"Yes! Yes! Call the police!" I screamed. JC instantly let go of me and slammed the door and slid the bolt. I ran out of the building without looking back at the other man. I sprinted up the block and into my own building and bolted my own lock. I was heaving and crying. I tried to take deep breaths so that I could focus. Would he call the police? Would they question JC? Would they come and find me?

I staggered to the bay window and sat on the sill. I watched and cried. I cried and watched. I examined the finger bruises already forming on my upper arms. I watched and cried until 2:00 in the morning. Nothing happened. Nobody came. So much for cross training.

# Mile Thirteen

The next morning was a "Vampire Morning." Most mornings are Vampire Mornings, no matter what the intensity of The Morning Dread. A Vampire Morning is when your skin is pale, your eyes are red, the daylight is painful, and you can't bear to look at your reflection in a mirror. At work I felt so weak and disoriented that I couldn't think how to begin. I went downstairs to the basement and waited for Helen to arrive. She came in and saw me slumped on the floor in the dark. I told her in a deadpan voice, devoid of all emotion, what had happened.

"You should call the police and make a report," she said firmly.

"No. I think he'll leave me alone now."

"Do you want to move in with me for awhile?"

"No, no. I think I'll be all right. I think I'll just start working now."

"Why don't you stay with me for tonight? You can calm down a little. We'll make dinner and just get calm. I don't think you should go home to your place right now. What if he's waiting for you again? We'll leave together after work."

"Maybe. Maybe that's a good idea." I was thinking how it might look to JC from his window. He would see me climbing onto the back of Helen's bike with a backpack crammed full of stuff and know that he was right about me all along. I was a cheating slut, running away to be with my multitude of boyfriends. Why should I care about that? I imagined the look on his face through the glass.

"Yes. I want to come and stay with you tonight. I decided. I think it's a good idea."

"Okay, then. Try not to think about it until then. Go and get to work before they start buzzing for you. Here, have some water." She stood up from where she was crouching down in front of me and went to her mini-fridge in the corner. She loved her mini-fridge. She could stay down here in the basement all day long without ever having to come up, even for lunch. She could duck into her darkroom as soon as she heard our footsteps on the stairs, and there was nothing we could do about it. The darkroom was sacred. I should have studied photography instead of studio art. In my office on the second floor, everybody was always in my face. I took the bottle of water and listlessly climbed the stairs.

I was staring at my computer screen, getting nothing done, thinking about what I should pack for an overnight with Helen when Mandala walked in with a stack of papers for me to proof. I didn't notice her until she was right beside me. I knew I was out of it, but I looked down to check out her shoes anyway to see if she was wearing something soft and leathery on the wooden floor. No, she was wearing chunky gray stilts with neon green glitter bands crisscrossed over the top. The heels and toes were tipped with shiny, silver metal, like horseshoes. I looked up to see her eyes staring into mine. She put the stack of papers on the desk to my right without taking her eyes off of me. Her eyes were both apologetic for the mound of work, and empathetic for the obvious misery that I was pouring out all over the room.

"You should move," she said quietly. Then she turned and walked away.

February was almost over, one of the coldest in recorded history for the state of Maryland. Fuck February. I'm ready to march into March. Tonight, the evening boasted a roasting 45 degrees. I went running. I made a pact with myself that anything over 40 was to be considered a doable running atmosphere. Anything in the 30s, I would squeeze into my Speedo and go for at least one trip to the pool during the week. Anything below 30, fuck it.

I called my landlord the day after I spent the night with Helen. Michael was a kind man, and agreed to help me move into one of his other properties in The Village without penalizing me if possible. Unfortunately, there probably wouldn't be anything available for a few more months, after graduation at the university in May. Every year, when the spring semester ended, the university spilled out its students and travelling professors into the world and "For Rent" signs popped up in almost every block. The best yard sales ever were when the professors moved away. All kinds of finely bound literature and funky artifacts were on sale for a fraction of their true value. I picked up an impressive hardcover, boxed trilogy set of Dante along with Russian and American masterpieces that I intended to read someday. I read the first 50 pages of *One Day in the Life of Ivan Denisovich* and had to put that book back down right away. I did enjoy wearing my Modigliani knock-off pins and embroidered scarves around town, though. Army ashtrays, lace doilies, and colored glass. You'd think I would have felt at home in those psychiatrists' offices with all their stuff and clutter, but it was different. My decoration felt eclectic and comforting. The offices felt stylish, planned, and worst of all, contrived. I didn't believe in them. I didn't derive any pleasure from the store-bought, poetically planted objects surrounding me. I wondered if they all hired the same decorator.

Michael was a flaming homosexual who was madly in love with JC, and hired him at every opportunity to repaint his properties in between new renters and leases. JC, the great artiste, considered straight painting beneath him. No pun intended. However, JC was also aware that Michael was in love with him and shamelessly used this fact to get his monthly rent knocked down. Michael lived on the corner of the very block we all lived in, and moving me farther away was in everybody's best interests. He was on the job.

Meanwhile, back on the farm, I was finishing up two miles on the track and debating whether to peel off into the campus for another two miles or stay put and plod on for one more mile, when the Army Air Force decided for me. A troupe of Air Force recruits, their status boldly printed across their chests and backs, descended upon the track and fell in jogging behind me. They were led by a female drill instructor who adroitly cleaned up the lyrics for the present clientele, and yet still kept it inspiring, if slightly macabre.

"If my parachute don't unfold," she boomed.

"If my parachute don't unfold," came the chorus.

"Box me up and send me home."

"Box me up and send me home."

My knees picked up. My pace picked up. I noticed other runners and walkers on the track begin to smile as the singing overcame them. I peeled off from the force of this unique cosmic ray and ran the campus loop.

Nirvana was crunchy and piled with snow hills on its borders. The sky was a sharp, dark blue like the thin ice itself. I didn't mind. The sky and the earth reflected my inner feelings. I felt fragile. I did not feel invincible even though I was taking actual steps to move on with my life. The ice cubes on the ground retained their solid form as the winter thawed beneath them. They looked like shattered glass strewn across the heavens that I ran upon.

I wake up in the morning, and I don't want to see the day. I don't want to hear it. I don't want to be in it. When I woke up Wednesday morning, after a good run the night before, I started sobbing when I finally had to get up, but I don't want to be dead. I know I don't want to be dead. Just exist for today. Get to work. Run tonight. Just keep running.

Thursday. I want it always to be night. Perpetual night. I want it dark and quiet. I don't ever want to have to open my eyes. I wish I could sleep forever.

Friday. I am really fucked up insane. I feel crazy. I'm snapping. I want to scream. I can feel the inner lining of my skull on fire. I can practically feel the nerve endings misfiring. I've been awake since 2:00 a.m., tossing about. Just get through today, and then get to the track. You have all weekend to flush out your craziness on the track. Run for the next three days. Run forever. Run!

Saturday. Once again driven with despair, I am out the door. I can do this. I can even out. I will be normal. I will run forever. I will run until there is nothing left to feel. I ran nearly six miles.

I didn't feel good about this. I don't feel good about anything. Running over five miles should make me feel something, right? The air was excellent, clean and cool. I only started sucking a little wind on the final hill. Air good. Soul black. I couldn't feel any lift. There was no flight inside of me, not even a glimmer, though my run was smooth and solid. What is wrong with me?

Sunday. Sick with depression. Soaked with it. Soaked, sodden, sullen, disabled, oozing, discharging, heavy, and thick. Every morning I feel like an anxious corpse, flat on a slab, shaking and dying. Move. Make yourself move. You must move. Do it. Don't call the doctor. The doctors will kill you all over again.

My knees and my ankles feel sore. My calves are aching. Go swim. Drenched, drowning, completely infused, dripping, and breathing deeply. I'm okay. I'm going to be okay. I thought about calling JC all weekend, but I didn't call, I made it. If I had cracked and called, things would ultimately have been worse. Things can always be worse. Think about it. And shave your legs for chrissakes.

Monday. Helen is brimming over with happiness. She formally introduces me to her new assistant, Adam, who started that morning. He is perfectly competent and a total stoner. Easygoing, with tousled, brown hair hanging into soft, brown eyes, he seems always to be smiling, even when he isn't. His eyelids are droopy, and crinkled at the corners, even though he is quite obviously a young pup. She sends him off into the darkroom so that we can chat.

"He is so great," she gushes. "He knows how to do everything. I didn't have to tell him hardly anything. He jumped right in and we're almost done with our workload for today."

It was lunchtime. I was on top of my workload as well, because I didn't have to spend any time running up and down the stairs or assisting Helen with the film runs. I was happy to gush right in.

"This is great. Where'd you get him from?"

"He's from Salisbury, on the Eastern Shore. He majored in photography and did some intern work at the hospital there. He looks like a beach bum, doesn't he? He's a real pothead. He already slipped me a joint."

"Yeah, you can see that a mile away. I'm surprised Richard hired him."

"This is his first job out of college, but he knows all the technical stuff. He was probably dirt cheap."

"Well, that'll do it, but be careful, I can smell him a little, you know?"

"I know. Here, smell my purse. Can you smell the joint? I'm going to have to leave him behind on my delivery run to the hospital this afternoon. I told him he'll have to clean up more when we go out on shoots." Helen was ecstatic. I actually started smiling back at her.

"Oh boy," I intoned like a swami, "I foresee some very long location shoots in the future. Can I come along and hold up the lights?"

"Very funny. Listen, I need to ask you something. You don't have to do it if you don't want to. I would understand."

"What is it?"

"My divorce is almost final. We've been apart for over two years now, but the paperwork is dragging on."

"Why on Earth?" I interrupted. "I thought you said you two weren't fighting about anything. You said you hadn't been married long enough to buy enough stuff to fight about."

"No, no, it's not about dividing property. It's all official paperwork and getting the lawyers to meet at the same time and all. He's going to keep all of the wedding things that his family gave us and I keep my family's stuff. We're selling some furniture that neither of us can use. It's the end now, and he's getting a little nasty, maybe because it's taking so much longer than we thought it would. I need someone to come into my lawyer's office with me as a witness. I need someone to swear and sign a paper as a witness that I haven't been with anyone else in the years we've been separated."

"What the hell? What are you talking about? Are you kidding me?"

"No, I'm serious. When you're getting a divorce, you're not supposed to have sex with anyone else while the divorce is in progress."

"You are absolutely kidding me. That is the most ridiculous thing I've ever heard."

"I know." Helen was very nervous, almost shaking. "Will you do it?"

"Of course I will." She collapsed into herself for a second and closed her eyes.

"Are you sure? You don't mind lying?"

"Hell no, I'll swear with a song in my heart. I've never heard of such a crazy, stupid thing. Neither of you are fighting, both of you agree that you made a mistake, there aren't any children, and I don't get it, what's the big problem? How the hell did Preston get divorced three times then? He's always screwing around. He never leaves one until there's another one on top of him."

"I think all of his wives screwed around, too, so they could never hold that against him. So you don't mind then?" she asked again.

"No, really. It's no problem. Just tell me where and when." The darkroom door swished open and we dropped the subject.

"Okay, I'll let you know."

"Okay." I left to go upstairs and eat lunch. I don't know why Helen was so nervous about asking me to lie for her about something so silly. No sex for two years because of some paperwork? It was silly in my mind, at least, but then again, Helen didn't know about the friends I grew up with as a good little Catholic girl. She didn't see the sickening tragedy I had witnessed when another best friend of mine had her young life destroyed by her parents' divorce. She and her teenage brother were declared "illegitimate," despite their obvious existence upon the earth, when their Catholic father bought himself an annulment so that he could marry someone else in the church. Their once-loving father dropped them both like hot potatoes for his even hotter new wife.

My other best friend's little sister was molested by a priest, and the family had to move to Virginia. I never heard from her again. The grief I absorbed from both of these incidents never died. It grew with every fresh offense, and the hits just kept coming. I never stopped smelling the ashes spill out from their bleeding, burning hearts. The ashes were stuck in my nose and on the back of my throat. I never stopped seeing the shock of disbelief and incomprehension in their eyes. Lambs at the slaughter. My friends were being slaughtered, and I was supposed to believe in a one, true God of wrath and vengeance. Give me a break.

I imagined the pen I would use to sign any document on Helen's behalf to be a sword of retribution in honor of them all. In honor of every child broken in the name of religion, I would have sworn on a bible without a drop of sweat. I mean it. I could have passed a lie detector test with flying colors, and let's face it, I'm a nervous wreck in just about every other aspect of daily life. Normally, I couldn't pass a lie detector test with the opening statement "My name is Grace."

In comparison to her listening to my constant crying over JC, and especially after she dragged me from the gates of hell on that awful night in October, I didn't feel the slightest twinge of wrongdoing. I was merely returning a favor, and a favor not even in the same realm of magnitude of the faith she had given me as a friend. I stopped in the kitchen to grab my lunch bag out of the refrigerator, and continued up into my office. I carefully cleared a space away from my keyboard so that I could eat and catch up on my emails at the same time.

**CAL:** Hi, Grace.
How are you? Feeling better, I hope. It's been a long time since I last spoke to you.
I'll be in Baltimore sometime in the beginning of April. Any chance we can put together a little reunion? Just let me know. I understand if you're not feeling up to it, but it would be great to see you.
Xx

**Grace:** I'm much better! I'm very well, and was just about to email Melanie and catch up with her. I'll find out if anyone is around town and let you know.

Okay, I'm lying through my teeth to Calvin once again, but getting together with old friends suddenly sounded infinitely superior to cracking up and begging for reconciliation with JC, and then crying for the rest of my life, guaranteed. Especially after the divorce conversation that had just transpired downstairs. I reached down to my purse on the floor and pulled out a small, folded piece of paper. I opened it up and looked at it.

"Please Just Talk to Me" were the words, written in JC's handwriting. I had found the piece of paper stuck under my windshield wiper blade as I walked to work this morning. Crumpling it up in my hand, I pitched it into the trash can.

**Grace:** Dear Melanie, what's up with you???? How is your job going? How is your love life? Mine sucks. I pretty much broke up with JC, and I'm bored and hibernating and trying to run between blizzards and not much else. Work is okay, I guess. I'm going to push with sending out the resumes this spring instead of constantly complaining about my job here.

Calvin has emailed me from California a few times. He says he's going to be in town in April and wants to get together with us. We could ask Diane and Abigail as well. I just thought I'd run it past you first since he said he got my email address from you. That's okay; by the way, I was just surprised he even thought about me is all. So let me know what you think . . .

**Mel:** YOU BROKE UP WITH JC??? AAAWWWEEESSSOOOMMMEEE!!! I wasn't allowed to say that while you were still with him. He was so bad for you! You are so much better off! How are you doing? Are you able to do any of your own artwork yet?

Thrilled to know that you are running again! That is great. My running is coming along slowly, but I am back up to an hour, and thinking about a marathon in the fall. I can't get lazy about my mileage just because of this winter.

Things with Eric are coming along. We've had a few differences over the last month, but have worked through the issues so far with fairly good manners. He took me to the Bahamas for my birthday, and ate strawberries off my back in the hotel room.

"Calvin from California," HA! Yes, I caught up with him briefly when I lived in San Diego. He drove down to take some photographs of a race event I was involved with for a television station he was working for. He asked about you, and I accidentally on purpose gave him your email address over time. Glad you're not mad at me! It was an innocent slip, in a professional setting, I assure you. So yes, let me know when this shindig will be set. I already knew he was coming to Baltimore from an email he sent me last week.

Missing you lots and lots.

Loved my birthday card. Thanks for thinking of me.

Love you much,

Mel

**Grace:** The Bahamas sounds like good manners to me! Professional slip, eh? No matter. I'll get the particulars and send out some invites to the rest of the gang. Can't wait to see you! Talk soon . . .

"Thinking about a marathon?" Bitch! Melanie was one of those natural runners who can run with both of her feet above the ground in mid-stride even when she's jogging. She had pleaded and cajoled and twisted my arm into trying out for junior varsity track in eighth grade instead of any other team because we were best friends forever before the acronym was even conceived, and for this I will always be grateful to her. She also talked me into one season of indoor track, for which I will never forgive her.

Melanie moved to California because of her father's job during our junior year in high school. I quit track that year, and, no joke, played lacrosse instead. Badly. In my senior year, I quit everything. I didn't know why at the time. I didn't feel like playing anymore. I rode off to college with my perfect credentials and my scholastic honors, and still didn't know why I couldn't feel anything. I was in classes and I heard nothing. I was in the middle of crowds, all over campus, and yet I wasn't there. I didn't feel the heat of anybody around me. I still don't know why I took a knife to my wrists in the wee hours of the morning on the dormitory bathroom floor. I didn't feel the knife. I can't remember if it hurt.

**Grace:** Hey ladies!! How is everybody? Diane, how are your beautiful children, and Abby, how is your hottie husband and why won't you give him to me? Listen up, Calvin Wright is flying into town this April for Easter, and

he wants to know if we can all get together for lunch. Melanie will be there, she's been keeping in touch with him over the years. Her mother still lives in the same house just one block away from his parents' house, and she even ran into him in California, however the hell THAT can happen. We've all got to get together and catch up. What do you guys think?
Love G

**Diane:** Hi Grace. I've been thinking about you and wondering how you were doing. I hope you and the family had a wonderful Christmas. Did you get a chance to spend time with your family? How are your mom and dad? How is your employment?
We're not planning on going anywhere over the Easter break, so be sure to let me know what you come up with. It would be lovely to see you. We all need to get together again.
Miss you!!!!
Love, Diane

**Abigail:** Sounds good . . . give me a schedule and then we can coordinate.

Diane and Abigail had both met JC in the early stages of our courtship over a few dinner parties and such. They heartily disapproved of him, as anyone in the civilized world would. They had sound minds and bodies, did everything by the book, married well, and lived as close to each other as we had lived growing up, except in an even better county of Maryland. I'm pretty sure Abigail had even turned Republican. She worked part-time in a real estate office, styled her hair, and seemed to completely forget that she used to wear Army surplus jackets with buttons that read, "Question Authority" in college. Diane was a rich housewife and did a lot of decorating.

The solid, predictable course of their lives both bored and frightened me. I didn't envy or covet their suburban lives, though I sometimes wished I were more like them. I don't know how this is possible, but it's true. They were safe. They looked beautiful. I was in the city, of course, and my stories of gunshots, corner bars, drunken art festivals, and syringes in the grass on my way to Wyman Park were horrifying to them.

"Why don't you move out of the city and closer to us?" they would cry. I looked at their sincerely shocked and loving faces in surprise. I thought my situation was about as interesting as it could get, aside from New York City, maybe.

Note to self: don't ever tell anyone what is really going on in your life.

Melanie was different. She was unmarried and worked as a marketing executive in D.C. We were the black sheep of the old gang. My stories made her laugh. Her stories were often worse than mine. Traditionally, there is no love lost between artists and marketing departments, but we never had a problem. I loved her more as we diverged together. I also had a vague idea what she might be up to with the sudden and very surprising reintroduction of Calvin into our lives. She would rather I bang anybody besides JC. She loved me, and would love to see him lost.

**Grace:** Mel, how about this - I come out to visit you and your mom and then you and I just pop over to the Wrights' house? I don't want to see the family alone, and I don't want to make a big thing out of it. I've never even met his father and barely know his brother. I can't do Easter week. Totally booked. Okay to tell him we're planning on stopping by, like, the weekend after Easter? Maybe have lunch around the corner if there's time. What's your schedule like? I've already contacted Abigail and Diane.

Any day in the week before Easter was completely out of the question. There is no getting around my family over any holiday, ever, with the possible exception of the Chinese New Year. I wouldn't be off the hook for a couple of days afterward either.

**Mel:** Your plan sounds great. End of the week would be better for me too. Let's stay in touch and we'll figure it out. I'm really looking forward to it.

**Grace:** Ball is in your court, Cal. Everything okay? Melanie and I thought it would be fun for me to meet her at her mom's, and then walk down to see you and yours. Maybe we could all have lunch around the corner at the Irish pub, say the Friday after Easter? Let me know. Would that be good? I'll wait to hear from you before I contact her again. I also contacted both Abby and Diane from the old neighborhood. You remember Diane, right? Let me know what your dates are and I'll try to set something up.

Love Grace

**CAL:** Of course I remember Diane. You, I'm a little fuzzy about. Aaahhh . . . it's all coming into focus now. You're THAT Grace. From the place near the thing where we went that time.

The Friday after Easter is perfect.

Xx

# Mile Fourteen

Nirvana is lush and green and overgrown and wet this morning. I didn't mind the wet shoes. I'm just happy that the dreariest winter in history is finally over. My progress is slow as I skip over the mud, but I feel really well. I feel like Miss America, trying not to topple in her stilettos on stage as I circumvent the deepest of the muddy pools. My defining new muscles and proliferating capillaries tingle as I set them into motion with the anticipation of a brand new run. I'm so into it, I've even started running at 6 a.m. before work sometimes.

If I were running for Miss America, I would definitely go the traditional route during the question and answer period, and carry on about how whatever I ended up devoting my life to would somehow involve furthering the cause of world peace. Down here in the real world, as a lonely, insignificant invader of space, internal peace is about all that I can strive for. But I've formed some ideas for those days when everything seems to be working against me, and let's face it, I'm not completely paranoid: everything in the world really *is* working against me some days. My alternative behavioral modification techniques are not traditional. *Runner's World Magazine* would never approve of them.

Sleep experts and relationship experts alike will warn you never to go to bed angry. Diet experts and nutritionists will tell you not to eat right before bedtime, much less go on a sugar binge. However, I find that both of these indulgences can add up to a highly successful, endorphin-releasing run the next morning, which in turn evolves into inner peace, which, of course, is one step closer to world peace.

Say I'm pacing the apartment in a heated mess around the same time I'm attempting to scrape my thoughts off the walls and get myself into bed at night.

Instead of freaking out and calling JC for some mind-numbing yet meaningless sex, I find that popping a beer along with a few spoonfuls of ice cream straight out of the carton can lull me into enough of a simmering silence to hide out for the rest of the evening until I'm able to fall asleep on my full and satisfied tummy.

The next morning, with nothing resolved, I leave the house in my running clothes while the city is still asleep and plunge straight off into a sugar-loaded run fueled with self-righteous fervor and determination to, you guessed it, save the world. I'm so focused on my arguments and so powered with sugar that, before I know it, several miles have already gone by and I feel the solutions appear before my eyes like the light at the end of the tunnel. I feel angelic, I can forgive everyone their trespasses, and I could just kiss the first person I see on the forehead.

At work, I am kind to my coworkers and understanding of my bosses. I arrive home with a smile on my lips, ready to tackle the disaster in the kitchen, the laundry undone, and the suspicious scraps of paper piled up in the corner behind the trash can. Can an endorphin rush really last past an eight-hour workday with the traffic in the streets and the work phone still ringing in my ears? The denial/reality portion of my brain agrees to say yes. And besides, there's always tomorrow morning alone at the track or swimming laps in the pool -- and there's still some ice cream left in the fridge.

In conclusion, I suggest that all spiritual leaders in the world be trained coaches as well. Exercise log books should be handed out with religious texts and referred to daily. The armies of the world should be required to do speed bursts and intervals while sucking on Tootsie Pops in team colors during boot camp. The resulting hormonal balance in the brain would then make it virtually impossible to attack anyone.

He is there, in aisle three, looking over the canned goods. Well, I had to run into him sooner or later. JC's reclusive, hermit style of living had worked in my favor so far, but the gourmet market is the only decent place to buy groceries within miles of our neighborhood, so here we are at last. I froze. He looked up and saw me, so I murmured a hello and walked over into the next aisle without a smile. He was beside me in an instant, but he didn't reach out to touch me. I stood still and looked blankly into his face.

"Don't be upset," he said softly and earnestly. "I'm not going to bother you, I'm happy to see you."

My face remained blank as I debated whether or not to keep walking as if he hadn't said a word. He spoke quickly, "I think it's better this way. I mean it. I think we'll be better just as friends. We're better now, aren't we?" I said nothing. "Why don't you let me take you out sometime?"

"No!" That came out easy.

"Not a date, but we can still go out as friends. Why can't we do that? I won't touch you, I swear." His eyes were full of dark emotion, turbulent and black with those thick, golden rims. I could feel myself getting sucked into their bejeweled and watery depths. His sleeves were rolled up to the elbows, and the black hair on his muscular forearms shot a familiar spark of desire down inside me. He was trying hard to control his own eyes, but they roamed and darted over my body, pausing at my waistline. We could never be friends.

"No, I really don't want to. Go out, I mean. I mean, sure, we're friends. I have to go now."

"Wait," he began, but I cut him off.

"I want to go now," I said. My voice was shaking. He straightened away from me. I turned and walked away, forcing my pace to remain even. I forced myself not to walk faster and concentrated heavily on keeping my footfalls light. I rudely left the parcels in my basket at the end of the checkout lane and headed out the door, straight for home. Outside, I glanced over my shoulder to make sure he wouldn't try to follow me. He didn't. I didn't see him. I walked home as quickly as possible without attracting attention and locked myself inside with my sadness. I was so sad, I could barely move. I was so sad. I weighed 300 pounds. I couldn't lift my arm to turn the lights on. My head was so heavy I couldn't hold it up. I tried to eat a leftover half of a sandwich from the fridge, but I couldn't make my mouth work. I couldn't chew. I put the sandwich back and walked to my bedroom in darkness. I crawled under the covers, fully dressed, and stayed there until it was time to get up for work the next morning. I didn't even get up to pee.

# Mile Fifteen

I flipped back and forth between the fetal position and the corpse pose all night long. When my legs started cramping up in the tight ball shape I was curled into on my left side, I stretched them out and rolled onto my back with my palms up, my arms straight down my sides, and my eyes on the clock. Not even midnight yet, good, good, close your eyes. I had plenty of time to be normal.

Breathe out, decompose. Breathe out, you're okay. Breathe out, plenty of time to rest. My heart starts to speed up anyway, and my legs and core are tingling. My brain begins to burn.

Flip to a ball on my right side. This is good. Much better. Breathe out, this is good, breathe out, you are comfortable, breathe out, slow everything down now. I doze. No good.

Eyes pop open and the clock says 2:30. Awesome. Plenty of time to get yourself together. Flip on to my back. No good, my legs are jittering. Flip back to the left side ball, okay. Breathe out, okay, breathe out, you're okay, breathe out, everything is okay, breathe out, you have all the time in the world.

Eyes open again, it's only 4:00. What the fuck? I thought I had slept for hours that time. Okay, no problem. I've still got plenty of time before I have to get up for work. Quick stretch and flip to the right again. Breathe, breathe, slow it down, it's okay, you're okay, everything is okay. This isn't working. Do I have any Xanax left in the house? No, it's all gone and I was afraid to ask for more. I was afraid of being referred to an actual shrink. I was afraid of being judged weak, incapable, unpromotable -- just the cute little graphics girl from down the street -- not the right stuff for a real job. "*Referred.*" I hate that word.     Okay, it's okay, you don't have any heavy deadlines today and you still have a couple of hours to rest. Okay, just rest. Breathe, you're fine. Breathe, you can do today. Flip right, flip left, flip right, flip left. Look at the clock. It's 5:30 a.m. and the birds are waking up to taunt me with their happiness. They jibber and jabber back and forth and laugh and chirp. Shotgun, somebody get a shotgun.

It's 5:45. I have to get up in 15 minutes. I go back to the corpse pose, prop myself up on all three pillows, and try to empty my mind and breathe as evenly as possible. There is nothing in my mind. Empty your mind. Not working. The Morning Dread is on my chest as heavy as a medicine ball. I've got to get it off and get to the shower. I start to reach for my vibrator so that I can blood-pump it off with an orgasm when I hear a chugging sound in the distance. Thank God. It's a train. It's a long train that rumbles along for what seems forever, with shrieking horns blowing from both ends. As it rushes by in all of its gloriously terrifying sweeping and clacking and pulling, I am finally able to get out of bed. I work quickly now to keep The Morning Dread at bay until I can physically get out the door. Don't stop to eat, forget about makeup, and just get some earrings. I can function as long as I have earrings. Now go.

The Morning Dread did not seem to be giving an inch, despite my gradually increasing success with my deadlines at work and my mileage at the track. Things were changing at work. Helen and Adam, as expected, stayed exclusively in the basement for most of the day, except when they were out on their very extended photo shoots. The equipment kept malfunctioning and the clients kept them waiting, and so on and so forth. The part about the equipment is probably true. I know, because I used to be the assistant for the larger, location shots, and our bosses would never invest in newer, better stuff. The suitcases weighed a ton and my arms used to ache as I tried to hold up the lighting poles for hours on end.

On top of all that, the ink on Helen's divorce papers was barely dry before she found herself in love with an important, blonde, upper-level executive from one of our big new accounts. The company manufactured a national brand of pharmaceuticals, and we were astonished when Preston landed the job, but I had great faith in Helen's ability to topple the blonde man. If anyone could blow over a real suit, a man seemingly out of our league, it was Helen, literally. I believe she would be willing to go further in a bedroom than JC, and he was pretty out there. I'm sure that is why he hated me hanging around her so much. He knew what she was up to. Sex freaks can read each other's minds, I suppose.

The best part about this new account was the mountains of swag she and Adam brought back from the shoots. Once the products were opened and rearranged under the lights all day, they couldn't be sold. They had to be thrown away. The photographers brought back so many products and perfumes and shampoos and body washes that the four of us girls couldn't even use it all. We divided the excess among ourselves, and I stashed mine away in boxes to save and give as the presents I could never afford for my family at parties.

Helen just wasn't around much anymore, period. Adam was so capable that she came in late and disappeared during the day even more than before. He was a good man, who silently bonded along with the rest of us as we covered for each other, day to day. This morning, I really wanted to see Helen, but she wasn't in. I felt tired and sad, and just wanted to hang out on her floor for an hour or so like I used to do on especially bad mornings.

I went downstairs to find Adam alone in the dark, standing over the light box. He looked up and read my face immediately. He was so laid back, he didn't ask a single question or give me any condescending, complicit looks of sympathy. He just said, "I have to go into the darkroom for awhile. Why don't you sit down." It wasn't a question. He walked past me, climbed into the cylinder door of the darkroom, and swished away.

I stood there for a moment, and then decided what the hell. I dropped my bags in the corner and sat down in the space between the light table and the mini fridge. I kept my coat on because the floor felt cold. Before I realized it, I had slumped to my side and was dozing off. I heard the darkroom door swish open, but I was half asleep, and I imagined it was Helen. I heard her feet walk quietly into the room and stop beside my body, all huddled on the floor. Suddenly, without opening my eyes, I tensed up inside. Adam was standing beside me, not moving, and obviously looking down at me. I was about to spring up when I heard the rustle of him taking off his coat. The dark room was always even colder than the rest of the basement. Then, before I could decide how to react, I felt him gently covering me with his coat. He turned, and walked even more quietly back into the darkroom.

A short time later, the intercom blasted out a phone call for me, line three. I got up and went to the phone. As I spoke to my client, I saw Adam come into the room with his arms folded tightly across his chest. He was positively white with cold. I hung up, thanked him heartily and went to work upstairs. What a gentleman. Too bad he was so young. Besides, no more artists.

Now that Helen was never around, I had taken to hanging out with the girls upstairs during breaks. Things were changing up there, too. Sandy had broken up with her verbally abusive, loser boyfriend and fallen into the arms of a former client. The former client worshipped and adored her. It was almost sickening. His puppy dog eyes followed her every move when he stopped by to pick her up, but we all agreed she deserved it after putting up with the sign maker for so long. His coddling and support had no effect on her workday style, just as the sign maker's hadn't. I reached the top of the stairs with my lunch in my hand to see her bending over the flat file, laying out some pages.

"Why am I doing this?" she bitched. "I just sent all of these pages over by courier and they couldn't possibly have looked them over yet. Why can't Robert and Preston walk down to the corner and hire someone else to bend over and take it on this table so I don't have to?" Mandala's face remained impassive as usual, but I burst out laughing. Sandy whirled from the table in a huff and went to pick up the line she had left blinking.

"I'm sorry," her honey voice crooned, "but Preston has taken the proofs to look over himself. Why don't I call you back in about an hour? You should have your copy from the courier by then and we can go over your changes together." The client must have agreed, because Sandy hung up without banging the receiver and reached for her sandwich.

"I can't talk to that asshole without passing out or puking unless I eat something first," she said calmly before taking a bite. Mandala was on a deadline, so she kept working as she ate and listened to us talk. Sandy took one more bite, pushed her food away, and turned back to her computer as well.

"I think I'll finish lunch while I check my emails," I say to the room, gathering myself up and going back down to the second floor. They are too busy for me today.

In front of my computer, I feel a twinge of unease as I open up my private email account. I am having second thoughts about the neighborhood reunion, and I half hoped that I would see an email from Calvin saying that he couldn't get away for the holiday or had cancelled his flight. There was no such email, and Easter week was drawing near. I decided to write to Melanie. She could always nail down a situation perfectly, even if she, herself, was at fault.

**Grace:** to Mel:  Subject:  **I Suck**

I don't know what the hell is wrong with me. This meeting with you and Calvin and Abby and Diane is less than two weeks away, and instead of excitement, I'm full of depression and angst. Why? I know who I am, and you know who I am, so why do I care what anyone else thinks about me?

I've been struggling with some heavy depression anyway these days. I'm not improving, I'm practically clinical, and I've been in a semi-crisis situation for weeks now, trying to avoid JC and/or end up on some powerful meds with nasty side effects. When I'm not at work or trying to run, I'm always on my back, lounging around, doing nothing. In short, I feel like a loser. And now I get to go out once again to meet up with my intimate high school pals to hear about their perfect "final" houses, their successful kids, their recent overseas trips, and their lovely husbands.

Jesus Christ, come on now. Can we really believe that I'm the only one of us that ever screwed up in a long-term relationship? Am I the only woman in our wild, old gang that ever thought about having an affair, a serious flirtation, or even some dead-end wishful thinking? Except for you, of course, you crazy bitch.

When I'm around them, I feel like they did everything right and I did everything wrong. I went through my closet last week because I have nothing new or cute to wear, and got so depressed at how I looked in everything that I left the apartment, went straight to a liquor store, bought a six-pack, came home, and guzzled one in front of my closet door. I popped open another while I rearranged my shoes and organized my jewelry.

On top of all that, I busted my left little toe on the edge of some furniture while pacing around in the middle of the night, and now it's all black and I can't run and I'm hobbling around and I can't even wear some cute boots to work tomorrow that I had forgotten about under all the shoe boxes. This morning I burst into tears at work when I finally found Helen alone. I told you about Helen. She's the one I ran off to the beach with for a weekend without telling JC and nearly ended up a homicide victim upon my return.

I don't wanna go to this luncheon. I don't wanna talk about myself, my work, or my monetary situation as Diane always seems so interested in, as if it's any of her fucking business. And she's the one who never worked a day in her marriage! She calls herself a "Work Widow" because her husband is always away on business, and you know her children are way past preschool and in elementary school full time now. She's all alone in that mansion for weeks on end. Can you really believe that no one ever hit on either her OR her husband as they live their separate married lives? Same with the others! I feel like such a loser around them. I was whining to Helen so she says, "Why do you subject yourself to this sham materialism and judgment? Why are you going? You have more than anyone when it comes to intellect and artwork and riches." Helen almost had me believing this for a minute.

I only really want to see Melanie (you) I cried, because we talk about life, love, books, running, our souls, and inspiration! We talk about ourselves and ask about each other, instead of parading about our families and our bank accounts as credentials.

So, see you soon! Can't wait!

Love Grace

**Mel:** Ha! I am feeling you, Grace. It's so familiar, your description of running out into the street in frustration and then doing something stupidly self-destructive, like guzzling beer over clothes. I feel like I'm there with you. The only cute shoes I have are running shoes. All of my other shoes are flats.

Of course, nothing good ever comes from comparing ourselves to our friends. As you point out, everyone's life is their own and nobody really knows what's going on out there. Everyone has secrets and skeletons. Believe me, everyone. And anyway, it's hard enough to deal with our own shit, let alone trying to figure out someone else's shit. It sounds like you really only want to meet with me and Calvin, so why don't we make separate plans from now on? If this reunion really bothers you, we won't do it again. Problem solved. Or . . . we could get really honest right in front of them and see what happens. I'd love to see THAT one play out! I'd back you up all the way and jump right in.

Whether or not Diane or her husband have affairs is beside the point. Guaranteed he has. I've been on the "other woman" end, and I guarantee it - no question. I don't even know her husband, but I know human nature -- that guy's had an affair. She probably has as well. But in any case, what does that mean to you? Nothing, either way. You do the things you do because they seem right. You're not irrational. You're not a bad person. You are an excellent person! We make choices and sometimes we feel great about them, sometimes we're ambivalent, and sometimes we're sorry, and then the sun comes up and you start over.

That's what this is, this life. The sun comes up and you do stuff. Stop keeping score, because everybody has a different scorecard and we're not all playing the same game. You don't hand in your card at the end of the day and get to choose something from the top shelf. None of it means anything, it's just stuff we do all day, and it all evens out.

Stop beating yourself up.

I'm still dealing with my last break up before Eric, even though it's been almost a year, and I see now, so clearly, how it continues to affect me. I may not be clinically depressed, but I'm still depressed, even with Eric around, and he's wonderful. I'll start thinking about my ex, and my self-esteem falls near to nothing. My desire to do things diminishes, and I'm nervous a lot. I'm not myself. So I kind of know how you feel. You don't get a break from it, there's no clear end in sight. I wish I had better advice, but all I can think of is to remind yourself that it's not really you, not the true you.

You are different, Grace. You are compromised, you are dealing with something other people can't even begin to understand, and you are alone in it. No one can climb in there and make it better. That you're surviving shows how strong you are. You're a monster! You're a machine! You must remember this! You can't save a family from a burning building, solve the debt crisis, run the Iron Man twice, and then show up at lunch and feel bad because your friend thinks her life is perfect. Fuck her new shoes and fuck her perfect husband. Every life has cracks in it that you don't get to see, it's far from perfect, and YOU ARE A MONSTER!! You are the Terminator!! Forget "you'll be back" . . . you ARE back!!

Buy something, bitch about something, drink a beer in a closet, masturbate twice a day, have sex without a future plan, flirt with someone, throw a tantrum. You carry too much pain around. You've got to let it go sometime.

Hang in there. I think we'll probably enjoy the lunch more than you imagine. Just remember, no one has to know anything about anything. We'll just go in there together, smooth as silk. We're all imposters. No one knows anything.

Save all of your words and thoughts. Write them down, and then send them to me. They are both creative and beautiful.

Can't wait to see you too!

Love you!

Mel


Melanie is my oldest and dearest friend in the world. She is the only person who knows and accepts that I am terminally depressed, and that there is no cure. She never tries to talk me out of it. She just talks me over it. She understands my running depression, and it's okay with her. She doesn't question it or make suggestions or try to get me committed. And what a pep talk! Spoken like a true marathoner. I think I really will enjoy this lunch. I think I'm even excited!

# Mile Sixteen

Easter was easy. I was surprised. Something must be changing inside of me, because Easter used to stress me out almost as much as Christmas. Well, certain facts did change a few things. The parties aren't as big and the baking is less extreme. The only thing I bake for Easter is one, big braided bread decorated with colored eggs tucked into the braids. Plus, I shone with the added perks of a few pricey perfume samples for the women in the family.

I guess the biggest change was that, for the first time, I didn't lie to my mother about attending Easter mass or where my boyfriend was. When she asked about the altar and the sermon and the decorations at Saints Philip and James Catholic Church, which, as I mentioned before, is directly behind my apartment, I didn't lie. Never mind that I could almost roll out of my bed in the morning and roll right into a pew, I just couldn't do it anymore. I tried to avoid the subject, but that never works with her.

I spoke calmly, "I didn't go Mom. You know, I don't attend mass regularly anymore. I don't feel right just showing up at Christmas and Easter every year." As I expected, she launched right in,

"No, no, no! You can go any time you like! You shouldn't think that way. You should attend more, but it's okay to attend any time. Did you even go at Christmas?"

"No."

"Oh, Grace." Her shoulders sagged. There was no time for a big display or a lecture with a house full of people, and we both knew it. She would never announce that her daughter wasn't attending mass anymore in front of her sisters and brothers and all of my cousins. I might taint their freshly confessed souls with my mere presence. She couldn't let it go though. She lowered her voice and whispered to me,

"Won't you ever go to church again? How will you treat this family? We have two weddings coming up this year alone."

"Mom, Mom, calm down, of course I'll attend mass for all family functions. I don't mind going with you and Dad on holidays, either. I just didn't make it out early enough this morning. That mass you attend at the crack of dawn is pretty, but I'd have to stay overnight here or something to make it on time for that one ever again."

"Well, you know the later masses get so packed on Easter and your father and I like to sit in our regular seats. We come all year round!" she ended indignantly, proving my point about the righteousness of regular, church-going Catholics. How dare we upstart, two-time-a-year heathens take up all the good seats?

People were crowding into the kitchen, and she had to stop talking. I smiled at her as the decibel level in the room rose to its family party pitch. I walked over and gave her a little hug to wipe the dour look off her face. Sadly for Mom, I felt relieved. I had one less lie to live.

"Don't worry, I'm fine," I promised, and gave her a quick kiss on the cheek before turning to scream at my cousins. Our family parties are always chaotic. Everyone talks at the same time and we're all trying to be heard above each other and over the shouting of the men in front of the games on TV in the next room. What can you expect from a house full of Italian-Slovaks? I never thought about it until two years ago, when I invited Sandy over to the house for the Christmas party. Sandy had just joined our firm, and was too broke to travel home to hang out with her friends. Her parents were flying out to Arizona for the holiday and didn't offer to buy her a ticket, even though they were rich and she was an only child. I didn't think she should be alone, so I asked her to come home with me.

She sat on a stool on the side of the kitchen for the entire evening, barely moving or speaking to anyone unless spoken to. I hoped we weren't boring her to death, but I found out at work the next day that she had been petrified. Sandy was not just an only child. She had no cousins, either. There was one estranged uncle she remembered seeing once or twice as a child. She had been absolutely overwhelmed with shock at the sight of my family in full swing. She never ate much, so that started things out all wrong right there. She spent a lot of time looking at the paintings on the walls and the doilies on the counter tops.

"Why do Italians like doilies so much?" she asked me after her shell-shocked confession. I had never really thought about that either. I had handmade doilies from my Slovak grandmother, and dainty circlets from Venice all over my apartment as well. What I did think about was a certain amount of forgiveness for JC, before he finally announced that he would not attend any more of my family parties. He never had a lot of extended family around growing up, either. This didn't let him off the hook. As a potential partner in life, he was expected to suck it up. No forgiveness.

It never stopped tickling me about Sandy though, that foul-mouthed, glossy-haired beauty getting frozen into place for hours over a little Christmas party. Poor Sandy.

**Grace:** Hey Diane, Yes, I still see my parents and brothers and at least two dozen other family members every Christmas. You know the deal. Mom and Dad even drove downtown to meet me for lunch at the BMA in January. Dad enjoyed the restaurant and even got turned on in the Matisse room. Mom liked the gift shop, but looked as if she couldn't wait to run for the door the rest of the time. Modern art confuses her and the city streets terrify her, so I must say that all is right with the world as it stands. Everyone is on the right track. How about you and the kids? Did your husband make it home for Easter? Did they get huge, ridiculously outrageous Easter baskets?

I've been trying to nail down everyone for Calvin's visit from California. I'll call Dad to see if the Irish Pub is still in business since we all know the area. Wait, let me call him right now . . .

GOT IT! It's still there, it's called McNeal's. It's in the main shopping center, just down the street from Melanie's parents. It should be super easy for everyone to find. Meet us at noon at the pub on the Friday after Easter, okay? Love G

**Diane:** Boo, I can't make it on Friday. My babies are still on spring break, and my mother isn't available to watch them. Can we pick a date in the next week or two that will work for all of us? I volunteer at the school on Tuesdays and Thursdays. Let me know, and give my love to your mom and dad. I want to see everybody!
Love, Diane

**Grace:** Bummer! Abigail told me that she always works Mondays and Wednesdays. In the meantime, the rest of us are going to meet on Friday anyway, because Melanie is driving in from Washington and Calvin is catching a plane back to California the following Monday. But don't worry, we'll work something out come summer. We'll talk soon,
Love G

**Grace:** Abby, we're meeting at McNeal's on Friday at noon. Sound good? Diane can't make it because she can't find a babysitter, but we can't change the date because Calvin is flying back after the weekend. I told her that we'd pick another date this summer, just for us locals. Looking forward to seeing you!
Love G

**Abigail:** I can't make it either. I won a trip for top sales in my office. Lance and I will be in New Orleans all week. Summer is better for me too. We'll get together then.

**Grace:** Okay, sorry to miss you. Wait a minute . . . aren't you and Lance doing this thing ass-backwards? Aren't you supposed to be in New Orleans BEFORE Easter? Just kidding!
Love G

**Grace:** Melanie, turns out neither Diane nor Abigail can make it. I am horror-stricken. I'll meet you at your mom's at 11:00 on Friday.
Love, your sorrowful, saddened, devastated, party-making friend, Grace

**Mel:** Pull yourself together girl! Buck up! I am absolutely devastated myself. Don't meet me at my mom's though, I can't get out of a morning meeting and will have to drive straight from work to the restaurant. I do have the rest of the afternoon off. I really can't wait to see you, it's been too long.
Lots and Lots of Love, Mel

**Grace:** I took the whole day off. In your face! Can't wait to see you too!

**Grace:** Okay Cal, we've finally got our acts together. Diane and Abby can't make it so you'll just have to settle for Melanie and me. Do you remember

McNeal's? It's right in the shopping center at the end of your road. We're meeting at noon. The menu has crabmeat on it, so you can get a little taste of home. I only picked that place so you wouldn't get lost. When is the last time I've seen you? I still have your cell phone number. We'll call you from there if you like.

Love Grace

**CAL:** Know it. It's been about six years. Looking forward.
Xx

# Mile Seventeen

It's Friday morning and I'm ready to go. There is still a little nip in the air, so I'm not wearing a dress, but I feel confident in the outfit I've chosen. I'm wearing a thinly knit, short-sleeve, mock turtle-neck sweater in a rich, dark brown. It shows off the lean biceps I've been working on, and the length of my neck. My corduroy pants are light tan, low rise, and slightly flared over high-heeled brown boots with gold buckles that match the burnished, gold buckle on my thick, heavily stitched brown belt. The combination makes my legs look long and my stomach flat. Getting stuck inside for half the winter with nothing but exercise videos was paying off. I left my hair down, the golden highlights glinting over the wide, gold hoops in my ears. Hoop earrings always flattered my diamond-shaped face, and earth tones went well with my skin. I felt like a warm, golden cloud. I felt fun and flirty.

I was ready early and started feeling nervous, so I decided to drive to the restaurant and wait around in the parking lot for a few minutes. I prayed fervently that JC was not at home that day to accidentally see me from his window as I walked briskly to my car. Michael had called me back, promising me a place in May, and May couldn't come soon enough.

There was no traffic, and I arrived at the restaurant fifteen minutes early. That's cool, I said to myself. I'll just sit here for a few minutes and enjoy the sunshine while I calm down a bit. My cell phone rang. What now? It was Melanie.

"Grace! I'm not going to make it! I'm so sorry! I'm stuck in traffic. I've barely moved an inch in almost an hour. There must be some kind of accident up ahead because this is insane, even for D.C."

"You are kidding me."

"No! I'm not! I'm going to have to take the nearest exit and get off the expressway before I run out of gas."

"Where are you? Can't you take another route and show up late?"

"I'm barely out of the city limits. I don't even see an exit sign up ahead. People are turning their cars off around me. I'll never make it. Listen, I've got to get off my cell in case this gets worse and my batteries start to go. Don't worry about me, just go ahead and enjoy your lunch. I'll call you later, when I get out of here. I'm so sorry. Say hi to Calvin for me."

"Okay, okay, I'll call you this afternoon to find out what . . ." but Melanie had already hung up.

I sat up straight in my car and looked at the dead phone in my hand. Now I was really nervous. Should I call up Calvin and just call the whole thing off? No, that would be so rude, after all the planning and, and, because I secretly, sexily, really wanted to see him. How the hell was I going to explain this without sounding like a total ditz? I looked at my watch. It was time. I looked out my front windshield to scope out the parking lot and there he was, heading toward the front door of the restaurant. That had to be him. Tall and handsome, with a slightly hawked nose and a straw fedora. Panic! No, don't panic. Just calm down, act natural, and tell the truth. I got out of my car and came quickly up behind him as he was reaching for the door.

"Calvin." He turned.

"Grace." We came together and awkwardly hugged.

"You're not going to believe this. Melanie just called and she's stuck in traffic. She says she can't make it."

He looked down at me, I had forgotten how tall he was, with a completely calm expression and a slight smile pulling at the corner of his lips.

"Okay," he said. His face was blinding me. I mean, the sunlight streaming into my eyes behind his face was blinding me, and I said, "Come on, let's go in. We can catch up inside."

The inside of the restaurant was so dark it took me a moment to get my bearings. A waitress in a flouncy green skirt led us to a booth all the way in the back, away from the front door, thank goodness. The atmosphere was already distracting, and I didn't want to contend with opening doors or tipsy people flashing in and out of my peripheral vision. She immediately brought us water, silverware, and menus, and then asked if we would like something to drink before we decided.

"Anything light on draft," I blurted without hesitation. How unladylike. I should have at least thought about it coyly first. "Do you have Bud Light?"

"Yes. Tall or short? That's a 12-ounce or a 16-ounce glass."

"Two talls, please," Calvin said evenly. She gave a tiny nod and turned away. I took a slug from my water glass to ease my suddenly dry tongue, and started flipping through the menu without noticing a thing on it. Why was I so nervous? Calvin and I had never dated. We had never been a "thing" and we hadn't even gone to the same high school. His parents sent him to a fancy, prep school in the area, but he stayed a part of our gang due to both history and location. We all grew up within a few miles of each other, and his childhood house was literally two houses away from Melanie's.

"It's good to see you," he said when she walked away. "You look good. Tell me about yourself," he said while looking straight into my face.

"It's good to see you, too," I exclaimed enthusiastically. "How are your parents? I used to see your mother around all the time before I moved into the city. She always stopped to talk to me. She is so sweet!" Jesus, I sounded like a stupid cheerleader. Plus, I was lying. It didn't feel good to see him. I felt totally stupid and ill at ease and wished I had bailed in the parking lot. I wished I had never agreed to this luncheon. The beers came, and I managed to restrain myself until Calvin picked up his glass.

"Cheers," he said, his eyes still strangely locked on my face. We clinked glasses and drank. I was able to see some words on the menu now. I politely listened to him comment on his parents and their retirement and how they shouldn't have retired so early because all they did now was fight and how eager he was to return to California. This was good. He really didn't want to be here either. He probably just wanted to get out of the house in any way possible. I relaxed.

"Wow, I'm sorry to hear that. My parents are semi-retired and travel all over the world every chance they get. They seem to love it, and can't wait to retire completely. You know, I don't think I ever remember them fighting in front of us."

"Well, what can I expect from a father that idolizes Charlton Heston? My father's bookshelves are nothing but nonfiction, and mostly political. I used to love hanging out at your house, we all did. Your parents were the coolest, and your mom was the most beautiful. You look like her."

I passed comment on that one as I pretended to study the menu. It's true that my house was the coolest, due largely to the fact that my parents worked so much and were hardly ever there. Mom always kept the freezer stocked with pizzas, just for our friends, and there were always plenty of soft drinks. The one thing that our household never lacked was food. There was a basketball net in the front of the garage, and a backyard big enough for a football game. Neighborhood kids were always knocking on our front door to ask if it was okay to shoot some hoops. The front hall closet was crammed with basketballs, so they didn't even have to bring their own. They rolled out all over the floor whenever someone opened the door to get their coat, just like a scene in a television comedy. The basement was turned into a clubroom, with a bumper pool table and a closet full of games. Yes, I thought a little proudly, our house was the coolest, as well as the loudest. Poor Sandy.

The waitress was back at our table.

"I'm having the crab cake sandwich special," I said to her as I closed my menu. I looked across the table to see that Calvin didn't appear to be looking though his menu at all. It was still open on the appetizer page. He glanced down briefly,

"I'll have the onion ring appetizer," he said and handed over his menu to the waitress. "I'm not really hungry," he said, turning his face back on me.

"Oh, come on! You come all the way from the West Coast and you don't even order a crab cake? I've never eaten a decent crab cake anywhere in the world besides here in Maryland. I don't believe there are any good ones in California. They're not even good in our border states. How can you pass this up?"

"Oh, I've had two already, while going out with friends. You go ahead, I want to watch you eat."

This statement was uncomfortable, maybe, but not weird, right? I mean, he had already stated that he couldn't wait to go home to California, and that he had already caught up with all of his prep school buddies. I was last on his list. I was only a courtesy call, a reason to get out of his parents' house, right? Then what was the weird vibe that I kept feeling in the air between us? Why had I felt weird emailing him, before? Why did he stare at me, unflinchingly, as we covered the requisite banalities of brothers and sisters and friends and work? And why couldn't I return his gaze? Every time I looked him full in the face, I felt flustered and looked away. His face was perfectly chiseled, with very pale blue eyes, short hair bleached blonde to almost white, and thin, but smiling lips. He had a light tan, of course, and his shoulders were broad and straight over the table. He was tall, strong, and light, whereas JC was small, dark, and wiry. There couldn't be two more opposite-looking men, I was thinking, when it finally hit me, what I was feeling in the air. It was sexual tension. I looked straight into his movie star face, and then I saw something else. I saw danger.

The food arrived. Calvin pushed his tiny plate away to the side and picked at an onion ring. I took a huge bite of my sandwich and tried to chew slowly to steady my nerves. I needed my carbs to calm down, I said to myself. Runners need carbs to handle every situation I inwardly reasoned, as I continued to eat alone at our table. When the waitress came back with more napkins, Calvin ordered another round, with his eyes questioning mine.

"Sure," I said.

*Danger! Danger, Will Robinson!* The robot in my head screamed while flailing its arms to and fro. The waitress brought our beers, and I launched into a funny story about how the teacher from my semester abroad had marched a bunch of us girls over to her boyfriend's restaurant in Venice one night. His kitchen staff didn't know how to pick the boatload of crabs he had acquired, and wanted to feature as a special on the menu the next night. She had Maryland girls! We had clacked over there in our new Italian shoes in the damp, deserted streets after midnight. Bruno couldn't have us in the kitchen until the dinner rush was over. We filed through narrow alleyways and crossed unknown bridges under a brilliant white moon until we reached the back door of Il Tulipano, Bruno's place. He had everything set up. His kitchen was huge and wide, with a long table covered in crabs in the center, beyond the stoves. His kitchen men leered at us with honest, good nature as they sat beside us at the table and watched us show them how to get the meat out cleanly. Bruno opened bottle after bottle of wine and kept the music playing as he danced around the table with our instructor. We didn't hobble back to our hotel near San Marco square until nearly dawn. The façade of the basilica was luminous in the early morning light, and appeared enormous over the empty piazza. I had never seen the piazza so silent. It was a wonderful sight, and a wonderful night.

"Did you know," Calvin said, "that I had a crush on you in the fifth grade?" I'm not even sure that he had been listening to my story. He was leaning back in the booth, staring at me, measuring something.

"Oh, that is so funny, because I had a crush on you, too, from the first moment I saw you. I never dreamed you even noticed me. That is too funny."

"Do you remember the party in our senior year, when I came in all messed up because I had wrecked my car on the way over? You didn't speak to me."

"Yes, I remember that party." He had come in wearing a long black overcoat, tall, muscular, stunning, and rattled. He went straight away to the host to ask to use the phone to make arrangements for his car. I hid behind a wall, because I was dressed in my usual eclectic style and I felt like a frump and a fraud being in the same room with his magnificence. I was too embarrassed to claim our acquaintance.

"I didn't know you even knew I was there. I never thought you noticed me."

"I was watching you. You were wearing overalls, and some sort of hat." How fucking embarrassing. He leaned forward and placed his arms on the table. "How about that? A fifteen-year crush. Over half of our lifetimes," he said in that same even tone, with his eyes boring into mine.

The waitress was there. We broke contact and turned our heads toward her at the same time. No, no thank you, nothing else, just the check please, no doggie bag, we're fine, everything was great. Calvin took the slim, black checkbook from her hand before she could lay it down on the table. He set it on the seat beside him and turned back to me. His intentions were perfectly clear.

"Can I see you again before I leave? I'd like to see you again, alone."
I felt weak and sad. I was madly attracted to him, but I was too fragile for a one-night stand. I was a little drunk, and he was leaving soon. The situation was safe, so I spoke candidly,

"You know, I've been imagining fucking you in a thousand different ways since we've been sitting here, but I don't think it's a good idea. It wouldn't do either of us any good. I think we should leave it alone." I saw his eyes change, but his body didn't flinch. He picked up the checkbook, glanced inside, stuffed it with bills, and placed it on the table.

"No, you should let me pay, or at least tip. You didn't eat anything." He shook his head and then stood before I could go on, extending his arm out to take my hand.

"It's my treat. Let me walk you to your car at least." He was smiling. He had taken no offense. I smiled back in relief, and we walked, hand in hand, out of the dark, cavernous restaurant and into the glaring sunlight. He walked me slowly to my car and then turned and took my other hand.

"You're sure I can't see you again?"

"I don't think it's a good idea," I said, bowing my head with apology. He didn't press. He could feel my mood. He let go of one of my hands and slowly, tenderly, lifted my chin.

"Can I kiss you, then?"

"I wish you would," I whispered. Still, he didn't rush. He lowered his face and pressed his lips perfectly onto mine. He started moving them slowly. He pulled my body against his. Our lips locked like Legos as he pressed his mouth more firmly onto mine and kissed me, and kissed me, and kissed me in the middle of a busy parking lot in the bright afternoon sunshine. Holy. Shit.

He pulled away slowly and smiled down into my eyes one last time.

"Goodbye," he said.

"Goodbye," I think I said. I got into my car. I didn't stay to watch him drive away. The next thing I remember was taking the Charles Street exit into town.

Veering left onto St. Paul Street, I drove right past my apartment. My brain had been buzzing the entire ride home. I felt like I had something more to say. I didn't know what I wanted, but I was floating in some kind of anxious, unresolved limbo and I needed to get onto my computer at work. I didn't have a personal computer at home like the others. I really didn't need one, and couldn't afford it anyway. I lived so close to work that there was no getting out of going into the office unless Godzilla suddenly descended upon the city.

It was late afternoon, and our whole staff usually bailed as early as possible on Fridays. The only exception was photography. They always had a doctor's deadline on a Friday night. When I pulled up in front of the building, I didn't see Helen's bike in sight, and the curb had plenty of free parking. One down. I let myself in with my key and the alarm didn't go off, so there had to be someone there. I heard a noise downstairs. That must be Adam. Upstairs I found Sandy at her computer, signing off.

"What are you doing here?" she said, already grabbing at her things to leave.

"I just wanted to check my emails before the weekend to make sure I didn't miss anything important today. Then I won't have to think about it all weekend," I replied casually, though I felt like I was sweating and shaking a little.

"Okay, see you Monday." She brushed past without taking me in. I rushed to my computer and sat down to write to Calvin.

**Grace:** You are really, really hot.
Maybe next time, when I see you again, I'll be feeling stronger and less afraid. Now, I've got to email Melanie and apologize for never calling her back. I actually didn't lie about her cancelling at the last minute, though it did occur to me to use her as a ruse in order to seduce you at one point.
Love Grace

I sat back in my chair and took a few deep breathes before hitting "send." I paused another minute, then powered down and got up to leave. I stopped at the top of the basement stairs.

"Adam? You down there?"

"Yeah," came a voice from somewhere in the depths.

"It's Grace. I just stopped in to check my inbox and I'm leaving now. Everyone else is gone. You're alone."

"Okay."

Outside, the sky was still beautiful and the sun was still brilliant. I briefly thought about hitting the track, but I was wiped. The beer that had made me animated and energetic before now made me feel woozy and tired. I decided to drive home and lie down on the couch until I got my strength back.

Dropping everything on my floor, I had just gotten comfortable with my eyes closed on the couch when the phone rang. Motherfuck!

"Hello?" It was Melanie.

"Heeeeeey," she crooned, "how was lunch?"

"Hey! Where are you? Are you back in D.C.?"

"No, I finally made it to my mom's. I don't know what the hell the traffic was about. I never passed any accidents on the road. I'm going to stay the night here and head back to D.C. first thing in the morning. There is no way I'm getting anywhere near my car again today. So, how was lunch? Did you go to McNeal's or somewhere else? I'm so sorry I ditched you. Give me the gossip!"

"No, we stayed at McNeal's. It was pretty strange and boring, I guess. I wished you were there. I mean, we really don't know each other after all these years and I could have used your wit at my side during this one, Mel. I'm afraid there isn't any gossip for you.

Well, wait a minute, it depends on what you mean by gossip. I have a little gossip. I had just pulled into the restaurant and parked the car when you called. I thought about cancelling with Calvin, but decided to go ahead and have lunch with him anyway because I was starving. After we hung up, I looked around the parking lot and Calvin was already at the restaurant door. Okay. I felt slightly stupid, but so what. I met him at the door and informed him of your cancellation, wondering all the while if he thought I was putting him on.

We went in, and he doesn't want to eat! I was freaking starving, so I ordered anyway. Conversation was the usual strangers who used to know each other kind of stuff, mostly about our jobs and all of you guys. He barely said anything. He probably gets sick of people trying to use him to get into the television station where he works, and so doesn't like to talk about it. He told me old friends and relatives keep flying out to flop at his place, thinking he can somehow just get them a job. I felt nervous because I really didn't know what to say to him, and it was hard to relax with him just watching me chew and trying not to be a slob about it. We wrapped it up and hugged goodbye in the parking lot. I got home just before you called."

Melanie laughed. "Yes, that sounds like him. He is strange. When we ran into each other in San Diego, he behaved in much the same way. I invited him to have drinks with my crew on the night before he left, when suddenly he stood up and announced that he had to go meet someone and put out some fires at work. It was almost 2:00 in the morning! Maybe he hadn't made hotel arrangements for the night and decided to start driving back before he got too drunk."

"TV people probably have to work all night, around the clock."

"Yes, maybe. Anyway, I decided it was silly for me to drive all morning and not even knock on his door. I went for a walk to see who was home and how his mother is doing. He answered, and I stood in the hallway for a few minutes, talking to his mom and his wife. I didn't know he was married, did you? It was a short conversation. I came home to call you and get a better scoop."

His *wife???*

"No scoop." I started trembling. "I didn't know he was married either until he mentioned it today. Um, so, are you going to stop and see me tomorrow on your way back?"

"No, I can't, I'm sorry. I need to go into work and catch up on some things. Eric and I already have plans for the rest of the weekend. I'll email you next week sometime and we'll set a positive date."

"That's okay, I have some stuff to catch up on, too." Boy, did I ever. "I'll talk to you next week. Love you!"

"Love you back!" We hung up.

His *wife???* Why on Earth didn't Calvin bring his wife to lunch with him versus leaving her at home? When and where had he married? Was he planning on divorce? If he was in the middle of a divorce, then why would his wife tag along across the entire country and stay alone with his parents while he ran around meeting up with old friends? Was she clinging on to a dead love? Why did he act like he wanted to hook up with me?

For some perverse reason, instead of feeling ashamed that I had flirted with a married man, my body was aflame. I was flush with a sudden, searing desire. I had never considered myself particularly attractive in the traditional sense. I never wore much makeup, my hair wasn't fixed, and my clothing wasn't trendy. I never understood what JC saw in me, unless it was the chance to exercise complete control over an obvious wimp-ass with low self-esteem. Perhaps he saw me as an artist's model: not too perfect, but with interesting lines. Girlfriends had pointed out to me that certain men were looking at me when we went out, but when I looked around, I never saw them.

Now, a married man, far from home, with a withering, unwanted wife in tow, had wanted to take an almost certainly large risk to have sex with me. I realized I was pacing frantically back and forth. All traces of fatigue were gone. I truly was on fire. On impulse, I made a decision, snatched up my purse, and headed back to work.

Everyone was gone. Good. I went straight upstairs before I could talk myself out of it. I didn't feel weak or afraid anymore.

**Grace:** Can you get away tomorrow afternoon, or anytime on Sunday?

"Send."

I walked home quickly, again. I honestly don't remember a thing I did for the rest of the afternoon and evening.

Saturday morning dread, 6:00 a.m., right on schedule. I wasn't feeling well at all. My body awoke with a start. I was full of compressed pain and suppressed screams. There was something bad ahead. Then I remembered what I had done. I felt really, really down. Just reeking despair and drowning in weakness, though my legs were twitching under the covers as if I were already on the track. I sprang up before I could allow myself into wallowing, and started talking myself into action instead.

First of all, adults have casual sex. It happens all the time. If everybody waited for the love of their life to appear, the world would be a very angry place. So, he's married, but it can't possibly be a lasting union if he's so obviously yearning to shag an old stranger. I'm not a home wrecker. His home is his own, private problem, right? What if he's just a total playboy and hits on any woman? No, no, I wasn't getting that feeling from him. His quiet manner wasn't calculating. His watchful eyes weren't philandering. There was sadness in his silence. Was I projecting so that I could rationalize having sex with a married man? How do I know he is still married to that woman? What did Melanie really know? If he were still married, he must certainly know that I would find out about the wife from Melanie. None of these thoughts mattered. I didn't even know if he'd seen my email, if he could get away, or if he still wanted to see me again. Remembering my email sent that bloody rush of heat throughout my limbs again. I had to move.

By this time, I was in my running clothes and left my apartment with a full set of keys in hand. First stop, I'll warm up by walking briskly down to work and taking a quick look at the mail. The street was deserted and the rowhouse was silent. There was nothing in my inbox. This did not deflate me. I felt a surge of safety and my energy was going through the roof. To the track!

I locked up, leaving my computer on, and flew up the street at a pace that was not appropriate for a warm-up.

Okay. Everything is okay. Yes, I wanted to have sex with Calvin Wright, but if I didn't, it was all okay. He's leaving on a jet plane. No harm, no foul. I didn't feel foolish for sending the email. I'm only human. I can laugh it off, make a witty joke of it. I rounded the last lap of mile three at the same steady pace and bounded off the track. The grass was wet. The moisture seeping into the toes of my shoes did not bother me. My progressively wetter and wetter socks did not slow me down. Nirvana awaited me, with the promise of cottony footfalls after navigating the soppy soil leading up to it. I glided through Nirvana with a wide, comfortable stride and splashed out onto 29th Street. The columns of the BMA gleamed with white magnificence in the strong morning light and I felt alive and wild and free.

**The math: no aggression + no fear + endorphin rush = perfect run.**

I decided to cool down by walking briskly back to work and shutting everything down. There was a message in the inbox.

**CAL:** Hi Grace. I'm just checking my mail now (couldn't sleep), so sorry for the late reply.

I'm a little tongue-tied, trying to say how much I liked seeing you yesterday. A fifteen year crush! And I drove away from there with that same feeling I remember having whenever I thought about you, even as a kid. Nervous. Excited. You're beautiful, sexy, interesting, a little weird. And yes, I'd love to see you again before I go. I need more time to explore you. It's going to be tricky, unless I have a good excuse. So let's think of one. When and where on Sunday?

Xx

Okay, he knows that I know. I started typing without hesitation.

**Grace:** The feeling I had as I drove away was also the same that I've had all my life: *I want him. But you can't have him Grace. So just forget about it.*

Then I couldn't stop feeling your kiss. Then I extrapolated and my face became hot and my legs became hot and I drove home as carefully as I could at ten miles over the speed limit just to get there as fast as I could before I had an accident.

Got home safe. All was well. Then my mind raced on. Where would we go? What would be the reason? How many people would I have to lie to or hide from before I felt too overwhelmed with the details to enjoy you at all? I put it out of my head once more, reminding myself that you are leaving on a plane on Monday for California and I ought to just get into bed and masturbate. The "enjoy you" part got stuck in my head again and I continued with my thoughts.

You leaving on a plane this Monday for California suddenly struck me in an advantageous light. Don't take offense at this! It's just that I am completely uninterested in changing anyone's personal or marital status at this time or any time in the near future.

I thought about how fleeting life is. I thought about how few good kisses I've ever felt. I thought about something I had read in a magazine article. The article was about a dying man, who said that he didn't regret the things he had done in his life. He regretted, more, the things that he hadn't done. I thought about how I live alone, and how empty the city becomes every Sunday. You could come and see me this Sunday.

Shit, my face is burning again, among other things. Where was I - oh yes, - seeing you. There is no one I expect to show up at my apartment tomorrow. There is nothing I am expected to do, and nowhere I am expected to be.

I have to stop for now -- your thoughts so far?

I ran down to the kitchen to get something to drink. I was craving an ice cube. I sat at the table and stared out over the tiny rectangle of a back lawn. I slowly sucked three ice cubes away, and then chugged down a glass of water and went back upstairs.

**CAL:** Subject: <u>Us</u>

I loved this note, Grace. I was feeling the same way all day yesterday. A little electric charge pulsing through me when I thought about you and kissing you and what I would do to you if I had the chance. And I confess, I thought about you through a very long shower. So yes, please . . . let's meet tomorrow. I only wish it could be today. It will be easiest for me to get away if it's around 10:30-11:00. I can say I'm going out to hit some golf balls with a friend I haven't seen yet. I made a decision recently to stop denying myself happiness. This is something between you and I, something I've thought about for many years, and something I really want to do. And I love how excited I am thinking about seeing you again.

Xx

**Grace:** I'll stay inside my apartment all day. I won't leave for a minute. I'm sending you directions.

**CAL:** See you then . . .

# Mile Eighteen

On Monday morning, I walked to work in a state of subdued suspension. I felt like I was somebody else, not myself. I felt really, really happy. This feeling made me extremely wary and uncomfortable, because I wasn't sure what to do with it. I didn't know how to act. It would probably be best for me to avoid my coworkers as much as possible, without attracting undo attention, until I could figure out how to land this strange feeling of floating from within. My feet weren't hitting the ground. I was watching myself in the third person as I slipped my key into the lock and walked into work. Luckily, the way our work was set up would make it relatively easy to avoid a lot of contact. I didn't expect to hear from Calvin. I knew he was on a plane. I didn't expect anything unusual to happen, and it didn't.

At the track that evening and ran as if in a dream.

On Tuesday morning, there wasn't any word from Calvin. I didn't expect any word, I told myself. He's just landed and has to get back to work himself. He's got to get back into his familiar groove. He's still married and living in the same house, though not for long he assured me. He didn't have any kids to distract him, but he certainly can't sit around mooning about me with a wife hanging over his shoulder, now can he? After work, I wanted to go to the track but couldn't. My legs were like rubber. I had run too far the night before, when I couldn't feel any pain, and now I was too weak to run again. I'll take the night off and catch up on my reading. Buy some beer on the way home, maybe a glass of wine, and just kick back and relax for the night.

On Wednesday morning, I started to feel again, just a little bit. I overcame The Morning Dread with anticipation in my heart, but there was nothing in my inbox when I arrived at work. What did I expect, a pat on the back? What did it matter? We came together knowing that there wasn't any future for two people that lived on opposite sides of the country, but come on now! He could at least send me a message to have a nice day.

I didn't go to the track again that night, either.

On Thursday morning, I was almost myself again. I could still inwardly smile at the memory of last Sunday, but the familiar gray cloak of dust that covered my life was settling softly back down into place, and my feet were once again on the ground. I powered up at work, and there was a message in my inbox.

**CAL:** Subject: **YOU**
Wow. That's all I have to say. (for now)
Xx

**Grace:** Ah! Thank God! I've been stewing and wondering . . . wondering what is the appropriate time interval that must pass in order for one not to be labeled an internet sex stalker. I decided not to tell you that all I can see while flipping through papers at work is the tattoo on your hip, and all I can see on the computer screen in front of me is your head between my legs and your lips over mine and all I can hear as the intercom blasts out behind me is you saying "Ah, there it is," when you saw my belly ring, as if you had been thinking about it. I decided not to tell you any of my rampant, rutting mind obsessions for at least one week so as not to frighten you into disappearance. Clearly that plan has failed. But you can take comfort in the fact that you are geographically protected and safe. (for now)

**CAL:** I've been trying to find a time to write safely, but keep having to abort. Only have a second now, but hopefully will find time tomorrow.

I went back into an elevated suspension, and back to the track after work. I ran as if I were in a movie scene. And then it was Friday.

**CAL:** Hi. So . . . I've been replaying that afternoon again and again in my mind. You on the bed, lifting slightly so I could undress you, the taste of you, watching you licking me. I haven't been that excited in a long time. It's going to sustain me for a while. It's funny also . . . I sort of wonder how it all happened. One minute we're catching up after six years or so, the next I'm devouring you on your bed. Man!

So now it's back to the grind, I guess. It is good to be back in California, I have to say. The hot air, without all that humidity, the lengthening days, and good to be working. I hope all's well with you and that you continue to get what you want out of life. You're so gorgeous and sexy, Grace, and obviously talented. It's very likely I'll be back there before summer's over. Maybe you could make a little time for me then.

Xx


Huh. Well, that was flattering, but also somewhat dismissive. Again, what did I expect? I wrote back something cheesy and suggestive about being available in the summer, and signed off with love. I worked furiously on my deadlines for the rest of the day. I couldn't get to the track fast enough. I needed to think, and I could only think calmly and logically after a mile or two.


It was warm enough for shorts, but I wore a long-sleeve T-shirt in case it grew cooler as the night approached. I didn't know how far I was going to run. My shorts were dark gray, and my T-shirt was a dull white. My attire was consistently loose and unobtrusive, as usual, compared to the neon Spandex get-ups of some of the other women on the track, but I was passing them. My ponytail no longer limped around between my shoulder blades. Now it flew about, and sometimes flew forward and smacked me in the face.


**Mile one:** Michael had shown me a cute little place, and I was definitely moving in the first week of May. Start grabbing extra boxes in the grocery store and get a jump on the packing. The new apartment was only a few blocks northeast of the old one, but I wanted to stay in Charles Village. I was comfortable here with my work and my track, and without any kind of commute. I had grown accustomed to rolling out of bed at the very last minute and walking to work, unlike the huddled masses, yearning to breathe free that I watched struggling in traffic as I waltzed by. The new apartment was on the second floor, again, but I only had the front, not the back, so I didn't have to worry about the alleyways. It was smaller, but the stained glass bay window was nearly identical to my current window, and the rent was only 15 dollars more a month. I was so close to the hospital I could crawl there if necessary. It felt lucky, and safe. I knew JC and his misanthropic ways, and I knew that I would not be running into him, despite the proximity. He never left his apartment unless he absolutely had to, he knew my schedule, and his pride would send him out for his errands during the regular workday in places where I wasn't around.

**Mile two:** The hospital. I wonder if I can get any more of that Xanax from the doctor without being forced to see a therapist. Moving is particularly stressful, and that stuff could come in handy. I'll be so close to the hospital that I'll probably be listening to sirens all night long instead of the familiar, soothing sounds of the train tracks. I'll miss the train tracks. I'll figure out how to play up the stress thing, and throw in some run-of-the-mill relationship and work stress to convince the doctor that I'm not just a nut case looking for a fix. I am just a regular person, just like everybody else. Move along now, nothing to see here.

**Mile three:** Who's that? It's Coach Dreamboat. CC has entered the track area and has moved his group of runners onto the end where they begin stretching. His group is larger now. There are some girls in it. I think I'll stay on the track tonight, rather than finish up on the campus, and watch his people run. That will keep me going.

**Mile four, or five, where am I?** Damn it. I forget where I am. Spacing out and reliving my fantasy over CC and reliving my fantasy weekend with Calvin and what mile am I in, again? Five. I'm in mile five. I am really out of it. I wonder if I would ever dare to talk to CC now that I am not a totally pathetic runner like when I first saw him on the track in the fall. Nah, I could never talk to Coach Cutie. Every time I look his way I am blinded by his dazzling cuteness. I would undoubtedly lose all ability to converse coherently in an instant. Seriously, he is just too damn cute. Alas! Coach Cutie will never know what an accomplished conversationalist I truly am.

**Mile six:** Hey, I could run a 10K. What's going on? One of his female runners is limping off the track and he is running over to collect her. Tragedy! His girl has injured her foot. CC is guiding her onto the edge of the infield, and makes her lie on her back on the ground. He picks her right leg up into the air and stands over her while he plays with her foot and her ankle and her shin. At the sight of this, I am practically coming in my pants and feel the need to leave the track immediately. It's late. Time to go home anyway.

Good workout.

# Mile Nineteen

Saturday morning. It's happening again. I feel the embers glowing in the center of my brain. I don't want the fire to catch. I've got to climb out of this fire. Remember the excellent run you had last night? You didn't even know you were running. Remember the excellent sex you had last weekend, play by play, it's never been better. I've never had an orgasm without a vibrator before. Calvin, the human vibrator. No good, it's not working. Good runs, good sex, good work, happy clients singing my praises, calling me a guru, friends and family with love in their faces, it doesn't matter.

It's there, every morning, that sickening depression. That sickness that sometimes hides for a tiny moment, but never leaves long enough for me to forget about it. I resolve to try harder, but I'm burning now. My brain is burning again. I feel a huge, hot hand clutching my brain. The palm almost covers my brain, burning it, while the fingers dig in and shoot shards of pain across the inside of my skull. I'll spend most of my day on the couch, sick and miserable. I'll resort to lying very, very still in order to keep the flames low, the pain dull and steady. Don't freak out. Just be still.

Sunday. I got up and cleaned the apartment for a couple of hours despite my slug-like enthusiasm level. I was gathering some books off the shelves to pack when I found an old photo album. Most of the pictures were from college. I pulled them out of the sleeves and threw them away as I flipped through the pages.

Then I came across some high school pictures from the ocean. There was one of me, smiling at the camera, sitting cross-legged on a towel on the sand. I was wearing a racing suit of dark blue, and even though it wasn't a bikini, it still made me look curvy and hot. The suit was wet. I pulled out the picture and tucked it into my purse. I threw the rest of the pictures, album and all, away, and then dozed all afternoon. I am way behind on life. I have no strength or motivation. I'm just inert. I've got to try harder.

Somehow.

Get up and run. Start running and don't stop until you fall down. You are seriously depressed.

I can barely move.


Monday. Okay, you can do this. Just get through today, and call the doc about that Xanax. I am at the end of my wits with this depression. This isn't right. This is ridiculous. Every day should not be a desperate struggle just to get through. Get up, go to work, call the doc, make an appointment if you have to, and be a robot until you get the pills. Function without thinking, and get some pills. Keep moving. I wish I could just evaporate, instead. I wish I could take a pill to send me into tomorrow.

Today, I just want to explode or implode or evaporate into thin air.


At work, things were humming along as usual when Mandala walked into the room with an armload of papers. She set them down on my desk and paused for a second. We could both hear Sandy swearing through the floorboards from upstairs, and she was obviously reluctant to head back up right away. She sat down in a chair beside the printer behind me. I imagined she was looking out the window, which is always entertaining in the city, or spacing out or something, but she must have been looking at me because suddenly she said, "Welcome back," with a little laugh in her voice.

"What?" I swiveled around in my chair to face her. "What are you talking about? I didn't go anywhere."

"Yeah, you did. You were like a ghost last week. It was like I didn't even know you. You okay?"

The room, with Mandala lounging backward in her chair, glossy as a supermodel on a magazine page, came down around me like a massive warm and cuddly blanket thrown across my back. The look in Mandala's eyes had knocked down the room.

"I had absolutely unbelievable sex with a married man two weekends ago, and I'm wondering if it was worth it," I blurted out in her face.

Mandala froze, and then lurched forward over her knees. She was shaking all over. She popped back up like a jack-in-the-box with tears streaming down her face and began choking for air while I observed her in a state of shock. She was hysterical! She was laughing hysterically and banging her heels on the floor. I continued to observe her antics with a frightened smile when she heaved herself up, hobbled over to me, still shaking, and embraced me. I patted her back and gazed stupidly into her face. She was calming down now, and she pulled back and smiled at me with her entire heart in her eyes. This was more emotion than I had ever seen out of her in all the years I had known her. My body flooded with relief as she staggered back to her seat, giggling, and said to me,

"It's about time!" She began wiping at her wet face with her long, bell-shaped psychedelic sleeve. "What're you upset about? Did he give you something?"

"No, no! Nothing like that. It's just that, there was obviously no future in it, and I kind of, well, I found out, I mean, I knew he was married before I invited him over . . ."

"So?" she interjected fiercely. "That's his problem."

"Yeah, I guess, but . . ."

"You say it was good?"

"Hell, yes!"

"You freak," she said, smiling. "You know how I feel about monogamy. It's not meant to work in this lifetime, and you only get one life. You need to be happy any way you can. Especially you," she waved her hand at me. "Besides, you needed something to get you over that other freak over there," she said, tilting her head toward my block. "So you had some good sex and you had a good time. Nobody got hurt, and you deserve it. What're you worried about?"

"Nothing, I guess."

"That's right. Nothing." She had rolled herself closer to me as we spoke and now she reached out and tapped me on the knee. "Nothing."

"Mandala!" Sandy screamed from her doorway as more phone lines started ringing. "Get the fuck up here!"

Mandala rose to go, grinning at me like I was a birthday cake in front of a toddler. She turned and walked away in a leisurely fashion, with perfect posture.

I felt okay. I never thought I would spill to Mandala, but I felt better. I watched her glide up the stairs in her platform heels. I had been dying to confide in Helen all last week, but she was so crazy in love with her executive boyfriend that I couldn't seem to do it. I didn't want to cloud up her magic spell of happiness. She had stopped telling me every detail of her love life, so I figured it was pretty serious. Plus, when she wasn't busy working or mooning or rushing to get out the door, she had Adam on her ass, and there was never a good time to talk. I don't know why I wasn't confiding in Melanie. The longer I took to confess to Melanie, the more surprised and confused she would be. She might even be hurt. Who was I kidding? I knew why I wasn't talking to Melanie. If Calvin showed up in the summer, I was planning on doing it again.

I picked up the telephone to call the hospital.

"Dr. Bellman's office, how may I help you?" the receptionist answered.

"Hey, Lisa, it's Grace. Is Dr. Bellman available? It's nothing urgent, I just wanted to ask him something."

"Just a minute, please," she sang, and put me on hold.

"Dr. Bellman," said a man's voice. I could always get the doctors. They always took my calls. I was the young, little female artist down the street who never let them down. I never did, either. I never missed a deadline and always went the extra mile, even if it meant waiting for hours and driving around at night to deliver a job. There was one Greek doctor who would stop whatever he was doing, with whatever patient he was with, to talk to me. There was a Spanish cardiologist who told me to have him paged, even if he was in surgery. There was a phone in the operating room, he informed me. The idea of a cardiologist taking a phone call about a slide presentation while he was in surgery completely creeped me out. I had Helen deliver all of my work for him.

"Hi, Dr. Bellman, it's Grace. I was wondering if, um, I mean," stop sounding so scared. Don't sound needy. "I was wondering if you could give me some more Xanax. The sample you gave me was very helpful." There, stop there. Don't go into any suspicious detail.

"I don't see why not." Dr. Bellman's voice was easy and light. "Why don't you come up and see me after work? I'll tell Lisa to send you straight into my office so we can talk."

Shit!

"Sounds great, I'll be there around 5:00, thank you." Shit! Well, I had to do it. I had to take the risk. The inner lining of my skull was snapping and I felt crazy. I felt crazy every day. I wanted to hide, but I had to go and talk to Dr. Bellman because I was losing my mind.

I climbed the back stairs to the hospital at 5:00 on the dot and breezed by the security guard with a wave. In Dr. Bellman's office, Lisa was on the phone and acknowledged my smiling wave with a nod as I walked through the waiting room full of restless, impatient people. I always felt a little guilty, jumping in front of physically sick people, so I disguised myself with tight, businesslike steps and important-looking packages under my arms. I didn't have a valid reason to be sick. I was ashamed over my weakness, so I tried hard not to catch anybody's eye.

I had just settled down in his comfy leather guest chair when he came in behind me and closed the door. Dr. Bellman almost always had a smile on his face. He was short and slightly stout, with a full head of dark hair and a perfectly groomed beard and mustache. His eyes exuded so much kindness that he reminded me of a young Santa Claus. He even had square, wire-rimmed spectacles. I had spoken to him many times before over different matters. He always took his time. He was never in a rush, whether I was passing him in the hallway or delivering some work. He had given me my mandatory physical when our company was based in the hospital, and treated me for bronchitis, twice, since then. I liked him very much, though I knew that, like the others, he could never cure me. I trusted him enough to lie about the extent of my depression as little as possible.

"So!" he said with a big smile on his face as he sat down at his desk. "What can I do for you?" He was positively full of joy to see me. He looked at me like I was a close relative he had been missing for a long time.

"I came to ask you for some more Xanax to help with my depression," I said matter-of-factly.

"Depression?" His smile faded a bit.

"Yes, I've been having some pretty bad episodes of depression lately (all my life), and the Xanax you gave me to try for my insomnia seemed to help with that."

"*You're* depressed?" He looked thoroughly confused now. "But you're always so . . . bouncy. I swear I see you running toward the track every day after work. What's going on? You say you're depressed?" His kind face was full of concern, and he stood up to walk around his desk and lean against it to be nearer to me.

I knew why he was confused. I liked him so much that I always came alive when we spoke. I often managed to sound intelligent, and once I had cracked him up with a perfectly timed quip in the middle of a crowd in the cafeteria. I had seen him, once or twice, observing me run from the driver's seat of his car at a traffic stop near the hospital as he made his way home. I knew that he thought I had it all together. I felt sorry for him, for both of us, letting him know that I wasn't all that.

"Yes, I really am. I know I don't seem like it, but I've been suffering (wrong word!), well, feeling very down lately, and I haven't been sleeping much at all (never) since I ran out of the Xanax. I know it's probably temporary (L I A R) since we've been crazy at work and I'm moving to a new apartment next month and all." He was watching me closely, and spoke carefully,

"Relationship problems?"

"I'm afraid so. I've just had a nasty break-up. I'm still upset about it." His face relaxed a little.

"You said that work was 'crazy.' Do you enjoy your work?"

"Oh, yes! I love my work, and no offense to Richard, but I have been thinking about looking for something that pays a little better at my age. He's a wonderful boss, and I do love graphic design. The people I work with are great, you know them." Dr. Bellman knew Richard very well. Don't talk about work anymore.

"Are you taking any other medications?"

"No, nothing on a regular basis."

"How about alcohol? Are you using alcohol?"

"No, not really. I drink a few beers when I'm out with my friends every now and then." Alone, all at once, in the space of a few hours on the same night, every other weekend.

"Nothing stronger?"

"No, mostly beer." Lots and lots of beer.

He was thinking. Then he spoke,

"You know, there isn't any stigma to depression these days. It's a treatable disease, just like high blood pressure or diabetes. If you had diabetes, you would take medicine to control it, right? It's merely a matter of finding the right medication for the problem. There is no reason for anyone to suffer from depression anymore. There are many, many options to choose from. Do you think you might like to try something other than Xanax?"

Here we go again.

"What you have is a chemical imbalance," he continued. Ooo, I like that one, "a chemical imbalance."

"I've actually tried a few antidepressants before. They don't work very well on me."

"Have you tried Prozac?"

"Oh, my God. That one was the worst. It made me even more depressed," and I had the scars to prove it.

"A lot of people like Zoloft, now."

"I tried that, too. It didn't make me more depressed, it just didn't do anything at all. Not even a side effect." I began smiling at him in a challenging manner, as if daring him to one-up me. He smiled in response, and we were almost like our usual selves.

"Yes, that would make sense. They both work in somewhat the same way, on the serotonin factor. What about Effexor? This is a drug that works on both serotonin and norepinephrine in the brain, . . ."

"Been there, done that."

"Okay, okay," he laughed, "you seem to know what you're about. So you want to stick with the Xanax?"

"Yes, please."

"What did I give you before?"

"You gave me a sample of 10, .5 milligram tablets."

"And that worked for you?"

"Yes, it worked well enough, better than anything else I've tried."

"Very well, then. I'll write you a prescription for 30 tablets of the .5 milligrams."

Jackpot! I had to force myself not to squirm around in excitement over this development. Dr. Bellman went back to his seat to write out the script. When he was finished, he didn't hand it to me over the desktop, but stood up and walked around the desk again. I stood up as well. We were almost the same height, so he looked into my eyes as he reached out to take my right hand in both of his and pressed the prescription into my palm. He held onto me as he said,

"I want you to come and see me if there's anything you want to talk about. Come see me if you feel that you need something stronger or want to try something else. You can call me anytime, okay?"

"Okay, thank you. I'm sure this will be fine for now." I gave him my most confident smile. He released me, and I smiled at him again over my shoulder as I exited the office.

Lisa wasn't at her desk. Good, no small talk. I went straight downstairs to the hospital pharmacy to have the prescription filled. I deserved a reward. I had shocked the shit out of two different people in the same day.

# Mile Twenty

I can feel them, the troops of anxiety gathering on the other side of the hill. They're moving up in waves, pressing their bodies closer together as they climb to the crest, readying to crash down upon me. I chopped a tablet of Xanax in half with an exacto from my art box in the front room, and climbed back into bed, waiting for it to take effect. I would have to chop as many tablets in half as I could to keep me going. I didn't have to be happy, I just had to avoid inertia and hysteria and doctors for as long as possible without asking for a refill. A half of a pill sometimes worked, just enough, but not always. I guess I could move the exacto back into the medicine cabinet now that JC didn't come over anymore. It would be more convenient.

JC had come out of my bathroom last Christmas with a strange look on his face. He stood before me without speaking, looking carefully at me, and then at all the space around me. He looked into my eyes without moving a muscle, and kept standing there, cool and alert. He was starting to scare me.

"What?" I finally demanded.

"Why is there an exacto in your bathroom?" he asked without blinking. It took me a moment to get it.

"Oh! That's for chopping my anxiety pills in half. You know how I feel about taking pills. If I take too many of those, the doctor will be sure to try and make me take something stronger. Or worse, make me see a shrink. You know that." His posture softened slightly, but he wasn't totally convinced.

"You sure?"

"Yes, of course. I can't risk getting caught up in all that again." He believed me. I thought it was rather amusing at the time, *me* scaring *him*. JC hated doctors almost as much as he hated law enforcement.

It wasn't working. My brain was burning and buzzing like three squirrels were racing each other up and down inside me. My brain was burning like a sick tumor. I got up and took the other half of the pill, pacing the apartment like a leopard on speed. I've got to calm down. I jumped back into bed and counted my inhales and exhales and waited.

Okay, it started working. The troops relaxed their weapons and lay down in rows. They didn't retreat. They just lay down. I still couldn't get up, so I jump-started my ass with a quick orgasm and finally got up to go to work, knowing that I didn't have time for a shower anymore. I raced up and around the block instead of crossing in front of JC's. I can't wait to move, I said to myself, though I knew it would not make a difference in <u>The Morning Dread</u>. It might make a difference in my worry over walking to work, but it wouldn't change anything that was fundamentally wrong with me. "The Geographic Cure," as we veteran psych patients call it, doesn't ever work.

I couldn't concentrate. My office as so quiet that I felt myself falling into a stupor as I stared blankly at my screen. I decided to be stupid. At this point, what could it hurt? I pulled the picture of myself in a bathing suit out of my purse, scanned it into my computer, and sent it to Calvin with no message attached. The response was immediate.

**CAL:** The source of a thousand fantasies! Man, what I would do to you right now!

**Grace:** You already did, this morning in my head, before I dragged myself out of bed. Everyone else on the beach disappeared. I put on my big, black shades and lay down upon my towel. I uncrossed my legs, spread them out in front of me, and imagined your head between them. I love the ocean.

**CAL:** I love this scenario. ESPECIALLY the ending. You know I almost feel guilty about how much I loved being between your legs. I think about it often. Your beautiful naked body, the feel of you on my lips, the taste of you, how wet you were, looking up at you as I ran my tongue over your pussy. I don't get to the beach enough these days, so I'll just think of you there . . . mmmmmm.
Xx

*Oookay.* Now I can get some work done. Get everything done. Go down to the basement and see if Helen has any empty boxes that don't have chemicals spilled all over them. Go straight to the track after work. Ogle Coach Cutie and pretend he is Calvin. Stop at some shops on the way home and ask for as many boxes as I can carry. Pack everything. Go.

The move was surprisingly easy. My family and friends were so thrilled over my breakup with JC that they showed up by the carload. They only wished I were moving farther away. My younger brother showed up with two beefy friends and a pickup truck. The atmosphere was like a party, and we had more cars and people than I needed, so my mother and her sisters stayed put, cleaning in the new apartment, while the boys and I did the loading and unloading. Helen showed up on her bike with Adam in tow, and they joined in the stair-climbing with boxes. In less than four hours, we were done. We all sat crammed into the front room in the sunshine of the bay window and ate the food that my mother prepared. The atmosphere was light and everyone was laughing.

Helen and Adam took off first. I had stocked up on cases of beer for my workers, but those two couldn't light up with my family around. The boys and younger cousins took off next, having all of Saturday night ahead of them. My mother was the last to leave. She wrapped her arms around me tightly and squeezed without letting go. Then she took my head in both of her hands and kissed me with tears of hope in her eyes.

"You want me to come back tomorrow and help unpack all of this?"

"No way. You've already done too much. I'm so wired, I'm probably going to stay up half the night unpacking and then sleep in all morning."

"How about food? I can run to the store and get you something."

"Mom! You've already brought me tons of food!" I exclaimed, gesturing to the grocery bags piled up in the tiny kitchen. "Just go home now, before it gets dark. I'll call you later this week."

"Okay, okay, call me tomorrow," she conceded, and hugged me again. I walked her to her car. My comment about the evening did the trick. Mom was afraid enough of the city in the day, forget about the night.

Alone now, I popped another beer and slowly started unpacking the immediate essentials: toiletries, clothes, and some food that shouldn't be left on the floor. My mother and aunts had already made up my bed and hung fresh towels in the bathroom. The bed looked so good compared to the rest of the place that I decided to sleep on the couch by the front window for the first night until I could get some more things in order. I drank beer and stared at the moon as midnight approached. I felt restless, which wasn't unusual of course, but I felt like something was missing or forgotten. In a sudden panic, I ran into the bedroom to make sure that my running shoes were there. They were. I carried them back into the front room with me for reassurance, and continued to drink on the couch by the moon. The feeling stayed with me. What was it? I ticked through the rooms of my old apartment in my head. We had done a final sweep before handing over the keys.

And then, I knew what it was. My angel. I couldn't bear to be the one to carry her broken body into the alley trash, so I had left her on the back porch, hidden behind the third-floor stairs to pretend I had forgotten about her. Now I missed her. "Botch!" I told myself. You left her there on purpose, because you knew you would never be able to forget the sight of JC carrying her in his arms across the lawn to you. You don't want her. I didn't want her.
He doesn't want you.
I missed her anyway.


On Sunday, I awoke with plenty to do and plenty of leftover beer to do it with. I didn't stop moving all day, then watched TV all night until I fell asleep for a couple of hours.


On Monday, I was on top of all emergencies by noon. I decided to eat lunch at my desk while I mailed out my new address to everyone I knew who had a private email on their computers at work.


**CAL:** Thanks for letting me know. How are things with you? I was a little worried that I somehow offended you in the last note. I hope not.
Xx


**Grace:** Offended me? You are certainly kidding. I reread your emails over and over again, masochist that I am. I get all hot and bothered, reliving the moment. No, no, you do not offend me. Instead I worry about pestering you with my never-ending filthy thoughts, and so I try not to write too much lest you begin to fear that you have made love to a crazy woman. I'm glad you wrote me back today.

**CAL:** Well, that's a relief. For the record, you can write me anytime you want. I like it.

I was looking at that photo again, of you in the bathing suit on the sand. Wow. I'm imagining an entire inner monologue based on your expression. Oh, to have had a crack at you back then!

I'm looking at YouTube cat videos. Yeah, I have a lot of free time these days. The new, "Special Interests" slot on the show is only getting started, so there isn't a lot of pressure yet. That leaves me with YouTube and cats.

Okay, may I just tell you how often I think about your perfect body, and having my lips and tongue all over you? Next time I see you, it might get a little dangerous for you. Since I started typing this paragraph I became instantly hard. And I mean hard! Now I'm stuck behind this desk until it goes away, which could be a while. Maybe I'll have to run along and relieve myself to the thought of it all.

Hope you're okay wherever you are. I think I'll be back there in August. Just saying.

Xx


**Grace:** You might get a little dangerous on me? Is that a promise? I love August. I can take the heat.

By the way, you're not the only one with dangerous and depraved thoughts on their mind. Once I get you alone again, I plan to rip your clothes off so quickly that you might consider investing in one of those theatrical tear-away suits in order to avoid destruction. Coffee or tea will not be offered beforehand.


Okay, this is getting out of hand. This is ridiculous. I never understood the concept of phone sex, so what is this? Would this be considered sexting? A long-distance affair? I'm not sure a one-day stand can be considered an affair, but the Internet sex is definitely doing something for me. Am I avoiding reality? Hiding from life? Well, the latter is obvious, but at least the diversion is keeping me from thinking about JC. This could be a healing phase. As long as I keep it in perspective, and expect nothing, which I don't. The two of us already made it perfectly clear to each other that neither of us has any desire to move across the country. We are harmlessly flirting with each other. Okay, we are pornographically flirting with each other. It's still harmless. We are not compromising national security while exercising our right to freedom of speech.

I begin sending dirty emails to Calvin almost every morning. I usually get an answer by noon, since his time zone is almost exactly three hours behind mine.

**Grace:** Subject: <u>**You Asked For It**</u>

Yes, you did, and it's time for another edition of "I Think Too Much about Calvin."

In this episode, our heroine found herself dog-tired at only 4:30 in the afternoon, yesterday. She had been up since 5:00 a.m. pacing the apartment at first, and then enduring and triumphing over the massive endeavor of getting her butt out the door. Unhappy phone calls, demanding clients, deadlines, rewrites, and several deliveries later, our beleaguered and unappreciated leading lady was feeling rather flagged. She decided not to return to work after the final delivery, since it was so close to the end of the workday anyway, and just rest on the couch until about 5:00 before heading out for the track. On the couch, alone in the living room, she allowed herself to relax, and . . . think about Calvin.

She imagines attacking his lips before the click of the door is even solid behind him. She has him nearly naked when he demands recompense and strips her as she tries to race across the kitchen. In the kitchen for awhile . . . then the bedroom . . . even talking a bit. They're at it again when he turns her over and tries a new avenue . . .

Our heroine bolts straight up on the couch. This will not do! There is still a workout in order, dinner to make and a neglected shower stall in the bathroom that smells pretty funky.

Quick inventory: where is everyone? Everyone in my building should still be at work -- no one will hear the buzz. The windows are cracked open to allow a breeze in against the heat, but the block is surprisingly quiet. She flies into her bedroom, strips, turns the batteries on high, and is done in thirty seconds flat. Quick recovery.

Wide awake now, and time to attend to the evening's agenda. Whew, glad that's over with. Thank you very much.

Love Grace

**CAL:** Man, I love these notes from you! I arrive at work without a shred of smut on my mind, but I'm not even halfway through that last letter when it's, "Ten-hut!" I love it. And I love the idea of taking you against the door or in the kitchen. I'll tell you now, anything you can think up, I'm game for.

Man! I'm hard as a rock again, just picturing you on that bed in that room and the moment I pulled your panties off. I can taste you and feel you on my mouth, lips, face. Those peach, cotton bikinis were cute, but we've got to get you into some black lace. Sheer black lace, with some rhinestones, maybe a thong. Every woman deserves sexy underwear.

I hope you're enjoying the warm weather, and know that when you're imagining me between your legs that I'm loving it, that's it's a constant fantasy these days. And the thought of you licking me drives me insane!! Aaarrrgh! Xx

Sexy underwear? See-through lingerie? Me and black lace? We'll let that one go for now.

Friday finally rolled around, and I felt like going out. Mandala never drank. Sandy had the longest commute and never hung around after work. Helen was already picking up her things to dash away when I reached the bottom of the stairs.

"I'd like to have a beer with you," said Adam in his gentlemanly manner. It briefly crossed my mind that he might not even be legal.

"Sure, let's hit the university pub, but I have to leave by 7:00. I'm supposed to meet a girlfriend downtown," I lied. I was uncomfortable around gentlemen.

We had a couple of beers and talked easily. I wasn't tempted to hang out with him any longer, though. He reminded me of awkwardly, accidentally bumping into my little brother and his friends at a bar.

Saturday morning I was wide awake at 4:30 a.m. I was so jittery. I knew there wouldn't be any more rest, even though I had been up every other hour during the night, as usual. I didn't have anything planned for the day, and I couldn't bear the thought of The Morning Dread on its way, so I popped a Xanax. It didn't work. At 5:30 I was so tense I popped another one. By 6:30 I was on the track. Might as well beat the heat, I told myself as I jumped out of bed. I ran five miles at a fairly good pace while thinking about a bagel for breakfast. Who the hell goes running after double-downing their tranquilizers? 'Something is seriously wrong with you,' I thought pleasantly as I ordered egg and cheese on a sesame bagel in a café on the way home.

I was trying to catch up on some reading in the afternoon, when the apartment started closing in on me. The heat could really build up in those subdivided rowhouses. My fan didn't help very much. It just pushed the wet air around.

The inevitable dread was coming down when I thought maybe I should go back to the pool. There was nothing to stop me now. It's hard to fuss and fret with your face underwater. That's it. I'll take up swimming again. I won't snark or sneer or whine or bitch or show any betrayal of emotion in my soul until I am submerged and moving forward. Then I can allow it all to flow down and away from my body in a world of blue. A thick, black line below me, and a world of blue streaming away. Bubbles disappear. Breath becomes usable. Goggles fog and I'll be where I'm supposed to be; living in a vibrant haze of disappearance.

Sunday. I wanna be dead. I wanna be dead. Sometimes I think I just need to wake up dead and get this over with and that would be okay.

No, no, you don't want to be dead. Then you would never laugh again, for sure. You would never watch the trees go by on the way to the ocean. I love looking at the thick, tall maples and birches and cedars and pines. I love the trees in Maryland. I don't want to be dead. It's just that I'm so bad at being alive.

Up past 1:00 a.m. last night and took the Xanax without waiting. Up by 5:30, with the morning panic setting in, but I'll be okay with this one. I was up late. I took sedatives. I don't have anything pressing today. I'll just relax, calm down, and breathe myself through this. I'll be okay.

Air in, air out -- it's okay.

Air in, air out -- everything is okay.

Air in, air out -- it's okay, everything is going to be okay, you're okay. The birds start chirping outside the window. I'm not okay. Breath starts coming in too shallow and it feels like two big fists are grabbing onto each lung and twisting them in opposite directions like a soggy dish rag.

No air, I need air. My thoughts are hurting. The despair is overwhelming. Now is when I think that maybe I should just die and get it over with. I need to be dead, maybe. Oops! There's my cue! I take another Xanax and get back to the work of breathing. In and out, slow it down.

After about 30 minutes, I can feel a little bit of warmth climbing up from my feet and stealing around my lungs and leaking into them, just a little. Keep breathing. The dish rag unrolls, but it's still wet. Okay, you can't die now, there is too much left to do. Hang on now. You have to get up.

I get up, head full of soaking, warm heat. You have to function. I start to function.

This is crazy. I'm existing on tranquilizers in order to function. I run for miles, swim forever, and still never sleep on tranquilizers. That's how fucking crazy I am.

I see the look of resigned despair on my face in the bathroom mirror as I brush my teeth. My body moves around in a trance of sadness. What's wrong? Nothing is wrong. I have nothing to worry about. Life is supposed to be fun. Nothing pressing, nothing to worry about, nothing as usual. Yet, I had to take a pill to get out of a panic attack and get out of bed.

That's okay. That's just me. I was beginning to calm down a bit when the solution hit me like a thunderbolt.

I needed to run a road race.

Flyers were all over town. There were races all around me. If I signed up for a road race, then I wouldn't be so alone every weekend. People who loved running would be all around me, and none of them would care a fig about my severely flawed and insufficient self. I could keep up: 5K, 10K, I could do it! I could fly with the eagles, run with the big dogs, take a bite out of life and all that shit. Start looking at the flyers as you walk around town.

# Mile Twenty-One

The next morning, I walked to work with a spring in my step. Hope was springing eternal. All I had to do was Google road races in Baltimore and I would be on my way. I was so hopeful, that I rambled on a little too long in my ritual fantasy email to Calvin, breaking the cardinal rule of never letting anyone know what was really going on inside my head.

**Grace:** Good morning, Calvin. My knees are hurting today, and unfortunately it's not because of rug burns incurred while you were kneeling behind me. Nor was I praying too much over the pyramid of leftover Sauconys in the corner of my bedroom. I love my Sauconys. I literally pile them up in the shape of an altar. No, I'm afraid I took a spill while running around my favorite course this weekend. *(STOP! Don't talk to lovers, friends, ex-lovers, or any non-runners about running if you want to hold their interest. I went on anyway.)* I was running downhill at full speed, in a lovely stretch of grass I like to call Nirvana. I was loving life and loving the sun and feeling as if I were in my true church when my left ankle hit a pothole disguised by the high grasses after a recent week of rain, and suddenly I was salaaming the asphalt beside the grasses like a Muslim in the morning. Upshot, knees all messed up today.
Hot and helluva humid here in tropical Baltimore. I was reading an article on the architecture of the Greek Wing of the Walters Art Gallery many years ago, where they described one of the obstacles as "Baltimore's semi-tropical atmosphere." Yes, I read that shit, if you haven't figured out I'm a geek by now then there's no use in updating you any further. Wearing my Speedo this weekend again as well. I don't like having my picture taken, but maybe I'll try to send you an updated shot of me in a swimsuit so that you can plan your

future moves on me. Maybe some moves involving water and/or other liquids, with or without the swimsuit.

A friend of mine is an acupuncturist, and she informed me that I am water. She keeps trying to cure me with needles. They don't work; however, in her holistic studies she tries to analyze me as well. She says I am water. That no matter how many stones are piled in front of me, I will continue to trickle through.

Compared to fire, wood, metal or whatever, I believe she may have a point. She is talking about the life I am living, but I am thinking about my running style. *(STOP TALKING NOW.)*

I run without music or headgear, and I swim the same way, for the same reasons: the isolation, the wall of **UN**sound, the hum of the world. As I turn my head for air in the pool, I enjoy the flash of light, the talk and the laughter of people hanging around the rim. I am equally lulled by the rhythmic thrashing and intensity of the swimmers beside me. I love the stream of the water over my body. How cleanly I can cleave through it. How the water rushes over my head, arms, and legs and loves me back. I surge and pull and try hard to maintain an efficient and linear aspect to my stroke, and the water loves me back. It pushes me forward, surrounds me and cradles me.

I would like to swim all over you. You cannot be impatient. You must allow me to swim all over you. I will flow smoothly and expertly over your body. I will suck you in and pull you out. I will possess you, just as the water has so expertly trained me to do, and you will dissolve.

You need to get your butt back to Baltimore for a visit before I shrivel up and wither away. The only social interaction I had all weekend was a beer with the Boy Wonder photographer at work. Poor baby. All of his friends are still on the Eastern Shore and he had to settle for me on a Friday night.

Love Grace


**CAL:** I like your description of your running and swimming styles. I can really see you doing it. Sauconys are awesome. Pray away.

I have had some success with acupuncture. I've had a few sessions for back pain. You should stick with that particular friend. I'd like to stick it to you right now.

And about the swimming - I will do anything you want, anywhere, anytime. I'll do whatever you tell me to do. But be careful Grace, be careful what you wish for. I can turn the tables you know. I'll force you to bend to my will. I will ravage you. I will use you up and leave you a broken, helpless thing. I'll take all the punishment you can give and ask for more. I'm so turned on by you it makes my head spin. It's great we rarely see each other. It would either ruin this thing or kill us. As it is, I think about getting you on that bed again and I feel like an out of control adolescent!

I absolutely must have more photos of you. Send more. You are officially smoking hot no matter what you're wearing, and the less you're wearing the better.

And here is something I can say with certainty. All those waiters, lifeguards, joggers, tennis pros, high school boys, college boys, all boys, and every man you pass by on a daily basis . . . they ALL want to fuck you. They fantasize about it while they masturbate. This is not a theory or opinion. Trust me on this. The men who meet you, day in and day out, lust after you. You are hot. And that's a pretty good thing to be. I've wanted to fuck you since I was twelve. I've dreamt about undressing you and imagined what you would look like naked. I imagined how I would respond to seeing you naked. I could see the rooms we might be in, the bed we were on, the lighting. I imagined kissing you, biting your lip a little, pulling it into my mouth. I thought about your nipples and licking them, and finally undressing you completely, and putting my tongue inside you. Since I was twelve, Grace. You are hot. That is all. Now I'm stuck with a fucking hard-on in a room full of people! Shit!

Xx

I am not going to be able to get any work done today. I am especially not going down to photography.

After work, I went to the market to find something good for dinner and stopped at the front window of the store to look over the flyers. There was music and theater and artwork everywhere. There were roommates wanted and couches for sale. I picked up *The City Paper* and kept looking. There was a race at Loyola and a race at Notre Dame and a race in Hunt Valley, and then there it was: a race at the Inner Harbor. A "Constellation Concourse," the flyer hailed. A road race beginning at the dock of the historic Baltimore warship, this 10K would honor our city, aid in the restoration of the ship, and benefit everyone and everything in general. The words *"festivity"* and *"fun"* sprang out at me alongside the word *"local."* Could I run a 10K? Maybe I should focus on the 5K flyers to find cures for cancer and leukemia and various other research facilities with loftier goals. I kept coming back to the Constellation flyer. It was so close. I loved the city. Could I run it?

"Are you going to run that race?" said a voice beside me. I looked over to see a painfully thin, older lady with cropped brown hair that I had seen before at the track. She was really fast.

"I don't know," I replied. "I've run six miles before, but not on a regular basis. I'm not sure that I could finish a 10K."

"Oh, you can, absolutely, if you can run even four miles. When you're in the middle of a crowd of people like that, in a race, the enthusiasm level just propels you along. You'd be surprised. I run it every year. It's easy."

"Huh," I thought out loud, and looked back at the flyer.

"You should enter," she said with a smile, and pointed to the stack of flyers with applications attached on the window sill beside the free newspapers. She walked out the door and down the street with her grocery bags.

Huh, I thought again, and picked one up. I wasn't sure I believed in her theory that a crowd of people could add mileage to my comfort zone, but decided to sign up anyway. The race was scheduled for the end of June. That was weeks away. I could do this! And maybe, since I often saw the skinny brown-haired lady at the track, maybe some other people I sometimes saw at the track would be there. Suddenly, I knew I could do this.

# Mile Twenty-Two

**Grace:** It's so hot here today. It's making me think about you. Over 90 degrees and the air is like gravy. I'm afraid I agree with you that it's best we don't live very close. I would be unable to resist you, even in the midst of this stifling heat. Flames and ruin for sure.

I was thinking about the paragraph you wrote where everyone supposedly wants to fuck me. You are so sweet.

Bye for now.

**Grace:** Subject: **Professional Consultant Needed**

So here I am, with dusk in the air, and I am no closer to blocking your body out of my mind than I was earlier in the day. I imagine kissing both of your tattoos, and everything in between, as I slam you back against the front door. I like to remember the feel of you all over me and inside me, every inch of you. I'm sure my eyes are glossing over as I vacate my surroundings and my attention submerges and my coworkers look into my face and say, Grace? Are you all right? My friends are always looking into my face and asking if I'm all right. Perhaps it is time for me to consult the self-help experts.

The Management Consultant Experts will tell me to do this:

1. When in fear, imagine that your audience is naked.

Yeah, RIGHT. We BOTH know what THAT is going to accomplish.

2. When overwrought, take a moment to become mindfully aware of your immediate surroundings. The examination and contemplation of the perfectly normal, familiar, and everyday objects around you will calm you down.

The only thing I want to go down on is you, and I'm mindfully aware that I neglected to stick my tongue up your ass.

3. Clear your mind. Enjoy the moment. Indulge in good food and the company around you.
Only one piece of meat I'd like to stuff in my mouth right now.
Not getting anywhere here. Damn.
Love Grace

**CAL:** Subject: **WOW**
Wait for it. Aaaaand there it is, another hard-on.
Do you realize there's a guy thousands of miles away who thinks about licking you for hours? You're probably leaving work or running some errand, completely oblivious to the fact that I'm picturing you on your back with your legs open, my tongue all over you, my fingers inside you.
God, you have no idea how much I want you in front of me on your hands and knees with your ass up in the air and my tongue inside and all over you. I am so fucking horny right now, Grace!! I can practically taste you!
And of course, as I'm writing this my phone rings, calling me to the set. Perfect. "Hey, Calvin . . . what's with the hard-on in the middle of the day?"
Nice.
More soon.
Xx

**Grace:** Ugh! You are disgusting. Talk later.
Love Grace

That night at the track, CC and company were already going about their paces when I arrived. There were six of them, and their legs moved in wide strides of perfect synchronization as they breezed past me, twice. I was in mile four, mesmerized by their form, when they broke off from the track to the campus, single file through the gate, without missing a beat. I felt fine. I finished my six miles and briskly walked home to fill out my application for the Constellation Concourse, write the check, and get a stamp on it while I was still high.

The next morning, I woke up and immediately thought about opening up the envelope and tearing up the check.

Don't do it. Don't die. Don't lie down and be dead. Stop ducking out.

Now, don't start crying. Don't cry in the bathroom mirror and don't go to work after you've been crying. It's so unattractive.

Stop wishing to be asleep at all times. Stop aiding this wish with alcohol and pharmaceuticals. Be a zombie, if you must.

Be a zombie in the beautiful, bright colors of June.

Become robotic. Do as you planned with your running. Make out a written list of what you plan to do, and then do it whether you feel present or not. Be a robot until you can feel human. You know you feel human sometimes. You will feel human again. You know that your humanity comes along sometimes, even if it isn't willing to stay.

You are supposed to be an artist and a runner, and whether you succeed or fail, it will not affect the sporadically rare and fleeting chances you have to be human in your own lifetime. Do not postpone the rest of your life.


I mailed the envelope on the way to work. I walked the rest of the way as if I were struggling against a riptide. My legs felt so heavy it felt like I was sinking into the sidewalk.

At my desk, I kept making mistakes. I stopped for a moment. Ah. I'm so stupid. Why didn't I think of this right away? I'll call Melanie and ask her to drive up and run the race with me! Why don't I ask her to stay over the night before?! I miss her so much. Even though she would obviously leave me in the dust during the race, I would feel so much better if she were there with me. Plus, I was doing wrong by her. I was keeping secrets from my greatest friend for fear of disapproval. In short, I was being a child. Why wait to call? I jumped on to my keyboard.

**Grace:** Hey baby! You are not going to believe this - I signed up to run a 10K at the end of this month. You have got to come up and stay with me and get me through it. I could get you an application in the mail tonight. Pleeeaaassseee!!! Please, please come and stay with me. Melanie, I am having serious panic attacks about the state of my life. I wish we could talk. I can't write down everything I have to say to you.

Right now I am very VERY distraught. Baltimore is simmering and I feel so alone. I miss JC. We were together for so many years. Then I remind myself that he is only contrite and loving me when I am in tears. He is forever incendiary, antagonistic, egotistical, and always inviting an argument in his passive-aggressive way. Yet I find myself wishing he were holding me in his arms. It's a constant struggle, and hard to understand, I know, but I got a little break a few weeks ago when Calvin Wright was in town and we fucked each other's brains out.

There, now I told you. Now you must come and run with me to take my mind off of things, and catch me up on yourself as well. I'm a bit of a wreck. I need you!

Love Grace


**Mel:** At work, so have to digest that interesting bit of news!!!

Will write soon.

Love you.


**Grace:** Mel, I'm having blabber's remorse. I know that I can trust you, but I really haven't talked to anyone about what's going on these days and now I feel foolish. I know that Calvin initially contacted you, trying to find me, but please don't send him any messages or anything at all, or things are sure to become all wrong.

Talk later.


**Mel:** If you can't tell me, who can you tell?

All of your secrets are safe with me. I have never told anyone, anything, not even Eric or my ex. That is what best friends, soul-mate sisters are for.

I also never initiate any emails to Calvin, he contacts me every now and then with a "what's up?" kind of note. Never anything personal. I do know, not directly but through a very reliable grapevine, that he has moved out and separated from the wife we never even knew he had.

Calm down until I can write to you at lunchtime.

Love you lots, Mel


**Grace:** Okay. I hope I didn't insult you. It's just that I haven't talked the whole thing through with anybody yet, and the shock of saying it out loud freaked me out. A gal at work knows, not Helen but Mandala, and she's not the gossipy type. She's a total realist and would only roll her eyes over my excessive analyzation and soul searching. I used to think she disliked me, but I don't think so anymore, and she's an excellent person to have around. Total realists are very hard to find in the art world.

On the bright side, if I can't talk to anybody I'm going to explode. You're in for it now. I feel better already.

Love Grace

I felt better, but not good. I never feel good. The terms "*bipolar*" and "*manic-depressive*" came up more than a few times in my sorry-ass history of therapists, but they could never make it stick because I was never really manic, just depressive. I didn't swing between unnatural highs and unhealthy lows. I was always just astoundingly low.

Now I felt heavily depressed, but not hysterical.

I felt despair, but not desperation.

See? Progress.

I was feeling stable, and getting a good amount of work done, when Melanie finally got back to me at about 3:00.

**Mel:** Okay. First of all, I believe you are allowed to fuck anyone you want, since I don't believe you have been given the attention you deserve in this lifetime. But let us not confuse sex with love . . . we need both. Best if they come in the same package. I wish you were both well loved and well fucked. You are worthy of both. AND I know Calvin had been into you since we were young. I also know that he wanted to hook up with you based on his messages to me . . . I am fairly certain he knew I was talking to you more than anyone else, not that I ever told him anything or even gave him your contact info right away. He was persistent though!!!

Sadly, I won't be able to run with you in the last week of June. Eric and I have already booked a quiet getaway in Belize, far away from the tourist traps. I am, I hate to say to you, in a good place, with a good guy. Eric and I run together a lot. Sometimes without a word between us, but often we work out some of our issues during those runs. I suspect it will blow up at any time. That is the pessimist in me. I often wish I had your positive outlook. We need to spend more time together. Cuz I love you.

By the way, you can tell me anything.

I will write more when I am not at work. I can't type here without somebody walking behind me every other minute.

I wish you could come and stay with me for a long, long time. But think of this as you run: consider the 10K to be your training race for the half marathon we will run in the fall at the Baltimore Running Festival. We will be a perfect team!

LOVE YOU,

Mel

**Grace:** Thanks, I needed that. I almost feel exonerated now about abusing Xanax. You have no idea what's going on these days and I don't want to tell you the whole sad story. Instead, you can give me training tips and advice. Forget about a half marathon, you've got to get me through this 10K first.

Do you run with music? Ever use a headset? Some guy at the track commented as he ran by that I was the only girl he'd ever seen on the track without a headset. So what, I thought. I don't wear hot pink spandex biker shorts either. Anyway, I've been compiling this "ultimate running playlist" in my head but the truth is that I never run with music. I don't like things clinging to me when I run and I don't like fussing with gear. I just wondered if you knew about some magical headset that all runners use that I don't know about because I'm a half-ass runner and I need to know.

Love Grace

**Mel:** There is no such thing as abuse of Xanax.

I do not run with music. Sorry, it is my time for my mind to relax and think. My thoughts are very loud. Running quiets me. Go forth into the good night and find peace my friend.

**Grace:** I've got too much in my head to deal with music while running as well. I just thought I might be missing something.

Back to Calvin. So! REALLY? Okay I sound like a teenager but I can't believe someone as hot as Calvin was ever that into me. Do you have any pictures of him from California? And you and Eric being too happy? FUCK YOU you pessimistic bitch. My turn to give advice to you. **Go home and suck his dick NOW!!!!!!!!!!!!!!!!!!!!!!**

Love Grace

Melanie wishes she had my optimistic outlook? Dr. Bellman, Calvin and now Melanie? Why do people keep thinking that about me?

I dove back into work to wrap everything up before 5:00. A local insurance company wanted three to five new ad ideas on their desks by 8:00 a.m. the next morning, or World War III would break out along with an epic pandemic that would paralyze the civilized world. I could feel Preston breathing down my back from behind his desk across the hall. Mandala breezed into the room and breezed back out again, wearing a floor-length, cream-colored, chiffon gown with gold trim and looking as if she belonged at either a wedding reception or a garden party. Her hair was a beehive of braids, and golden hoops gleamed from her ears, wrists, ankles, and toes. She smiled at me, with the smile in her eyes as she exited the room on the fluttering wings of her chariot of angels. Why did she like me? She is so perfectly together and I am such a perfect storm. Suddenly, I felt even calmer. I watched her flowing train as she floated away and decided that from now on Mandala was no longer the Logo Queen, or the Smoky Witch. She was the Zen Spirit.

Almost immediately, Helen burst into the room,

"Hey! Want to go to the beach this weekend? I want to get out of here. I'm sure I can find us a place in time, even if we have to sleep in Salisbury for one night."

"Sure." There was no one waiting at home to murder me for having a good time anymore. "I'd love to! Just tell me when you want to leave and what I owe for the trip."

"Great!" Helen bounded back down the stairs to start making phone calls.

What was with these people? How come I had so many girlfriends? I even used to have male friends before JC came onto the scene. I thought about it.

Well, I really only had two major S.H.I.T. T. friends: Melanie and Mary. Melanie was in D.C. and might as well have been on Mars for as much as we got to see each other, and Mary had deserted me to make boo-coo money in Boston. S.H.I.T. T. stands for "SHovel In The Trunk" friends. Basically, it means that no matter what day it is, no matter what time of the night, no matter what the other person is doing, and no matter how important it is, if I showed up at their doorstep with a body in my trunk, the other one would say,

"Wait while I grab a shovel" without blinking an eye.

It's like the old joke about bailing your friends out of jail. A really good friend would show up at 3:00 in the morning to bail you out of jail, but a

REALLY good friend would be sitting right next to you saying, "Boy, did we ever fuck up."

I had known them both for most of my life, and even lived with Mary for a few months between apartments, so they really knew me, and yet they still loved me. To be fair, I knew everything about them too, and I was always on their side, giving advice, comfort, and support that I was unable to give or take myself. I had a shovel in my closet for them as well, and they knew it. Hell, I had the shovel in my trunk at all times with the engine running. I had friends for secrets and friends at work and friends for fun. I had a huge and unabashedly loving family. Maybe I wasn't so bad after all. I felt serene as I finished up the layouts, printed them out, and crossed the hall to leave them with Preston. Powering down my room, I grabbed my things and went down to the basement before leaving work. Helen was hanging up the phone as I walked into the main room.

"What are we doing?" I asked as she turned to face me.

"I got us a room on the beach side way up north for Friday night, but we're going to have to stay in Salisbury on Saturday night at the Sleep Inn. That's okay though, because we can leave right from the beach on Sunday."

"Fine with me. I'll go to the bank and give you the cash to cover my half of the rooms before we leave. You had to charge the rooms, right?"

"Yes, and I couldn't get much of a break because it's the weekend and so last minute . . ." she began to apologize.

"That's okay, it's okay. I'm not doing much of anything else this summer, so I can get the money." She looked relieved.

"What's up anyway? Are you alone for the weekend?"

"Yes, John has to go away for an entire week. He's leaving right away. Some big, important, emergency meeting in Las Vegas, of all places." She paused, obviously thinking about saying something else.

"And what? You're so in love you can't bear to stay at home without him for one, single weekend?" I teased.

"You know, he's not completely divorced yet, himself. He has about a month to go."

"I didn't even know he was married. You don't tell me anything anymore." Thank God, because for some reason I didn't feel like confiding in Helen anymore either. I didn't care to talk about myself in general. Look how long it had taken me to tell my greatest friend in the whole wide world that I had just recently been magnificently laid.

"Yes, but it will be over soon. They're done fighting."

"Good!" I replied with a solid upbeat. "I can't wait for Friday!" So, her lover was still officially married, I thought as I ascended the stairs. Whatever. People in glass houses. I forgot about Helen and John and Calvin and everyone and started thinking about getting to the track and checking out the scenery.

Thursday morning. The Xanax I took at 5:00 to ward off the 6:00 a.m. panic attack was already wearing off. As I lay there, feeling it leave, I could feel my brain begin to tap into the side of my skull.

Tap, tap. Not sharp. No knocking sound, but not a gentle nudging either.

Tap, tap, like a tapping through a pillow onto a wall. Like a child trying to signal her playmate in the room next door, telling her that the coast was clear to sneak over and play. But there was no fun. I'm dark and it hurts.

Busy day today. All you have to do is get as much work done as possible so that you can make a speedy getaway tomorrow with Helen. Work hard, run long, pack up, and then you only have to get through one more night before you are at the beach.

The sound of the waves at the beach work on me like the sound of the trains and the traffic do in Baltimore. Soothing. Sedating. I'll be okay. My depression doesn't disappear at the ocean, but it seems to subside and become almost manageable.

I remember during Senior Week after high school graduation, I was sitting on a couch at the beach with four of my girlfriends bouncing and chattering around me in circles as they pulled on their suits, slathered on sunblock, shrieked over their tangled hair, and prepared to walk down to the water. I watched them silently from the couch, with an unopened book in my lap.

"Come on, Grace!" they yelped as they filed out the door.

"Right behind you, I just want to finish this chapter."

"Finish it on the beach, come on!"

"Okay, okay." I listened to them tromping down the stairs. It was a brilliant day. The day could not have been more absolutely perfect. There was a cool breeze coming in from an open window beside the couch where I sat, and the wind smoothed over the sweat on my brow. The sky was a cloudless, light periwinkle blue. My friends were charming and they wanted me with them.

I was viciously depressed. I couldn't move for the depression. I think it was at that exact moment that I realized that something was very, very wrong, but I wasn't ready to accept it yet. I got up and put on my suit. It was also then, at that exact moment, that I became the Great Pretender.

# Mile Twenty-Three

**Grace:** Subject: <u>**Wave Therapy**</u>

Good morning, Mr. Wright. The photographer and I are ditching work at the earliest possible moment tomorrow and heading to Ocean City for the weekend. Jealous? The photographer is a woman so forgetaboutit, as we Italians like to say. I can't wait to get away. I can't wait to feel the heat of the sun all over my body as I stretch out on the beach, and I can't wait to backstroke out into the water as far as I can without upsetting the lifeguards, and just float on my back with my face to the sky.

I've been stressing too much. The waves always help. I plan to lose myself in the waves.

Love Grace

**CAL:** Oh yes, I am jealous. Yeah, a weird week for me as well. I split with my wife. I guess you already know that.

Obviously I'm doing a lot of thinking lately, going over every permutation in my head. I wanted out years ago, but I made up my mind to stick to it, not give up, not take the easy road and run away. And then it got into my head, the idea of quiet desperation. Do I want to spend the next fifty years silently grinding my teeth and fantasizing about the life I wish I had? Is it a bigger mistake to leave or to stay? And the funny thing, the thing that finally pushed me to act, was asking myself, "If you had a million dollars, would you stay or go?" The answer to the question was clear.

I'm in some kind of twilight zone, but not about the divorce. I'm okay with that. I'm suddenly really ready to move on to something else, relationship-wise. But fuck, it's complicated! Have a great vacation. At some point imagine what I'd be doing to you if I were there. I certainly will be.

Xx


**Grace:** Oh, I know all about quiet desperation. I know what you are feeling. Friends might give you sympathetic looks, admit they can't imagine what you're going through, and then take you out for drinks to divert you. Or maybe they think they do understand because they've been through a divorce themselves, but every single person is different.

When I finally broke up with my boyfriend of several years, my girlfriends were dizzy with delight, they were so sick of seeing me sad. My cousins called constantly. My brother called to say he saw the Renaissance in me. My work was impeccable and my bosses were satisfied.

I believed I was really okay too, just like you, until pools of misery bubbled up from the earth and formed around my ankles and made my feet stick to the ground. My chin fell down onto my chest and I became frozen with pain, even though I knew it was for the best. I didn't even have a million dollars to dance around.

That empty, sucking pain in the pit of your stomach that tries to tell you you've thrown too much time away? You haven't, you know. Everything you did at the time you did it was right. You had to follow your heart. You deserved to fall in love.

You may think that you are fine over the divorce, but I can assure you, you are not. The only person I have met who truly doesn't care about anyone besides himself is my ex-boyfriend JC, and it took years for me to believe it. I still can't get over it, and I know now that there is something missing in him. I don't believe that there is something missing in you. No, we don't know each other very well, but this is a big thing and you are not missing this particular piece of heart.

I don't presume to know your life. Just take care of yourself, and only yourself for a little while.

I fear that you will find me flip, inappropriate, or uncaring if I try to cheer you up with some fumbling prose or inept comedy. So you tell me. Is it okay to write to you right now, or should I just shut the fuck up?

You're not going to hurt my feelings.

Love Grace

**CAL:** Thanks for this. I didn't sleep well last night, with so much shit running through my head, and I needed to be spoken to directly. Your honesty is all I ever want, and I appreciate it. I don't really need cheering up, or anything at all actually, but I do like to know what's what.

I feel a little bit like we're two life rafts tied together by a very long rope. Now, off you go, into the great beyond.

Hang in there, enjoy the sand and sea. Take at least one long shower where you play with yourself and think about me eating you. That scenario is my go-to jerk off fantasy!

Xx

That night at the track, I decided to really push it since I wouldn't be doing much of anything besides sitting around at the beach and drinking for the next three days. I was going for the "tempo" run I had just learned about, in which I push myself slightly over my comfort zone and just under "race pace," and then hold that pace for as long and steady as possible. I learned these words from *Runner's World Magazine*, which I had allowed myself to buy at the corner deli because I was finally beginning to consider myself a real runner. Never mind that three-quarters of the text in the magazine flew right over my head. I still managed to find some inspiration in the paragraphs that I was able to understand.

Coach Cutie and crew were going about their usual routine. Sometimes when he passed me, I could see his eyes flick over, but his eyes probably flicked over every lane along the laps to make sure his posse wasn't in danger of trampling over anybody. I wondered if I would ever say hello to him.

"Hello!" a happy voice said from behind my left shoulder. It was the thin and swift brunette from the grocery store.

"Hi!"

"Did you sign up for the race?"

"I did!" I had to keep my sentences short or I was going to muck up this run. I was determined to have a good run this evening. Plus, I didn't have enough VO2 max to talk and run at the same time. See how savvy a single copy of *Runner's World* had made me? I had no idea if I was using the words correctly in a sentence.

"Excellent. My name is Jane. I'll look for you!"

"I'm Grace . . . thank you," I managed to say without losing my rhythm before she took off on her regular pace and then exited the track. For some reason, it made me feel very, very good that someone at the race would be looking for me. I finished up four miles without slowing and went out to run the two-mile campus loop. I fantasized that I would soon become as fast as Jane. Jane and I would become good friends, and I would have someone to hang out with all the time in the city. I fantasized that while searching for Jane in the crowd at the starting line of the race, I saw CC instead. We were so pleased to see each other that we took off, side by side, at the sound of the gun, and somehow I stayed with him the entire race.

Before I knew it, I was in front of the museum, finishing the campus loop. Where had my run gone? I decided to run it again. I was invincible tonight! I was going to *subscribe* to *Runner's World Magazine*, but I began to falter in mile seven, and had to stop and walk for awhile in mile eight. Once I was in the middle of the campus loop, I couldn't exactly cut it short. A high hill and a wall of trees cut the road off from the campus on my left, so it was impossible to cut the running loop short and take a short cut home. At least it was lighter out late in June, and who was I kidding? I wasn't going to fall soundly asleep no matter how many miles I ran.

At home I took a shower and packed my racer, two T-shirts, sunblock, and one change of shorts in a small duffel bag. I would throw my toiletries in after I washed up in the morning. I checked my wallet, not much left after I paid off Helen, but it would do. I had a credit card for emergencies. My sunglasses were already in my purse.

I went to bed in a pretty good mood after running for well over an hour. I could finish up my workload by noon. I did have some ballistic clients who went crazy on Friday nights, but I didn't have any jobs going on for them at the moment. I was full of pleasant anticipation for the beach.

Friday morning. I awoke to do hand-to-hand combat with my anxiety as I lay in bed, struggling to get on top of my opponent. The birds were chirping away like the mob at the gladiators' ring. A heavy sadness at my inadequacy as a person began pushing down on my chest. Don't do it. Don't give up. Live longer.
You are never going to be a super happy person. So what? You're depressive. So what? You don't have to want to die over it. You live in America for chrissakes, not in the Middle East covered up in a burka.
I thought about the miles and miles of trees that I loved to look at on the way to the ocean. I was up.

At work, as I had hoped, everything unavoidable was finished up by lunchtime. I went downstairs to check in with Helen. Adam was working away while Helen was stuffing some lenses and film into a bag.

"How are you doing?" I asked. "Please tell me you are taking that camera with us and not heading off for a shoot."

"No, I'm taking this. Preston is gone for the day, but I think Richard overheard the other girls talking about us going to the beach, so he's probably going to hang around longer than usual just to keep us from taking off early."

"Shit!"

"I know. He's never here after lunch on Fridays, but now he's going to stick around just to piss on us."

"Shit!"

"I know. What did you bring?" When she wasn't on a motorcycle, Helen drove a two-seater Pontiac Firebird convertible, in fire-engine red, of course. Helen didn't mess around with her machinery.

"Just a duffle bag and my purse. It could all fit under my feet if you have a lot of stuff."

"No, I don't have a lot, but I wanted to stop at the farm stands on the way back for a bunch of cantaloupes and corn."

"Ooo! Me, too!"

"What kind of bathing suit did you pack?"

"My Speedo."

"Why don't you wear a bikini? You've got the body for it."

"Hell, no," I blurted out, embarrassed. From the corner of my eye, I could see Adam smirking in an unobtrusive, benevolent way as he leaned over the film on the light table.

"We're buying you a bikini at the beach." I was about to say hell no again, when I thought about Helen maybe getting some pictures of me in a bikini that I could send to Calvin.

"My Speedo is skin-tight, and very sexy." I replied saucily. At this, Adam sniggered out loud.

"Shut up, Adam," Helen said. "Well, I'm ready to go as soon as Richard leaves."

Sure enough, Richard stayed at his desk, obviously killing time while Helen and I pretended to work until almost 3:00. We were out the door and stuffing our things into her car almost before he turned the first corner.

"We're going to get stuck in traffic," she moaned.

"Maybe not."

"When should we start drinking?" she asked as we pulled out and headed south.

"We'd better wait until we're over the Bay Bridge at least. If we do get stuck in traffic we'll end up smashed by the time we get there."

"You're right. Let's get some sodas now and use the cups for beer after we cross the bridge."

"Sounds good."

True to form, it took us two hours to get over the bridge, a trip that should have taken less than one hour.

"God damn it!" Helen moaned again, as we nudged at a snail's pace up to the tollbooths for the bridge, but I wasn't impatient. I loved going over the bridge and looking out over the water from such a height that it seemed as if the car were flying, and knowing all the while that the beach was at the end of the trail. Eyes on the prize.

"We'll be okay as soon as we get over. Rush hour isn't even in full swing yet."

We finally made it up to the tollbooth and took off on our flight. The traffic was moving steadily, if not speedily.

"See?" I said when we were almost over.

"Yeah, we're good, but I've got to pee like a racehorse. Let's look for a place that sells beer and has a bathroom."

"I've got to go, too."

The minute we were over the bridge, there was beer stop after beer stop, and we easily found one with both restrooms and ice. We filled up the empty cooler behind the seats, and filled up our empty soda cups before resuming our journey. The traffic was still moving steadily, and now we could relax and go into cruise mode until we reached the ocean.

"Sooo," I crooned suggestively as I leaned back into the wind of the fiery-winged sports car, feeling mighty slick. "What's going on with you and John?"

"We want to get married as soon as everything is settled between him and his ex-wife."

"*What??!!*" I bolted upright and faced her.

"He wants to start a family and he knew he could never start a family with her. She's still driving him crazy with phone calls and last-minute demands." Helen's voice was not full of emotion. I couldn't get a read on the situation.

"Wait a minute, wait a minute. You've barely gotten through your own divorce and he's not even through with his and I thought you told me they were past the fighting part and I thought you told me you never wanted to get married again and what the hell is going on?"

"We're in love. We're old enough to know exactly what we want. He's already in his 30s and wants to start a family. I want to have kids right away, too. I guess we just know." She paused. Was she finished?

"I'm in shock," I said. "Do you realize that anybody in their right mind, no I take that back, that anybody anywhere would say that this is a classic rebound scenario?"

"I know, I know, but I'm telling you this is it. This is the man I want to have my children with, my life with. He's so together and he is absolutely incredible in bed. He made me come three times just eating me out before he left for his conference."

Now, this was the Helen I could understand, but I was still in shock about the rest. I just stared at her from behind my black Ray Bans. The sexy sunglasses were my last Christmas gift from JC.

"It's going to take some time, it can't happen right away. We both have to get an annulment on our first marriages to get married in the church . . ."

"*What???!!!* You're going to get remarried in the Catholic Church? After all the shit you've been talking about how your ex-husband's heavy Catholicism was a sham that was ruining your marriage? I don't get it. You're already planning the wedding?" I took a heavy slug from my soda cup.

"That was his own, personal problem. It has nothing to do with me and John. We want to get married in the church. We want to start a family, a big family. I'm going to quit work as soon as possible after we marry and hopefully get pregnant right away." Her voice was even, but it wasn't very strong. I still didn't feel a loving rush of emotion in her voice as she ticked off these details. Hell, she was happier, practically exultant, when Adam came on board as her assistant at work. Was she only settling because he was rich? What could he possibly see in her that signaled "stay-at-home mom? What was I missing? Well, we hadn't talked in a long time. I realized that I had allowed an unsupportive silence fall between us. We had never been unsupportive of each other.

"Wow. I don't know what to say. I'm really, really happy for you!" and I meant it, even if I wasn't sure I believed it. She could hear the sincerity in my voice. She finally smiled -- the first smile of our trip.

"Thanks! God, I can't wait to get to the beach. Only about an hour or so to go. Now, what about you? Aren't you seeing anyone? Anything on the horizon?" Funny she should use that choice of words.

"Nothing. Nada, zip, dead zone. I'm going broke on Duracells." She burst out laughing.

"Come on! Isn't JC stalking you at all?"

"No, not at all. If he is, then he's very good at it, but I know that he isn't because his massive ego would never allow it. It's always the girlfriend's fault. He's had so many ex-girlfriends I keep getting them mixed up. We are all such heartless, unfeeling creatures! He still hasn't figured out the common denominator."

"Well, I'm glad to hear it anyway. He's pretty scary."

"Yes, that is the general consensus."

"But come on now, no one is asking you out? I see men looking at you all the time."

"What men, where?" I pretended to be hot on the idea. I was thinking about what Calvin had said.

"Just everywhere we go, or used to go. People that come and go at work, too. You're looking fabulous these days. Your figure is all perfect. If you're not seeing anyone, then how come you look so good?"

"Jesus, now you sound like JC. I have been working out a lot. I've been running more to try and clear my head. I've even signed up for a 10K race downtown on the Sunday after we get back. I've been trying to lay off the booze and train for it so that I won't feel like a fool when I can't finish the race." I took a dramatic sip of my beer with a flourish to my wrist and a smack of the lips. Why can't a woman work out just to feel better about herself? Why does everyone assume that a woman only works out to look good for a man?

Helen laughed again. It was just like old times, but it wasn't. This time we were both pretending. I could feel it in the air between us. I wasn't telling her about Calvin, a conquest I would have gone over in elaborate detail for her in the past, and she wasn't telling me something else.

"Will you finish?"

"I'm pretty sure I will."

"That is awesome!"

"Hold that thought for the Monday after the race."

"Maybe you'll meet somebody there."

"Now that you mention it, I'm all hot and bothered over this one guy I see at the track a lot."

"Why don't you talk to him?"

"Because he is way out of my league, and he runs by me so fast that the only way I could get a word in edgewise is if I stuck out my foot and tripped him as he flew by."

"You are buying a bikini tonight," she firmly stated.

"Bring on the bikini! But people don't wear bikinis at the track, you dunderhead."

"Why not? Be a trendsetter!" We laughed about almost everything and everybody we knew for the rest of the trip.

At the hotel, we threw everything unceremoniously on the floor of the room and washed up quickly to drive down to the boardwalk. We walked along as Helen picked out one outrageous bikini for me after another. Finally she pointed to a plain, black string bikini that looked okay except for all the strings hanging down from the hanger like a bowl of dripping spaghetti.

"That's it," she said.

"I don't know. I don't like the thought of having to fiddle with all of those strings. The bows will be too big. I'll look like a French poodle."

"Oh, no, this is definitely it." She had taken the hanger into her hands and discovered that the top was thickly padded on the inside, turning the cups into a push-up bra.

"Are you making fun of me?" I was reminded of an exercise class I had been allowed to take for free up at the hospital in the physical therapy gym. I had to admit my job was full of perks that, unfortunately, never showed up on my paycheck. During the class, the male instructor had us do push-ups with our feet balanced behind us on an exercise ball. A lady in the back row was very well endowed, and when she put her feet up on the ball she plopped right out of her skimpy workout tank. All of us in the group just got hysterical while the poor college boy up front turned red. I was in the front row and said, "Good thing it wasn't me, I'm in the front row!"

A lady near the back said, "If it was you, Grace, no one would have noticed!" Sigh.

"Let's move on to the saloon, and I promise to think about it."

"Okay, but you're buying it." She checked the tag and showed me the numbers: size S, $19.99. I could do that. We walked down to the Purple Moose Saloon.

We sat at the bar and caught up on each other some more, but the details were light, and we were just having a good time drinking with a view of the ocean and the breeze coming in from every angle. Finally, I was drunk enough to buy the bikini. I always have to be drunk to go shopping. I hate shopping. I don't know why. I hate trying on clothes. I never believe I look good in anything. I don't like looking at myself in the mirror. If it weren't for my mother, I would be wandering around in rags. She takes me out for my birthday every year and insists on buying clothes. She's very good at it. She keeps me in staples and always throws in one expensive, snappy outfit that I end up using for every occasion until the next birthday. Even with Mom, I have to order a tall beer when we start with lunch, as her eyes signal her disapproval of my day drinking from across the table. She gets over it quickly though, when after lunch I agree to try on almost everything she picks out. Shopping is exhausting.

Just like my mother, Helen jumped at my decision. We paid our tab, and she marched me back up to the shop on the boardwalk where she had seen the bikini, and I bought it without trying it on.

"Are you sure I should get the small and not the medium?" I asked in line.

"Yes, positive. The strings make everything adjustable."

We made it back to the hotel without incident and passed out on the beds. Well, Helen passed out. That girl didn't move a muscle all night long and she didn't snore either. Good thing. I'd been to the beach with her before, but I always worried that my pacing and tossing would bother her in the small hotel rooms at night. We never had a problem. I still paced and tossed, but I wasn't full of anxiety at the beach. It was that weird, scientifically impossible energy that kept moving some part of my body at all times. Hey! Maybe I wasn't left behind on the caravan of the ancients, because I was left behind by aliens instead! I concentrated on the sound of the ocean waves and dozed for a while.

The next morning, Helen started moving around 10:00 a.m. I had already been up for hours, of course, looking at cable channels with the sound turned off.

"What time is it?" she mumbled in pain.

"Ten o'clock. We don't really want to get down the beach this early in the day anyway. No amount of sunblock would save us from an entire day on the beach."

"Why the hell are you so cheerful? I feel like shit. You don't even look hungover."

"I'm okay."

"You fucking bitch."

"Good morning to you, too." I actually giggled. I love the beach!

Helen stumbled into the bathroom and didn't emerge for about half an hour. She was ready to go though, when she came out, wearing a star-spangled, American flag bikini top and navy blue trunks instead of the matching bottom.

"That's cute," I said, "and perfect for a biker bitch like you. Don't you have the matching bottoms?"

"I do, but I don't like how they look on me." She went straight to the cooler and popped her first beer of the day. I jumped up, annoying her even more with my perky step, and grabbed one for myself.

"Get ready while I set up the camera and slather up," she said. "We have to check out of here and throw everything we don't need on the beach in the car."

"Okay, boss!" She glared at me in a friendly way. I sipped at my beer while I tried on the suit. It was, without a doubt, the skimpiest thing I had ever owned, but I loved it. I loved it because my flat chest suddenly had boobs. The top actually gave me a totally fake rounded bosom. What happens when a date takes you home and discovers the deception? But that didn't matter right now. Calvin already knew what I looked like naked, and he totally approved. This bikini was only meant to torment him and make him want me even more again in August.

"Let's go," Helen said. We threw on oversized T-shirts, guzzled the last of our beers, grabbed our towels, and headed for the check out desk.

It was a perfect day. We lay around and then got in the water. We lay around and got in the water some more. We walked back to the car, ate the snacks we had bought, and drank another beer from our leftover soda cups. We went back to the beach and lay around and got in the water again. Helen was snapping pictures all around. I saw her focusing on me a few times, and heard her snapping in my direction when my eyes were closed. It was late in the afternoon when she said, "Let's walk down the beach a little bit." I got up and followed her. She was walking down the middle of the beach on the hot sand instead of in the surf line.

"Let's go down to the waterline. It's cooler and easier," I said.

"I'm looking for Dr. Greene," she replied. He said he would be in this block this weekend with his family. I just wanted to see if we could find him and say hello."

"Okay," I said. Don't. Say. Anything. I had to say something. "Why? What's he doing here, three blocks away from us? Isn't that kind of creepy? I don't want to see his wife and kids."

"Oh, his wife and kids won't be out this late on the beach, he told me. They are way too white."

Not the answer I was looking for. We kept walking, laboring through the sand. My mind was racing. If his wife and kids were with him, then she couldn't have been expecting to hook up with him at his rental. If she wanted to hook up with him in her rental, then why was I invited along? Why would she want to hook up with him ever again if she was so madly in love with someone else that she wanted to march around in a church for the second time, and start popping out as many kids as soon as possible? Was she trying to make him jealous with her double-crossing talk of a wedding with someone else? Did she believe he would leave his family for her? Was she secretly in love with Dr. Greene? If she wanted to make him jealous then, again, what was I doing here? I guess I was supposed to make her appearance on the beach seem accidental and unplanned, just in case his wife was around. This was clearly not unplanned, because there he was, stretched out on his stomach, alone on the beach.

We said polite hellos, and then the two of them started making small talk about some project she was doing for him. I watched them both talking. The sun was so bright, I could see his eyes checking me out from behind his sunglasses. And that was another thing! Why would she drag me along in front of this notorious letch? Why did she so strongly encourage me to buy a bikini? Helen had at least 50 pounds on me. Her shape was boxy, not curvy, and her body was soft, without muscle tone. I was in pretty good shape, with plenty of muscle tone, including a well-defined four-pack that was almost a six-pack, thank you very much, Mr. Holland, Ms. Smith, and the unwittingly inspirational Coach Cutie.

On the other hand, I was no match for Helen's double D's, even in my push-up top, and some guys really go for that kind of thing. I felt so awkward just standing there that I forced myself to stare casually out to the sea, instead of obviously wishing I were anywhere but where I was. Wait a minute. Was I some kind of bait? Was she testing her love for John or was she testing Dr. Greene, trying to see if he would betray her with some inadvertent show of interest in me? Did she suspect John of lying about his business trip in Las Vegas? This whole thing was fucked up.

"See you Monday," they were saying. We turned and walked back to our towels. Helen was quiet, almost morose. I seriously had absolutely no idea what to say. I couldn't wait to get back to the car and drink another beer. Maybe Helen would explain a little more over dinner. We would have to wear our clothes over our suits, since our next shower stop was in Salisbury, but you can do that just about anywhere in Ocean City.

We ate crabs at a shack on the strip, and I drank more beer, while Helen switched to iced tea. She'd had too much to drink the night before was all the explaining I got that night. We didn't go back to the boardwalk or out again after dinner. We had to drive into Salisbury anyway, so we left the city early, at about 8:00 There was still a little light in the sky, all beautiful over the bay, as we drove out of town.


The next morning was cloudy and overcast. Helen had slept like a dead thing again, while I sat around on my bed, watching silent cable and thinking sad thoughts. Helen was a party girl. She had ditched her first marriage mainly because it got in the way of her being a party girl. Now she was planning on marrying a suit. A real Corporate Joe, with a lot of figures in his income. I worried that she was marrying him for his money and his job security. She was afraid of the future that her current lifestyle had in store for her. That's why she had to go and look at Dr. Greene, I surmised. She wanted to prove to herself that she was over him and all the rest of the men in the world. It didn't appear that she had convinced herself. Or maybe she really did love John, and was going through some kind of mourning for her relatively short stint as a bachelorette. That could happen. I wasn't convincing myself.

I was also afraid of my future, deathly afraid, but I sure as hell wasn't going to marry myself out of it. Helen and I had initially bonded over the partying and our codependent escapism, but now we didn't seem to have much to say to each other. The sad part was that neither of us seemed to really want to have something to say to each other. We were moving in separate directions.

I wasn't interested in her direction any more, and she wasn't interested in mine. What had happened to us?

Helen was awake, so I turned up the sound on the TV. Yep, rain moving in unexpectedly from the south.

"Maybe we should just head out," she said. "If it starts raining really hard, we won't even be able to stop for our produce."

"I agree, let's go. I've got a bunch of stuff to catch up on tomorrow," I lied. We checked out quickly and piled into the car.

Three hours later, Helen was pulling up in front of my building. We hugged each other, and lightly kissed cheeks. I gathered up my bags and my melons.

"Goodbye, see you tomorrow," she said as she began to pull away.

"Goodbye, thanks for driving," I called after her. Goodbye, Helen, I said again, to myself.

Monday morning at work, I was trying to figure out how to get a look at the pictures Helen had taken of me without being too transparently selfish. Helen was bustling about, all busy, when I went down the first time, so I said good morning to her and Adam and went back upstairs.

The second time I went down, she was sequestered in the darkroom. Adam smiled at me from the light table. I had an idea. I moved in close to him.

"When you have a minute, could you come upstairs and talk to me for a sec?"

"Sure," he replied, surprised, but still unruffled.

I went all the way upstairs to the third floor to kill some time with Sandy and Mandala. I really didn't have much going on that day. Sandy's eyes were unflinchingly glued to her screen as usual, but Mandala looked up.

"How was the beach?"

"Oh, it was okay. We came home early yesterday because of the rain." It had barely sprinkled all the way home. "Get this, we ran into Dr. Greene on the beach."

"Yeah, right," Mandala spat, sounding disgusted and just like JC. I don't know why, but I laughed.

"Yeah, that was pretty much my feeling as well. I'll catch you two later." I got up and went back down to my room. Adam was already there, sitting in a chair, waiting for me.

"How busy are you guys today?" I asked him. He shrugged and mugged a little.

"Not too bad. Totally manageable. What's up?"

"Well, Helen took some pictures of me at the beach, and I wanted to get a look at them. I might want to send a picture of myself to a friend." I sat down next to him, and he continued to look at me in that calm, yet intense way that his soft, brown eyes had. I leaned in and confided, "She took some pictures of me in a skimpy little bikini." His eyes sparked up. "I want to see if I look good in any of them so that I can send one to a man I like."

"I'm on it." He rose to leave.

"Don't worry about it if you're too busy. Don't make a fuss."

"We're not too busy. I'll find them, and," he paused in the doorway and looked over his shoulder, "you'll look good." He went downstairs. What a nice guy!

Adam came into my room with a half a dozen prints in his hand before lunchtime.

"There's a ton of shots, but I thought these were the best ones for now," he said, handing them over.

"Oh! Thank you! Don't worry about the rest, I'm sure these are fine. I trust you."

Adam smiled and walked away. I looked through the shots. Ooohhh, yeeaahh. These were good. Trust a man to pick out a bikini shot. I chose two shots to scan: one of me lounging on my back on the beach, and another one of me frolicking around in the surf. The shot of me on my back was really sexy. Helen had positioned herself behind me and taken the shot over my shoulder. Only a part of my face was in the shot, the rest was a landscape of my torso. Very artsy-fartsy.

**Grace:** Ahhhhhhhhh. Better now. Eighty to ninety degrees every day, and I just bought a new string bikini for the summer. Maybe you'll get to see it in August?

I woke up this morning, and my equilibrium must be off, because I swear I could still feel the rise and swell of the waves rocking me awake. I feel great! I hope you are happier, too.

Our photographer, Helen, brought along some equipment from work, so I finally have a picture of me without a bunch of family around. The one where I'm on the towel is me while watching the sea. Permission to come aboard.

**CAL:** Subject: **Beach Pics**
You are fucking killing me!
I just popped off the set briefly while they change camera angles. I opened my email and bam! You hit me with that! The shot of your belly is so sexy. I just want to slide my hands down in that little space, lift that bikini bottom up, and slip my fingers inside you. As for the ocean shot . . . I throw my arms around you and you jump up, wrapping your legs around me. What is it about water and salt air that makes one so horny? At least it does me.
Keep having fun. Keep stealing shots like that. And if the bottom falls down a little . . . well, accidents happen, don't they?
And next time I see you I'm tying you down. I'm going to need some time to do what I want to you.
Xx

**Grace:** Sounds like a plan.

# Mile Twenty-Four

Tuesday. RACE WEEK. I'm okay. I can do this. I know I can do this. I can easily run six miles. I've done it many times before. Just take a few easy runs his week and save yourself for Sunday. Stay calm.

Wednesday. Nice, easy four-miler last night. Taking it easy. Taking tonight off. Do a little core work. No high drama here. The track was pretty empty. Am I supposed to take off the whole week before a race?

Thursday. I had only planned on running the campus loop once tonight, but I had too much energy and I ran it twice. Another four-miler, that's okay. Three days before the race without a run is going to be tough. Maybe a little swim on Friday night? Whatever you do, don't take too much Xanax. Don't reach for the solution. Be the solution. You've got to go into survival mode. Walk around the block. Shut yourself off. Be the zombie.
You don't like yourself? Well, now is your chance to be someone else. You know you can run this race.

Friday. Panicking, just a little. This is no biggie. For chrissakes, you can run six miles. There are always a few walkers in a race, right? You can't possibly come in dead last. You don't even have to go to the race, you know. There is no pressure, no one is rooting for you. Nobody will care if you sleep in on Sunday. You don't matter in the grand scheme of things.
Panic climbing higher. I get busy with deciding which pair of shorts and T-shirt and running bra and socks I will wear to the race.
The phone rings.

"How's it going, champ?"

"Melanie?"

"That's right."

"I thought you were on an island somewhere."

"I am. Wait until you see the shots I'm taking from the front porch of our cottage. This place is awesome. There is hardly anyone else around. We have a whole white beach and oceanfront completely to ourselves. I never want to leave. I just thought that maybe you could use a pep talk for your very first race. I'm so proud of you! You're the whole package, girl: looks, brains, creativity, and now a runner!"

"Oh my God! Thank God you called! I'm having second thoughts. Okay, I'm fucking panicking. I don't want to run the race. What was I thinking? Isn't this phone call going to cost you a fortune?"

"Stop right now. Take a deep breath. You are going to run this race, because you can. You *want* to, and I'll disown you if you crap out. Just kidding. Now listen, have you picked up your race packet yet?"

"No, I have to pick it up tomorrow at the running store on Falling Rock Road."

"Excellent! You're going to love the running store, and you're going to love the race packet. It will get you all psyched up. You'll be on fire! You'll see. I guarantee it!"

"I am kind of psyched to get the free T-shirt. And I know I can run the distance."

"Yes you can! Now go to bed -- oh, I forgot who I'm talking to," she said with good humor. "Now try to rest, and dream about that race packet. But first, go to the video store and pick out something completely stupid or romantic and watch it. Get *Gone With the Wind* or anything with Mel Brooks in it. I got it: get *Chariots of Fire.* These are your coach's orders. Once you get the race number in your hands, you'll be fine. You'll *want* to wear it!"

"Okay, okay, I'll do what you say. I do want to run this race!"

"That's better. I've got to go. Hang in there. Don't stop running. Keep pushing that finish line every day until you get want you want. Never stop fighting until the fighting is done!"

"You stole that from another movie. I feel better! I love you! Goodbye!"

"Love you too! Love you LOTS, goodbye!"

She's right. I can do this. Piece of cake.

The next day at the running store, I could barely find a place to park. Inside, the store was crowded and full of noise and excitement. I got in line for the packet pick up and started looking around. Lots of very cool gear, including some things I had never even thought of before, like hydration belts and a multitude of gadgets to clip onto every part of your body. The men and women around me were weathered and finely toned and already wearing expensive, brightly colored running gear. They chattered loudly about times and races and training schedules

I don't belong here, I thought. But the line was long and I had time to look around some more. I saw a group of ladies who looked like middle-aged mothers talking as loudly and happily as the weathered runners. They were wearing gardening shorts and corny cotton T-shirts with flowers and elementary school logos on them. They were not slim. They were all slightly heavy. I even saw a rather dumpy, balding man in a polo shirt standing in the line. I'm good. I am not a sham. When it was my turn to step up to the table and sign my name, I willed myself to sign with confidence. Another person behind the desk passed me a plastic bag and I was off.

The drive home was short and the parking was easy on Saturday. I parked in a restricted zone right in front of my apartment since I planned to drive downtown early the next morning anyway.

Inside, I dumped the entire bag out onto the floor. I picked up the shirt first. It was beautiful, bright white, with an enormous drawing of the Constellation in full sail over a turquoise sea with red and yellow accents. The back was covered in logos. I set it aside and started rummaging through the rest of the stuff. I saw a Power Bar and opened it up to eat while I looked. I picked up my race number and stared at it. My number was in the two thousands. Oh, boy. Yes, I'd better get an early start tomorrow.

On impulse, I jumped up quickly and grabbed my purse and walked out into the sunshine. I needed to stay calm, and I couldn't do that in my sweatbox of an apartment. I decided to walk east toward Greenmount and see who was still open at the Farmers Market. There were always some truckloads of farmers who stayed on a little later in the morning and sold off their produce for pennies just to unload it all before driving home. The produce wasn't the pick of the lot, but I was a patient picker and I always found an armful of treasures. I would find blueberries, tomatoes, and leafy greens in a half-rotten state, but sold for only a dollar a pop, which was really an excellent deal. I would go home and pick and wash and discard and end up with a feast of goodies that would last for several days. I would go and get the produce first, then drop it all off before going to the video store and taking Melanie's advice to distract myself with a couple of movies.

A perfect plan. I was going to do this.

Sunday morning. I was way up and in a high-energy mode by 6:00 a.m. The race didn't begin until after 8:00, but I wanted to get going right away. I washed up, brushed my teeth twice, and fixed my hair three times until my ponytail was perfect. It took several attempts to get the number pinned onto my shirt so that it was even and unbuckled. It didn't dawn on me until afterward that I should have just taken the shirt off and pinned the number on first. I wrapped a few dollars around my license to leave locked in my car along with my apartment key, and took only my car key to hold in my hand as I ran. I ran with my apartment key in my hand all the time at the track, so I was used to the feel and I knew I wouldn't drop it. Maybe I would buy one of those cute, Velcro key pockets that lace onto your shoes that I had seen in the running store, or maybe a wrist-wrap pocket. A whole new world was opening up before me!

I drove down St. Paul Street and parked easily at a free Sunday meter near Redwood Street. This way, by walking a few blocks to the starting line, I could beat the crowds trying to leave the Inner Harbor after the race. I immediately saw groups of other runners wearing matching T-shirts and covered in numbers heading down from all directions. There were girlfriends, and guy friends, and even some families with kids with numbers on. My spirits rose even higher.

The crowd thickened as I crossed Pratt Street, and I began to blend in and follow the mob. In the distance I could hear music coming from Rash Field, where the race would end. It was only 7:30 and it looked like the party was already starting. I had plenty of time, so I walked up to the field and milled around the booths, looking at the merchandise and the food and the jewelry.

Mostly, I looked at all the people. Everybody, I mean *everybody* looked so freaking happy! I was so glad to be here, I almost felt like crying. There wasn't a sad face in sight. Old, young, fat, thin, light, or dark, everybody was smiling silently or grinning while chattering away. I felt like I was in Oz.

I couldn't wait to run. I was bursting to run.

Finally, a voice was booming from a microphone somewhere, calling all runners to the start line. I followed the thickening throng and wedged myself somewhere in the middle of the mass of happy humanity on Light Street. My legs and feet were shuffling back and forth with impatience while a welcoming speech that I couldn't hear a word of was belted out over our heads. A gun went off. We began moving slowly forward. By the time I went under the starting line's arch of balloons I could hear Ray Charles loud and clear singing "Hit the Road, Jack." My legs started moving faster. I had neglected to find out anything about the course route, but I wasn't worried. I figured I wouldn't be anywhere near the front of the pack and so I would just follow along like a sheep.

We were heading north up Calvert Street, familiar territory for me, and I was pretty good with hills. My pace felt good. Some runners started passing me, but I was passing people too, and it felt mighty fine, I must say. We passed block after block on Calvert Street. Then we passed more blocks after blocks, heading straight uphill, and my thighs were beginning to feel it, but not very badly. 'I wonder where we'll turn,' I mused as we continued uphill.

We didn't turn. At the first mile mark, we were still heading uphill. I tried to look above and beyond the runners' heads in front of me to see if the thick line of color was turning at any point. They were not turning. We passed North Avenue. We kept going. My breath was starting to come in harder, but I concentrated on controlling it and keeping it even while adjusting my pace.

We passed 25th Street. Holy Shit! We're still going uphill. I'm going to run right past work. I did. It was deserted and dead. I was pushing it, but some strange inner fire was keeping my legs pumping upward. I was not going to stop.

We passed my apartment. Holy Shit! I was not going to stop. I was not going to walk. Fuck it, I was not even going to slow down. We were headed for the hospital. This was good. If I pulled a muscle now, they could just wheel me on in. But wait! The crowd of color was finally turning. I could see them turning left at the hospital. I passed in front of the hospital and glanced over at the crowd of men and women in blue scrubs cheering us on from the corner. Was there anybody I knew? Nope. Hey! I hadn't seen Jane, either. I didn't know anyone around me, but wasn't alone, and I didn't care because now I was on 33rd Street and it was blessedly, blessedly flat and the pain in my thighs eased up without a cramp and suddenly I was heading down St. Paul. Holy. Shit.

All of the pain left my body. The downhill was so steep that all I had to do was pick up my knees and keep putting my feet forward. My breathing slowed and evened out. I was going to make it.

And then a very sharp pain hit my heart. We were passing JC's apartment. I couldn't stop myself from looking over, but there was no sign of life at his window or on his porch, and I was over him in a flash.

I continued downhill. I was feeling no pain. I forgot about my breath. I forgot about my knees. My head floated up above my shoulders. I forgot where I was. I think I was going even faster, making up for that long uphill, but all I could sense was sunshine and color and the wall of white noise in my ears like the long trains and the waves at the ocean.

Before I knew it, the finish line was coming up. The elevated screaming alerted me up and I realized that the finish line was near. People were picking up their paces and coming up from behind me. Ooohhh, nooo. We'll have none of that. I picked up my pace as well.

Breath coming in harder. I was feeling it now. *Don't stop.* I looked up and saw the finish. I saw the digital clock high up on a pole. I was coming in at under an hour. Unbelievable! The screaming was hurting my ears. The microphone was blasting incoherently over the screams. I crossed the finish line and everything in my head went silent.

Holy. Fucking. Shit.

I couldn't believe it. I walked down a corridor made of ribbons and I just couldn't believe it. I did it! I ran a 10K! Someone was tearing off the bottom of my race bib as I exited the racecourse. The tears started pushing up again and I pushed them back down. I did it! I couldn't believe it! I couldn't stop not believing it!

I made my way back to Rash Field to join the party. I drank two bottles of water and ate a banana and a half of a bagel. I wandered around in a daze for almost an hour, listening to the music and the laughter and looking around for a familiar face and not finding one.

I was alone, but I was okay. I felt truly okay for the first time in a very long time. I walked back up to my car, drove home, showered, and put on a pretty sundress for no reason. I walked into the Village and bought a six-pack from the package store at the university pub to celebrate.

Home again, I sat in on the seat of the bay window and sipped and watched the world. I drank two beers in the hot window, went into the bedroom where it was only slightly cooler, lay down on the bed, and passed out for four hours.

# Mile Twenty-Five

I had decided way beforehand not to bore my fellow coworkers with every interesting, spectacular, unparalleled detail about my race the day before, but I couldn't contain myself. In the basement, I talked rapidly and happily to the air while Helen completely ignored me, and Adam tried very hard to look interested. He almost succeeded. I went upstairs and carried on to Sandy and Mandala. Sandy, unlike Helen, acknowledged my presence but had no comment to add to my narrative. Mandala looked over at me like a warmhearted mother indulging her child. No problem. I would go home and blast it all out to Melanie tonight.

First, maybe a little dirty email to California to deflate some of my excitement and allow me to concentrate on work.

**Grace:** I can't get any work done today because I am burning up in my chair. I am burning up inside when I think about your talents and your hot, hot body. I have a ton of projects to work on, and one print job I have to deliver in my own car in all this heat. Our salesman is on the other end of town, and my car doesn't have any air conditioning.

I'm in a really hot spot right now, and I'm not talking about the heat wave in Baltimore.

I am, this minute, writing to you between editing files for the printer. I'm supposed to be out there for a press check in about an hour.

Breathing audible, heartbeat hitting chest wall and vaginal twitching begins. One of my many daily improvisational scenarios begins:

I'm pulling up at the printers', preparing to step out of the car when my phone rings, just as it did that day when Melanie called only a moment before I saw

201

you pull up at the restaurant. It's you. You're so sorry you didn't give me any advance warning, but you are in town for a broadcasters' meeting that was scheduled at the very last minute. Any chance we could meet? What a coincidence! I am already in my car, and this client is notoriously picky and known to take forever to sign off.

The "press check" is going to take awhile. Maybe all afternoon.

It's so hot here, I've taken to wearing my bikini around the house to try and stay cool. Maybe I'll take some more pictures for you if you're a very good boy.

Are you still planning to visit in August?

Love Grace


**CAL:** I'm a good boy!

Keep enjoying the sun, write me all your dirty thoughts, and know that I'll be thinking of you in the shower tonight. I've been really swamped here lately, but I wanted to tell you that I had a little dream about you last night. I can't quite recall all the details, but there was the inevitable oral sex. I cannot tell you how much I think about it and how much I look forward to getting my lips and tongue on you again. Happy Monday from beautiful, smoggy Los Angeles!

Xx


I noticed that he didn't answer the question. Luckily, I had too much work to do to dwell on it.

It was near the end of the day, and I was getting ready to power down when the phone rang, lighting up my line. Damn! I thought about not answering. I was wilted and wiped, but it wasn't exactly 5:00 yet, so I had no choice. I took a quick slug of ice water, sat up straight, and answered in a perky, professional manner. A deep, gravelly man's voice came over the line.

"Is this Grace?"

"Yes, this is Grace. What can I do for you?"

"This is Dr. Whitacre. Are you able to talk in private?" I recognized the voice now.

"Yes, sure, just give me a second." Preston was still away from his desk across the hall, but I got up to close the door anyway. I was pretty sure I knew what was coming. A lot of the doctors asked us to do small jobs for them on the side, off the company books, which was financially beneficial to both parties as long as we didn't abuse company resources. I walked back to my seat and picked up the receiver,

"Okay, now, what can I do for you?" I repeated.

"A little bird whispered in my ear that you are looking for a new job," said the quiet, rough voice. "Are you?"

A little bird? Dr. Whitacre was a prominent figure at the hospital. I was surprised, and I answered cautiously,

"Well, yes, it's true that I've been sending some resumes out. I love working with Richard, but the company has been considering relocating, and I'm interested in finding a job with better benefits." Or any benefits, for that matter. Our company only offered one week of vacation, which we were never able to take all at once due to the size of our staff, and a health insurance policy with a deductible so high I could be dead before any money showed up to save me. The only reason we had any health insurance at all was because it was the law. Also, Richard and Preston had been talking openly in front of us about moving somewhere safer. We were all a little freaked about this, because they were talking about far away exotic lands like Catonsville and Owings Mills. We assumed it was mainly because they were tired of their fancy BMWs getting dinged on the sides of North Calvert Street.

"I have a new position opening up here that I want you to fill. It's a publications management kind of thing. My department is taking on a lot more residents, and I don't have time to deal with all of their paperwork and presentations and other foolishness. I'm launching a long-term research project of my own, and I need you here to organize the whole thing with editing and pictures and all that aggravating PR stuff. What do you say?"

"Um, wait a minute. Would I be working for you or for the hospital?" This position sounded fantastic, and I had always enjoyed working with Dr. Whitacre. He had an enthusiastic, blustery, no-nonsense style, but if I were working for the hospital, then Dr. Whitacre would ultimately not be calling the shots. He couldn't promise me anything.

"You would be working for me, and only me," said Dr. Whitacre, interpreting my question correctly. "Don't worry about HR, I can take care of everything."

I believed him. Dr. Whitacre was a well-known and well-respected physician. He had been at the hospital for a very long time, and the hospital would bend over backward to keep him there.

"Why don't you come up and see me after work hours?" he went on. "I don't want to cause you any early trouble, and I know your bosses are up here almost every night. How about Saturday? Can you come to my office on Saturday and I'll lay the whole thing out for you?"

"I'll need health benefits," I boldly blurted out.

"The hospital has excellent health benefits. Don't worry about that."

"I'm looking to make at least forty thousand a year." I don't know where I came up with this figure. This was almost double what I was currently making, but hopefully would sound more like a drop in the bucket to someone in his position. Besides, I loved graphic design, and wouldn't want to abandon being a full-time artist for anything less.

"I can do that," he replied. I instantly regretted not asking for more. Don't push it, Grace. Besides, by this time I was standing beside my chair and beginning to tremble. I needed to wrap up this conversation before somebody walked in the door.

"What time would you like to meet on Saturday? Shall I bring my portfolio?"

"No, no! No need for that. Just bring a copy of your resume for me to hand over to HR. How about 10:00?"

"That's fine. That's great! I'm looking forward to it."

"Good. You're going to like this job, Grace. You're perfect for it. Dr. Bellman and I both agree. See you Saturday." He hung up without waiting for a goodbye.

So! Dr. Bellman was the little birdie. I was so excited I was temporarily frozen. The bleating of the dead phone line shook me awake and I replaced the receiver. I gathered up my things and raced home to the tune of "Take This Job and Shove It" playing in my head.

Calm down, girl. Don't say anything to anyone until you are locked in. I wanted to go running immediately, but my legs were tired and my shins were burning slightly from yesterday's total road race. I had never run that far on asphalt alone. I was so jazzed up; I knew I would go stir crazy in the apartment. I dropped everything and put on my suit and drove straight to the pool without even thinking about dinner.

The next morning, I had the worst panic attack I'd had in months.

I was awake by 5:30 a.m., right on schedule. I knew I was already in trouble because I felt it. The brain burn. It's not a headache. It's not a stabbing pain. It's the canvassing, complete burn of the inner lining of the skull. The burn concentrates and radiates up from the base of the skull in the back. This is it. I'm losing it. I lay perfectly still on my bed, trying not to explode in a blast of hyperventilation. It felt like pieces of my brain were burning up and falling out -- just falling out like ashes. My brain was an active volcano, with a layer of skin that was my skull stretched over the top, trying to hold back the explosion of dissolution that was myself.

I struggled upward to get my Xanax. I took one and fell back down.

Sleep, sleep. I want to be asleep. Forever asleep. Deeply asleep. I wish I were asleep.

I had to go to work. I got up and brushed my teeth and fell back down.

I got up and took a quick shower and fell back down.

Finally, finally the drug seemed to kick in, and I got up and made it to work, only 20 minutes late. How on Earth was I going to take on a new and better job?

I had to do it. I knew I could do it somehow. After all, I could run a 10K.


Everyone at work was busy. Good, there was nobody to play pretend with. I didn't feel like playing pretend with myself anymore either. I knew that Calvin wasn't coming back to the East Coast in August either, if ever.

**Grace:** Subject: **Spider Sense Tingling**

I can feel the winds of disappointment blowing in from across the country already. I must come up with a plan of action to drive away these waves of sadness and longing.

First, I will book another trip to the ocean. I'll lose myself in the water, and use the sand to scrape away the shreds of anxiety that cling to the inside of my brain.

Then, I will return home and devise a course of punishment for you.

You should never have made love to an Italian. Southern Italian at that - Calabrese - one step away from Sicilian. But wait! I am only *half* Italian; therefore, I will let you live. I will sexually torture you over the internet with my filthiest fantasies and the dirtiest illustrations I can create. What are you going to do about it, eh? You're in CALIFORNIA. Ha, ha. I will prolong and continue this torture until you break, beg for mercy, and fly home again. This sounds like much more fun than pining away, don't you think?

Hmmm. Where to begin? First I will order that high-powered vibrator I've been reading reviews about over the internet. The "Hitachi Magic Wand." Playboy Magazine hails it as the gold standard, and the reviews practically guarantee a fast and furious orgasm, even for the inorgasmic. I'll do that today. I've needed to replace my old, regular plastic model for a long time now. It's at least four years old, and the end cap is cracked and held together with duct tape. The inside screw keeps shaking loose, so I keep a small screwdriver in the drawer of the nightstand beside my bed. Because of the duct tape, the vibrator can only be turned on and off by screwing on or removing the end cap. When I'm through, and reach down to remove the cap, the force of the spring inside the cap often shoots it across the room. I'm always crawling around, naked, trying to find the cap. Once I heard it ping off the wall and I leapt over the side of the bed to keep it from rolling down a hole in the hardwood floor beneath the radiator on the side of the room.

**STOP LAUGHING!!!!**

This is supposed to be a terrifying preview of your upcoming long and painful penance.

Let me get myself together.

What next?

Next, upon the delivery of my new toy, I will practice. I will practice with the aid of audiovisual stimulants. I will choose my favorite "Double Penetrators" video clips. No one-on-one porn, no gang bangs, only double penetrators . . . starring Australian surfers, no Californians.

Gotta get to work now.

Love Grace


**CAL:** A duct taped vibrator? That is pathetic! It's also hilarious, and I think it might end up in a script at some point. Great story as well. I alternated between laughing and being horny - always a good combo.

I'm swamped here as usual, so nothing fun to report. I'm going to have to think of a dirty little scenario and send it to you soon. Right now I'm picturing a hotel room, clean white sheets, beer on ice, a bunch of toys at the ready . . . you on your back, possibly tied down, soaking with sweat . . . me playing with every inch of you, licking your pussy, your stomach, your nipples . . . flipping you over and lifting your ass in the air . . . licking your lower back, your ass, reaching under to play with your clit . . . slamming you down on the bed for being a bad girl and not obeying . . . flipping you back over and putting some fingers in you - both ends - while I lick you some more and some more and some more . . . until you beg me to fuck you . . . me on top of you holding your hands over your head, grinding into you, sliding our slick bodies together.

It's a start.

Xx

**Grace:** Subject: <u>**Trumped**</u>

FUCK! Fuck, fuck, FuCk!, fUcK, fuCK, FUck, fuCK!, FuCk, FuCk, fUCK, FUck, FUCK, fuck, fuck, Fuck, fuck, FuCk, fUcK, fuCK, FUck, fuCK, FuCk, FuCk, fUCK, FUck, FUCK, fuck, fuck, Fuck, fuck, FuCk, fUcK, fuCK, FUck, fuCK, FuCk!, FuCk, fUCK, FUck, FUCK, fuck!, fuck!, Fuck, fuck, FuCk, fUcK, fuCK, FUck, fuCK!, FuCk, FuCk, fUCK, FUck, FUCK, fuck, fuck!!

I'M supposed to be torturing YOU.

And your sweet little hotel scenario, just off the top of your head, happens to be a modern classic, already on the back shelf of the library and I DO beg you to fuck me near the end of every chapter. Damn it!

**CAL:** One time, and I LOVE YOUR PUSSY!!

Xx

Okay, maybe verbal sex was just as good as real sex sometimes, because I suddenly felt as light as a feather. I threw myself back into work, with the stimulating knowledge that I might not be here much longer.

All of a sudden, I stopped working and stared at the wall behind the computer. Look at me. Look where I was: alone in a room, with only six other people at any given time, at best, in the entire building. The only romance in my life was a virtual sex partner who lived over 2,000 miles away. Think about it, if you take the job up at the hospital, it's a completely different world of people out there with unlimited possibilities. There are hundreds of departments, hundreds of rooms, and hundreds of different ideas. No more isolating.

Things are going to change.

The next morning was the same. When my eyes were forced to admit that it was time to face another day, I felt that familiar wave of desolation. My brain was aching, and my pores were flooding with anguish. I felt the waves rising, and waited with sad, but practiced containment as they washed up over my head. Like having your hands full with a burning plate of food, while over your shoulder you watch, helpless, as the sink overflows from the faucet you left on.

My imaginary butler was there, his tray extended with a new menu item of "D&D." Desperation and Despair. I waved him away with determination.

New plan. It was getting too hot to run in the evenings anyway. In your new job, the job that you are going to nail down with aplomb, you might have to work overtime for awhile in the beginning until you get yourself in tune. This will interfere with your evening running routine. From now on, you are going to get up as soon as your eyes are open for good at 5:30. You are going to put on your running clothes like a good little zombie, and you are going to start running in the morning before work. Every day will start out on the right track.

I implemented my new plan the very next morning. It worked. I missed my "friends" Jane and CC as I ran alone in the quiet, dew-crunching stillness, with only my breathing to punctuate the cool silence of the morning, but this is what I needed. The solitude was peaceful. The winding campus loop and Nirvana were both calming and invigorating. It was a perfect interlude. I was high as I kite as I dashed off to work. No more morning dread.

I am going to change things.

# Mile Twenty-Six

On Saturday morning I squeezed in a run before my meeting with Dr. Whitacre, and showed up feeling beautiful, breezy, and confident.

Dr. Whitacre moved his plush, leather swivel chair to the front of his desk so that we were sitting knee to knee, while he leaned back and detailed what would be expected of me on the job. It was all too easy. I could handle every aspect and more, and I told him so.

"So, is the job mine if I want it? Are you interviewing anyone else?" I asked.

"No, no! I want you on board. I could use you immediately. You just need to decide how to tell Richard. We're all friends here. How much notice will you need to give him?"

"Ah! I've been with them for so many years, as you know. I would feel terrible just giving him the standard two weeks. I'd like to give a month at least. Can you wait until the middle of August?"

"Sure, sure! I'm putting you down to begin on the second Monday in August. Give me that resume. I'm going to have to haggle with HR anyway, and you're going to have to come in and fill out their applications and paperwork for the record books. Don't worry about any of that, either. I've already squared it all with the department head."

"Wonderful! I'll wait to hear from you then." We stood up and shook hands. He walked me toward his office door.

"You'll probably have to take some kind of damn orientation course, even though you've been here before," he continued in his blustery manner. "Don't worry about any of that crap. I'll call you next week, and if you need to jump ship sooner after you tell Rick, then that's no problem either."

"Thank you."

"Have a great weekend!" he practically shouted.

"You, too! Goodbye."

I bounced down the stairs and into the soggy, sunshine streets of Baltimore.


On Monday, I decided to tell Mandala and Sandy first. For some reason, I knew they would approve.

"You whore," Sandy declared. "Now we're going to have to train some retard straight out of school to take over your job, and end up doing half of it ourselves for the next year." I laughed.

"My job isn't that great, you know. Richard will hire another little girl, just like you said, and she'll be dumb enough to accept the salary, just like we did."

"I've been looking around closer to home too, you bitch. My commute isn't worth my paycheck." Sandy abruptly turned and began furiously tapping at her keyboard.

"How about you?" I said, turning to Mandala.

"I'm okay here." Mandala was smiling that motherly smile again. "I've been doing my own thing on the side, and making enough money for now. You should go though. You should definitely go. You'll be better off, and I think you'll be happier too."

"How can you say such a thing? You know that I love you!" I teased, waving my arms about like a drama queen. "I'm going to have to tell Preston and Richard this week. Should I tell Helen and Adam?"

"No!" they both intoned simultaneously, Sandy from behind her back.

"Helen wants to marry that executive guy, John, run away from here, and start having babies."

"We know," Mandala answered, as if it were of no consequence. It wasn't really. The photography department didn't affect their work very much.

"Okay," I sighed. "I guess I'd better go downstairs and psych myself up to present this in such a way that Richard won't hold it against Dr. Whitacre."

"Don't tell him today," Mandala said with quiet force.

"Why not?"

"Tell him on Friday, near the end of the day. That way we won't have to listen to him storming around all week, and he'll have the weekend to cool off." Wise as always.

"Good idea, I won't." I got up and went to my room.

**Grace:** Subject: **<u>Break is Over</u>**

I hope you enjoyed your little break from my cyberstalking this week, but don't get used to it. I've just had too much going on, culminating last weekend when I accepted a new and better job offer at the hospital near my apartment. I am on cloud nine!

Back on the farm, my fancy new vibrator arrived last week. I was so intimidated by the size of the box and its weight that I didn't even open it for a couple of days. Practice is not going well, progress reports are pending. Who would have thought to check the dimensions and weight of a device advertised as a hand-held massager?

Calvin didn't answer that day. On Tuesday I wrote him again.

**Grace:** Subject: **<u>A "B" Novel</u>**

This morning in my dreams, we were in a mad rush. You were on a short trip back to Baltimore, and you warned me that you wouldn't be able to get away the next day, but we were on fire. We couldn't stand it, being so close and yet apart, and the magnetic pull between us, across the evening sky over our two houses, was far too strong. We emailed each other as everyone was asleep. We wouldn't have any time but we didn't care. We agreed to meet, even though our excuses could only cover about a half an hour or so.

The moment the door was closed behind you, I rushed to latch onto your lips but you pushed me away and said, "Don't waste any time, get your clothes off." "My thoughts exactly," I breathed, and we stripped ourselves and left a line of mingled clothing behind us as we made our way to the bed. Then it was no holds barred. You grabbed me before I reached the edge and we fell naked onto the bed together. Our lips glued together, we ran our hands furiously up and down each other's bodies until you pushed me away again and we dove and grabbed and sucked and came up for more air like some divers in the ocean.

You looked at your watch, then looked into my eyes and kissed me quickly goodbye. You were gone.

I got out of bed and reached for the vibrator. I'm getting the hang of the new thing. I'll have to send you a picture because you would never believe what I'm up against. It looks more like a weapon, a policeman's baton or a lamp base than a vibrator. But I'm surviving.

Love Grace


**CAL:** Subject: **The Dream**

I love this little dream. I have my version of it all the time. I can almost smell your skin when the image comes into focus. You lying stretched across a bed with the sun slashing into the room across your body. I roll you a little onto your side and kiss you behind one knee. I don't move away though, but let my eyes move up and over you toward your flat, tanned stomach. It rises and falls as your breathing gets heavier. I have both hands on your legs, just above your knees. I'm holding you still, on your back now. I won't let you touch me yet, but make you keep your hands at your sides, gripping onto the sides of the bed, curling the sheet around your hands so you won't give in.

I run my hands slowly up over your legs. My thumbs come so close to your pussy, which is getting wetter with every breath. But I don't touch you yet. More the promise of a touch, delayed. I run my hands over your stomach and up to your breasts. Your nipples are hard, sensitive, waiting for the touch. My fingertips brush lightly over them, both at the same time, and then I pinch them, delicately at first but then harder. It puts a little shock through you, this contrast of hard and soft. But you take it. You want to open your legs, to let me in, to feel that first touch of the tip of my tongue. But I don't let you. My arms are still holding you where I want you, but I reach one hand toward your face. You instinctively open your mouth and I put my finger inside. You make it wet with your tongue and then suck on it. You're treating my finger like a cock, tasting along its length, wrapping your lips around it, pulling it into you, pulling me into you, devouring me, everything that is me.

I take my finger back and at the same time force your legs apart, not gentle anymore. A subtle wave of air hits you between your legs, sending a shiver across your body and making you inhale sharply. I run my still wet finger over your clit and down into you. I love this wetness. I'm hungry for it. I bring it out of you and all over you, making your pussy wetter and ready for my mouth. You can't wait anymore and neither can I and your hands reach for my head, pushing me into you, making me eat you. Taking you by both ankles, I push your legs up and open, so I can get all of you into me. My mouth on you, my tongue licking and slurping and drinking you, my mouth kissing your pussy, the greatest make-out session of our lives. I lick along your lips, I suck and lick

212

your hard little clit, and I drive my tongue deep into you, as deep as it will go. I'm fucking you with my mouth, with my tongue. I can't get enough. I can't . . . get . . . enough. And now I put two fingers hard into you, slamming into your pussy, fucking you in a rougher way while my tongue keeps a gentle and wet pressure on your clit. You can barely breathe, barely keep up with this energy coursing through you, beckoning you to orgasm. You can feel my breath against you as my excitement is almost uncontrollable.

You stretch one leg down until your foot finds my cock. It's so hard and hot and you know it's going to be in you soon. Our rhythm builds. I fuck you harder and deeper with my fingers while my tongue sucks your clit. You're getting close now, almost coming. My other hand moves up and you feel my finger, wet with you, sliding toward your ass. I play around the opening, not going in yet, putting gentle pressure on you. I can feel your back beginning to arch. You want it. You want me in you, in your ass, in your pussy, fucking you, sucking you, licking you. I'm crazy with desire for you, burning to drive my cock into you. You begin to moan. It's not under your control, it's just coming out of you. You begin to scream as the orgasm lifts you up, like a wave that's taken over you, that will throw you over its edge. My fingers, my mouth, my tongue, our bodies. You come so hard you're lost for a moment, tossed around on this little tempest. The images and feelings flutter by as the orgasm tears through you. Sweat on our bodies, light through the window, a salty taste of skin, muscles clenching, a gasp for breath, fingers grasping in the sheets, toes curled. The feeling slowly begins to let go and you feel your muscles releasing. You become heavy with exhaustion and contentment and you lie fully on the bed trying to catch your breath. You look up, finally opening your eyes, to see me sitting up, still between your legs, a smile on my face. You get it, what I'm saying. I haven't come yet, I'm still hard as a rock, I'm ravenous for you, and it's about to start all over again.
Xx


**Grace:**  Oh, you're good.


I need to stop this email affair immediately. I am becoming foolish. It is all wrong. This direction will have no fruition, and you are full of impossible hope and unnecessary sadness. Neither of you will ever move across the country. So stop it now.

Oh, forget about it. I already know all of that. I don't imagine any future with Calvin, and I'm just enjoying the fantasy until my love life moves on in reality. Fantasy, hope, and dreams have their place. They are good. Obsessive behavior is not good, unless it's in a lap lane or in a pair of running shoes. You'll stop fantasizing so much when you're busy with your new job. Check it out -- he didn't even ask about your new job! We're not seriously interested in each other. It's okay. It's all good, for now.

The next morning, I am so nervous about my upcoming announcement on Friday that I am at it again. I had snapped a (headless) picture of myself the night before, displaying my new toy on the bed sheet between my legs.

**Grace:** Subject: **Out With the Old**
This is what I'm up against.
It's your fault you know. Investing in a new vibrator was imminent, but not imperative until I had you.

I attached a picture of my Hitachi Magic Wand, entitled "The Problem."

**CAL:** Subject: **WHAT?!**
Man, that thing is like a mini jack hammer! What's that thing on the side, another handle? Is this a two-hander? Must be powerful.
Now, the next step is for you to take a photo of you using that thing and send it to me. Immediately!
Xx

**Grace:** No, silly. The little tan thing near my right leg is the old one. Note the unattached cap with duct tape around it. The new one on the left is so unmanageable that I can barely wield the thing and concentrate at the same time. It's heavy too. Then there's the cord. Sometimes I have to hold it with two hands but it's been paying off in both method and practice.

**CAL:** Subject: **Hot**
I don't think you understand how fucking horny I am right now, after seeing your crotch in that shot. At least, in my mind that's your crotch. And then I start thinking about it, and how nice it would be to pull that material aside and run a finger over you, or a tongue.

**Grace:** It's my crotch. Black panties.

**CAL:** Or even better . . . a shot of you playing with yourself. (tell me if I'm crossing the line)

**Grace:** Nope! You're doing great. I've already come once this morning, but as I read your responses I'm starting to melt off the seat cover on the chair in front of my computer. I'm going to have to walk away. I've got things to do today.

**CAL:** Please! Pull them aside and take a photo of that beautiful pussy! I'm too hot and bothered to be polite about it.

I didn't respond.

**CAL:** So I'm not going to get to see more of you today? I'm about to walk out of work, go home, and jerk off thinking about what I would do to you! The only problem is, I can't stand up until this thing goes away.
Have a great week!
Xx

Finally, Friday rolled around. I was very nervous. Everyone was in their respective rooms all morning, and it looked like it was going to stay that way for the rest of the day. Everything was quiet. I didn't want to wait until the very last minute. That just seemed rude. I would aim for around 2:00 or 3:00, I told myself as I tried to swallow my lunch.

**Grace:** Subject: <u>Today</u>
I'm trying to tie up all of my loose ends at work today, but I can't get anything done because I'm thinking about fucking you.
I really need to call a new client about his logo design, but I can't seem to pick up the phone because I'm thinking about fucking you. Very unprofessional.
I have to compose myself in order to inform my boss about my plans to leave the company, but I can't get my thoughts together because I'm thinking about fucking you.
I can't get ANYTHING done efficiently so far today because I can't stop fucking thinking about FUCKING YOU! FUCK!

**CAL:** Later tonight there will be a shower. My hard cock will be sliding in and out of my soapy hand while I think about fucking YOU! That is a fact.

Okay, I was ready now.

First, I walked across the hall and pulled Preston's door closed behind me as I sat in the chair in front of his desk. He looked up without interest.

"Preston, I came to tell you that I'm leaving the company. I'm starting a new job in about three weeks. I really need better health benefits, and they've already agreed to pay me forty thousand a year."

Preston's face was completely slack, but I could hear his brain ka-chinging inside his head. Preston was always after the almighty dollar, tacking on as many extraneous expenses as he could make up onto every client's bill. I knew he was already calculating what he could do with my salary if they could manage without hiring a new person. When he heard me say the words "forty thousand" his face became intact.

"Well, we certainly can't compete with that. Have you told Richard yet?"

"No, I'm going down the hall to tell him now."

"Well, I can only wish you the best of luck then."

"Thank you." I walked out. What an asshole. There was no way they could run the graphics with only Mandala and Sandy. Best of luck to *you* asshole. You didn't even bat an eye over the news. I guess a man on his fourth wife is used to this kind of conversation. Things went down differently in Richard's office. When I got to the part about the health benefits, he jumped up from his chair and shouted,

"*We* can give you better health benefits!"

"They're also paying me a starting salary of forty thousand a year."

"*We* can give you forty thousand!"

At these words, I became so shocked and angry that I became completely calm. I had been asking for a raise, not even a big one, for the past two years, and had been met with nothing but whining excuses over expenses and long, moaning tirades about how difficult it was to run a small company. Now, all of a sudden, just as I was leaving, he could hike up my salary and increase my benefits. I knew he didn't have that kind of money. I knew that whatever counteroffer he could actually come up with would be the last raise I would ever see in that place for the rest of my life. I felt insulted that after years and years of underpaid service, my worth was only acknowledged at the moment I was leaving.

"I've already accepted the other job," I said coolly. "I'm starting three weeks from Monday. I'm sorry, but I really need to be doing better at this time in my life. You know you can always call me if you have any problems while you're hiring a new girl. I'll help you out in any way I can." I threw in that last part because I had been with him for so long, but mostly because we would inevitably be running into each other sometime in the future.

"Who are you going to work for?" he was still standing, and still shouting.

"I'd rather keep that private for the time being. I'll leave you now." I got up and left the office. Richard followed me and slammed his door so hard that the walls shook. Preston brushed past me in the hallway without meeting my eyes and went into Richard's office. I turned to watch him, just in time to see Richard pulling at his telephone wire and slamming his phone into the wall across the room. The building shook again.

I raced upstairs, heart pounding, to find both Sandy and Mandala staring at their doorway with their eyes glued wide open.

"Did you hear any of that?" I gasped.

"Fucking *shit*! We heard the whole fucking thing!" Sandy said loudly. Mandala had already gotten herself together and was shushing us both, but Sandy was even more furious than I was.

"Where the *fuck* does he get off saying he could pay you more money and give you better benefits? *Fuck* this place. I'm so *fucking* out of here!" She was grabbing at her things and marching out the door. "They can both *blow* me!" she hollered as she exited the building. Mandala turned to me, "You'd better go for the day, too. Don't worry about Sandy. She'll be okay. She's always like that."

Sandy *was* always like that. "Don't worry about those two, either. I'll keep it cool until you're gone." I took her advice. I powered everything down and grabbed my things as quickly and silently as possible, but was stopped at the front door landing by Helen.

"What the hell is going on?" she whispered feverishly.

"I'll tell you later. I'll call you tonight."

"Tell me now!"

"I just gave notice. I'll give you all of the details later. I've got to leave right now."

"You lucky bitch! I'm jealous! Okay, okay, I'll talk to you later."
I was out.

That night, the heat storms began. The heavy heat and humidity of the day often broke into thunderstorms by sunset. How appropriate, I smiled to myself, as I watched the lightning flashes from my window. The phone rang only once. It was Helen, of course. When I let it go to the answering machine she either got the message or was too busy with John to bother calling back. My parents already knew about my plans, and were thrilled beyond belief. Now, if only I would just move out of the city . . . I could see the thought behind their congratulatory smiles.

The only problem with the storm in progress was that it was supposed to last until midday tomorrow, and I was busting to run.

"Scattered clouds and thunderstorms," said the beautifully groomed weatherwoman, "tapering off around 10:00 a.m." Not good. I wanted to run now.

I watched the storm go on until midnight, and then lay down to rest, just in case I could somehow get out between the clouds in the morning.

Five o'clock. The sounds of the storm kept me dozing peacefully until 6:00. That's it for me, as always. I got up and dressed slowly, while drinking leftover coffee as I watched the rain continue outside. At 7:00 the rain seemed to slow down to a very light drizzle. A slim ray of sunlight shone through for a second, casting a shadow of a tree onto the sidewalk below my window. That was all the encouragement I needed. What's a little drizzle?
Sauconys on, I was out the door.

It was nice. The sun peeped out intermittently as I jogged to the track, warming up. A few flecks of rain touched upon my shoulders, face, and torso every now and then, keeping me cool and steady. I entered the track. It was completely deserted. There wasn't a soul in sight or a car on the road. Perfect.

I began my quantum level leaps in an atmosphere of sublime and splendid solitude. My stride had never felt so exquisite. My arms had never fallen so comfortably. I felt classical as I mentally projected my run past Nirvana and over the illustrious portico of the BMA. I fell into my other world.

I was floating into mile three and dreaming of ionic columns when the thunderclap from Hades sounded out in the distance. I actually stopped running, nearly falling over my feet, the sound was so loud. I looked out over the track and saw a massive curtain of rain approaching me like a tsunami in a movie scene. The sight was so surreal that I stood stupidly in place until the curtain of rain was upon me. I woke up and dashed beneath the bleachers. Thunder roared as I shivered in the shadows. It was like a waterfall! I swear I felt as if I were tucked away in a rocky crevice behind Niagara Falls. What to do? The snappy-belted, bright lip-sticked weatherwoman's words came back to me as I pondered my situation: "Scattered thunderstorms."

I was wondering how long I should wait, when a new sound of pounding came into my ears. It was the sound of someone running. I looked to my left and there he was.

CC was hurtling across the infield toward me. He ducked under the bleachers, and stopped on a dime, not two feet away from my startled and immobilized presence. He was grinning from ear to ear at our combined foolishness, proving beyond a doubt that he had dimples to die for.

"Hi," he grinned, catching his breath, and leaning down over his knees.

"Hello." That was all I could come up with. CC straightened up, and was looking right into my face.

"They weren't calling for anything as bad as this," he said, almost apologetically, like the thunderstorm was entirely his fault and he was so sorry that I was stuck underneath the bleachers with him.

"No, no, they weren't," I answered moronically.

"I've seen you on the track," he said.

"Yes, I've seen you, too. You're a coach for the university team, aren't you?" I finally remembered that I had a brain in my head.

"Yeah, yeah. We're a small team. I'm not here most of the time. I mostly work in the Sports Medicine Department at the hospital over there. I'm a physical therapist. My name is Noah," he said, extending his hand.

"Then, this is all your fault," I quipped, pointing to the sky with my left hand as I shook his hand with my right. "I'm Grace. I work in graphic design for the hospital from a small firm on North Calvert, but I'll be moving into the hospital with Dr. Whitacre in a few weeks."

"Dr. Whitacre? He's great! You'll love it."

"Yes, I've already worked with him for several years. I'm looking forward to the job." An awkward silence fell over us as we watched the rain falling steadily, with no end in sight.

"You know," he said, "we probably shouldn't be waiting it out under here." I looked up and around at the metallic cave we were standing in. "Where is your car?" he asked.

"Oh, I don't have one. Not with me. I only live a few blocks away."

"I'm parked on the other side of the athletic building. I could run around and get my car and we could go grab some coffee. I mean," he stumbled, "I mean, would you like to go and have some coffee with me?"

"Yes! Absolutely." Now I was the one grinning from ear to ear. "If we can find someplace that will accept us like this." I gestured to our soaking wet condition.

"I'll blast the air on in my car. We'll be fine. Wait here while I pull around the circle in front of the building. I'll lean on the horn and then you come running."

"Okay," I said. I think I was beaming. I might have looked like a fool, but it didn't matter because he was already off and running. Less than two minutes later, I heard the horn. I took off from under the bleachers and rounded the building to see him leaning over to open the passenger side door for me. His car was a black Jeep.

Now, I don't know if I'd subliminally seen him getting in or out of this Jeep around town, or if karma is for real . . . and I didn't really care. I jumped into the seat beside him, and slammed the door closed.

# Point Two

In the past, my panic attacks were so sorry and fierce that the mere thought of getting behind the wheel of a car was a terrifying gamble. I was afraid I would have a panic attack and decide to drive over a cliff or into a tree or something. My routes were carefully planned around the availability of supermarket parking lots and rest stops.

When JC and I got together and moved into the same block downtown, my panic attacks became so severe that JC would bring me a paper bag to breathe into until I calmed down, like a scene in a sitcom. The paper bag works, by the way.

Running is another thing that works. Running pisses on the pain, the fury, and the sadness. Running throws a bucket of water on the shame, the regret, and the hate. It's hard to get enough water sometimes, or the bucket isn't big enough, but it works anyway.

I still have panic attacks, and live with them and through them with the experience to know that there is an end in sight. Somewhere, sometime, somehow it will end. I will laugh again, watch the trees go by on the way to the ocean, buy new shoes, go for a run, and stuff my face with chocolate totos once more.

The depression will never end, but knowledge is power.

With this knowledge, and in spite of it all, I still believe that there is nothing in the world that a couple of miles can't cure.

59421503R00124

Made in the USA
Middletown, DE
21 December 2017